Strange
Way Home

Strange Way Home

Nancy W. Faber

HENRY REGNERY COMPANY

Chicago 1963

TO MY HUSBAND

B. S. F.

WITH ALL MY LOVE

Acknowledgments

The author, with deep appreciation, wishes to thank the following for making this book possible. Without their help it would have been impossible to authenticate many of the details of the story.

Mr. John Selby, Novelist, Fire Island, New York

Father Hendricks, Church of the Good Shepherd, Rhinebeck, New York

Father O'Malley, St. Patrick's Information Center, New York City

Monsignor O'Brien, Catholic Archdiocese, Madison Avenue, New York City

Rabbi David Gersten, Temple Shearith Israel, 71st Street, New York City

Father Armand, Capuchin Monastery, Ste. Anne de Ristigouche, Gaspe, Canada

New York Historical Society, Central Park West and 77th Street, New York City

New York Public Library, Research and Music Departments

Miss Elizabeth Sutherland, Canadian Tuberculosis Association, Ottawa, Ontario, Canada

New York Tuberculosis Society

New York Telephone Company, Public Relations Department

New York Central Railroad, Public Relations Department

Canadian Consulate

Canadian Pacific Railways

J. J. Vallee, Mayor of St. Anne de la Perade, Canada

New York Botanical Gardens, New York City

CHAPTER
1

Late Sunday afternoon, September 18, 1904, on their way home from a visit with the Nordlanders, Mr. and Mrs. Auguste Fath paused at the northeast corner of Washington Square Park, their eyes searching for their three children, with their nurse and tutor.

"*Bien*. There they are." Belgian-born Mr. Fath started toward the fountain, arm in arm with his wife.

As they passed through the white marble arch, there swelled about them the sound of children's voices raised in play. And tops and balls seemed everywhere; tricycles and doll buggies flashed past the gray sycamore trees. Beyond, the nurses in their starched uniforms sat gossiping on the benches.

A sturdy five-year-old boy, blue-eyed and brown haired, limped exaggeratedly at the head of a line, to the beat of his toy drum. He piped an old tune in a high key:

> Hip, hip, I lost my leg in the army . . .
> Here I come with my rusty gun
> To shoot the British army
> Hip . . . hip . . .

"Well," Mr. Fath surveyed their second son with interest, "I see Charles has put himself in his usual modest place."

They watched as their chubby, curly-headed girl ran up to Charles, crying, "I want to be in the army, too."

"Armies aren't for girls—go away, Emilie."

Charles gave his sister a little push. Emilie sat down hard in the middle of the path.

She started to wail, more in indignation than pain.

At once a beautiful boy, their older son, darted forward.

"Don't cry, Emilie," he said, bending over the little girl to brush off her dress. "Who wants to go around shooting people anyway? Here." He handed her his hoop and stick.

Mr. and Mrs. Fath exchanged a proud look.

"That Henri, he is an unusual one." Their French tutor startingly spoke from beside them, his dark gaze full of pride too.

On her second try Emilie hit the hoop too hard. It rolled out of the park.

Henri sped after the hoop and for an instant was hidden from view. The thin, stooped figure of the tutor moved rapidly after the boy. He returned in a few moments, leading him by the hand. They were chattering happily.

"Thank you, Monsieur," said Mrs. Fath warmly. "Thank you for being so careful of my son."

Monsieur Dupier bowed with the humbleness that was his chief characteristic. "You may rest assured, Madame, that I intend never to lose sight of him even for an instant." He paused and added softly, "He is one of God's chosen children."

"It is warm for September, Henri." Mrs. Fath smoothed the heavy hair back from his moist forehead. "Did you have a nice day?"

"Oh, yes."

The sun's rays had caught the ends of the tiny blue feathers on his mother's hat and made a blurred halo around her head. To Henri she looked like an angel.

"Well," said Mr. Fath, "start at the beginning. What did you do the first thing this morning?"

"The first thing? Well, Monsieur took us to Mass—"

"Again!" Mr. Fath glanced angrily up at Monsieur Dupier.

The tutor stood with bowed head, hands clasped in front of him.

Henri's full mouth trembled. "It was not for very long, Papa. It took no time at all."

Mr. Fath took the tutor aside. "You will please come upstairs to my study the instant you are back at the house."

Monsieur bowed his head again.

Henri gazed at his father, made a motion as if to go to Dupier's side, then remained standing irresolutely.

"Run along, Henri," Mr. Fath said. "Tell Fraulein it is time for everyone to go home. We will see you back at the house."

The boy turned to obey, and Mrs. Fath, strolling up, took her husband's arm. They left the Park and walked slowly west along the north side of the Square.

As far as Auguste Fath was concerned, the incident was over: Dupier would leave and that was the end of it. Mr. Fath had no patience with incidents; he dealt with them swiftly and surely, then forgot them.

Indeed if Mr. Fath was successful—and he had all the

security and worldly goods that a reasonable man could ask for—it was because he always acted swiftly and surely.

Back in 1869, on his seventeenth birthday, he left Antwerp for America: he did not like the way his family's lace manufacturing business was being run, and he'd not stay there under the circumstances. He landed alone in New York, quickly found work. After a year, his knowledge of Dutch, French, and German helped him find a good job with an importing firm.

When he was in America six years he felt ready to go into business for himself. And ironically, he found himself in the business of importing lace.

His dealings led him to make the acquaintance of the Kohlins, a cultured Viennese family. Their daughter Edith was eighteen years old when Auguste met her; and the moment he saw her he thought of her as a red-headed doll. So he renamed her Dolly, and just before her nineteenth birthday they were married. Henri was born soon after she turned twenty-one. Now they had a fine family, a fine brownstone, good friends, a comfortable life— everything a reasonable man could ask for.

They reached their house and Mr. Fath rang the bell. The park was suddenly empty now, and the sound of children's voices stilled. On distant streets trolley cars clanged, but here on the fashionable Square only horses hooves and the occasional rattle of carriage wheels broke the silence.

Fraulein opened the front door, and Mr. and Mrs. Fath entered their home.

Mr. Fath climbed the stairs to his third-floor study. Monsieur Dupier was waiting for him, his black hair brushed straight back. His heavy lids drooped over large black eyes sunken in a sallow face.

4

Mr. Fath lit the Welsbach burner of his desk lamp, and addressed the tutor without preamble: "I warned you, Dupier, that if you took my children to Mass once more, you would have to leave!"

"But sir—"

"I hired you to tutor my children in French, not in the ideology of your faith!"

"You said"—Dupier's voice was low but stubborn— "that you were putting the little ones in my safekeeping. What better way to keep them safe than to teach them God's ways?"

"You forget," snapped Fath, drawing his shaggy brows together, "that we have our own religion!"

"You have nourished your children's bodies well, Monsieur, but we must remember the Lord's admonition. God has told us that each can receive the never-ending happiness of Heaven, but those who do not obey His laws will be punished with the never-ending torments of hell."

Jolted by such an attitude, yet restrained by a sudden compassion, Fath said equably, "Let us just say we don't see things in the same way."

"You dare to speak of God as *things!*"

"For God's sake!" Fath's face reddened. Then, with a noticeable effort, he collected himself. "I'm sorry, Monsieur Dupier. In these few weeks, you have been devoted to the children. Especially to Henri. They will miss you. Your month is up this Saturday. You will have to go."

Dupier stared at him. When he could finally speak, his voice was barely a whisper. "You cannot mean that, Monsieur. To take me away from Henri—"

There was the sound of footsteps in the passage.

"Papa—" Henri's eager voice preceded him. He paused just inside the doorway, sensing something wrong. What had happened to Monsieur Dupier—patient Monsieur, who always had time for his questions? Bewildered, he turned behind him to his mother.

Quickly she took in the situation. "I think that Fraulein would like you to help her with Emilie's bath," she said.

Henri shook his head, not in disobedience but in perplexity. His eyes sought his father's stern face, his tutor's stooped form, and finally the grave face of his mother.

"Better go to Fraulein," his mother urged gently.

Henri stood off one more moment, then turned and was gone.

"Come in, Dolly," Mr. Fath said. "Monsieur Dupier is leaving us."

Mrs. Fath nodded.

The tutor, his eyes still fastened on the doorway through which Henri had disappeared, groaned, "Henri, Henri. *Mon petit, cher* Henri."

"Come now, Monsieur," Mrs. Fath said. "It's not so bad as all that."

Dupier looked at her dully, as if he had not heard.

"There will be other children. Many other children will need and love you, Monsieur."

"There will never be another Henri!"

Mrs. Fath felt as if she had been dealt a physical blow. To think that a mere stranger should share her most private feeling. She loved her children equally, of course; it would be wicked to have a favorite. But there was something about Henri!

She busied herself with a decanter of Courvoisier. "Take this." She smiled at Dupier. "It will make you feel so much better."

But Dupier ignored the glass. His lips moved slightly as if in prayer.

Mr. Fath caught a few words that sounded like *"L'arc du bois . . . gopher."* But they made no sense to him.

Suddenly an odd, wary expression crossed Dupier's face; his eyes widened; he stared straight ahead at something Fath could not see. Then the heavy lids hooded his eyes once more, and he bowed to Mrs. Fath and reached for the brandy. He drained it in a single swallow.

"You are very kind, Madame."

The chambermaid knocked softly, came in and lit all the gas jets. The light flickered uncertainly at first through the multi-colored glass chandelier, and as it grew stronger the Bokhara rug came to life under the monotones of the green plush furniture. They remained motionless and silent until the maid withdrew.

The tutor started to leave the room, then turned back. "One favor, Monsieur. If I may be permitted to tell the children in my own time—"

"Well—"

"In my own way, Monsieur. It will be easier."

Mr. Fath sighed. "Don't take too much time about it, Dupier."

"Merci beaucoup, Monsieur. Thank you. Thank you very much, Monsieur."

Fath was startled at the effusiveness of his gratitude. "But no more Mass!"

"Between now and the time I leave, no Mass. I swear it."

"Very well, then."

Dupier moved silently from the room.

CHAPTER
2

$\mathbf{D}$UPIER left the Fath house and went to his modest room. He spent the remainder of the evening writing a long letter. It was late when he finished, but he went out to mail it before turning in.

The next day, Monday, September nineteenth, was Yom Kippur, the Day of Atonement. The cook, nurse, and maid worked on as usual in the Fath household, but there were to be no lessons, and Dupier had been given the day off.

Dupier rose at his usual hour and went to Mass. Afterwards he walked to a Fourteenth Street clothing store and made several purchases. These he took home and packed together with the rest of his clothes, in a large shabby valise. Then he locked the emptied closet and set himself to wait. When his landlady left the house, he picked up his valise and traveled by Third Avenue elevated to Grand Central Depot. He went to a ticket window, made his purchase, and received a baggage check.

He attached one half of it to his luggage and sent it off. The other half of the check he put into an envelope and mailed.

Instead of boarding the train at Forty-second Street, he walked down Third Avenue, stopping off at a pharmacy along the way. At Thirty-fourth Street, he boarded the elevated again and got off at his usual stop. Once more he made his way to the church at which he worshipped. He remained there a long time.

Then he went home and prepared for the lessons he gave in the evening.

Late Tuesday afternoon, Dupier went to the house and met Mr. Fath as he came home for dinner.

"Have you told the children?" Mr. Fath asked.

"I was not here yesterday."

"Tomorrow then!"

The tutor bowed humbly.

On Wednesday, Fraulein's day off, Dupier took the children for a walk.

"How would you like to go to Wanamaker's instead of the Park?" he asked. "They have a wonderful display of toy trains."

Emilie clapped her hands, Charles looked delighted, and Henri radiant. Trains were Henri's passion. He would spend hours playing with them, running them up and down with his hands, making up stories all the while.

Dupier brought the children back in ample time for supper. He was still there when Mr. Fath came home. Henri hurled himself at his father, and began excitedly to tell him of the wonders at Wanamaker's. In the hubbub, Dupier slipped away.

Thursday passed uneventfully.

On Friday, September twenty-third, Mr. Fath was delayed at his office. Fraulein had taken Charles and Emilie to the dentist. Dupier spent a long time alone with Henri, but he left before Fath arrived home. Mrs. Fath and Henri said good-bye to the tutor at the door.

Mrs. Fath bent down and hugged Henri. Briefly the child rested against her breast. He rubbed his face against her velvet collar and wriggled a little in pleasure. He loved the feel of velvet. Besides, Mama always smelled so nice.

"Time for bed." Mrs. Fath released him.

"Come and tuck me in, Mama?"

"As a special favor," his mother answered gravely. Each evening Henri asked the same question; each evening his mother gave the expected answer. But tonight Mrs. Fath sat beside Henri a little longer than usual.

"You have been so quiet all day, my little one," she whispered as she smoothed back his unruly hair. "Is anything troubling you?"

Henri hesitated. "No, Mama."

Mrs. Fath leaned forward and kissed him lightly on the forehead. "Tell me about it, Henri. I can keep a secret." She waited a moment but Henri remained silent.

"No. No, Mama. It is nothing."

"Good night then, my darling." There was the slightest rustle of her skirts and she was gone.

For a long time Henri lay awake, gazing up into the darkness. He hadn't told a lie. Yet he knew he should have told his mother of the treat Monsieur Dupier had promised him.

He slept fitfully.

The next morning seemed forever. Henri squeezed his eyelids together and tried to imagine he was giving the day a tremendous shove, so that it would move faster. It seemed years to lunch time.

An hour later, the Faths retired upstairs to rest. Fraulein took Charles and Emilie upstairs for their customary nap, and Dupier was left alone with Henri. He smiled down at the boy.

"Have you kept our secret, Henri?"

"Oh yes."

The tutor nodded, handed Henri his cap, put on his own hat, and quietly they slipped out the front door.

"Emilie and Charles will be so disappointed," Henri said. "Perhaps we should have taken them with us after all."

Mama's friend Madame Liebling turned the corner, saw them, and waved. Henri waved back.

"They may be disappointed," Dupier agreed, "but remember the last time we took them to see some trains? It really wasn't much fun for them. Remember how tired Emilie was? And Charles was interested only in the guns."

Mr. Dowling the janitor, wrestling with his ash cans, saw them come down from the stoop.

Dupier, holding Henri's hand tightly, crossed the street and walked diagonally east across the Square.

Fraulein, standing at an upstairs window, saw them.

At the corner of Eighth Street, a ragged shoe shine boy watched them approach. He noticed the boy's fancy clothes.

Henri was breathless as they completed the climb up the steep stairs to the Third Avenue elevated, where a train was just pulling out of the station.

"Monsieur, Monsieur, we missed it!"

The stationmaster tore off the tickets and pushed them

11

through the wicket. He saw the boy standing back to him at the edge of the platform.

In a few minutes another train throttled down into the station. Dupier and Henri stepped aboard. The doors shut, the platform trembled, the whistle screamed. A series of small chugs, and the train clanked off along the elevated tracks.

Henri sat transfigured. Finally a conductor appeared between cars and announced "Grand Central Depot." The train slid to a halt.

Monsieur Dupier took Henri firmly by the hand and stepped out onto the platform.

As the train gathered speed, casually the conductor's eyes swept the platform. The last thing he saw was a lean dark man moving toward the exit with a small boy beside him.

Dupier and Henri hurried through the exit and down the stairs. What a long way it was to the street. The elevated was so high, thought Henri. He wondered if the trains at Grand Central were high, too.

At the bottom of the steps, Dupier asked, "How would you like an ice cream soda, Henri?"

"Could I!" Henri's voice stumbled in excitement. "Could we go to Huyler's, like Mama and Papa do?"

"That would take too long. But there is one right here at the corner. It will be quite as good."

Dupier ordered a soda, too. Carefully he stirred Henri's for him.

When they'd finished suddenly Dupier seemed to be in a hurry. They walked west to Lexington Avenue at a pace almost too fast for Henri's short legs. Then Dupier stopped.

"Look Henri, we are here!"

Henri lifted his head skywards in awe. He had heard much about the wonders of the station. There it stood, six stories high and just six years old, a miracle of modern architecture.

Then they were inside, and Henri cried out in amazement at the vast dome of steel and glass high above him. He hurled questions at the tutor as they hurried along. How had the workmen ever climbed to the top? Who cleaned the windows? Where were the trains? But Monsieur was too impatient to give him but a few answers.

Finally they reached their goal. There, under a shed hundreds of feet long, stood a train with a giant locomotive belching smoke.

They walked the entire length of the platform to get a front view of the locomotive. The engine, black, shining and huge, seemed to Henri like an enormous animal, resting its face on its paws, lying in wait.

"Where does this train go to?"

"This one?" Dupier paused a moment. "I believe it goes north."

Dupier had learned a great deal about trains and he told it all to Henri. Henri listened as intently as he could, but suddenly he couldn't help feeling dreadfully sleepy. It was an effort to keep his eyes open.

"Perhaps you would like to inspect the inside?"

"Could we?"

"Why not?"

"Would they really let us?"

"I don't see what harm it would do." Dupier glanced about them. "Let us walk back a way first."

They passed a few cars. Dupier took one last look

around. No conductor was in sight. There were no passengers in the car as yet. He hoisted Henri up to the platform.

It seemed strange and wonderful to see the inside of a real train. Still, Henri thought, it did not look very different from his own little trains at home. Only much, much, much larger. Too large, almost.

They were standing in the middle of the aisle when Henri almost fell. His legs felt awkward. It was hard to walk, and he felt sleepy.

"Slide in here." Monsieur placed him in a seat. Soon Henri became conscious that they were moving. He opened his eyes and jumped up.

"The train is moving! We must get off, Monsieur!"

"So it is. But there's no need to worry." He patted the boy on the head. "We will get off at the next stop."

Henri remained standing, swaying dizzily. "We'll be longer than one hour. Mama will be very angry."

"Perhaps a little. But think how happy she will be when she knows what an adventure it's been."

"I don't know." Henri's head felt so heavy, he could barely shake it. "Why don't we ask the conductor to stop the train and let us off?"

From a great distance, Henri heard Dupier say, "That's impossible. Why don't you just sit down and watch the scenery until we get off? Think of it—a real train ride!"

"I don't want to . . ."

Then Henri felt he was falling, falling from a great height.

Dupier caught Henri as he toppled over, gently laid him on the seat with the curly head resting on his lap.

MONSIEUR Fath woke from his nap. He stood up and stretched. He called and his wife came in from the next room.

"The children are so quiet," he said. "Are they still in the park?"

"At five in the afternoon? They're home by now."

"And so quiet?" he persisted uneasily.

"You're being silly."

"Of course I'm being silly," he agreed, but together they hurried to the nursery.

Charles and Emilie were sitting beside Fraulein. She was showing them illustrations in a German song book.

"Where is Henri?" Mr. Fath demanded.

"He is out—with Monsieur," Fraulein answered.

"What!"

"Monsieur Dupier took him to see the trains in Wanamaker's. But it is two hours now, and he has not returned." Fraulein began to reflect their uneasiness.

"How foolish to be so frightened," Mrs. Fath tried to

15

comfort herself. "Wanamaker's is still open. Probably Monsieur Dupier couldn't persuade Henri to leave the trains."

Mr. Fath was already at the nursery door, putting on his coat. "Of course, but I'll just go over and hurry them along. That Dupier! Taking the boy without permission. Lucky he's going tomorrow."

"I'll go with you," Mrs. Fath said, and sped down the stairs before him.

"We'll take a cab," Mr. Fath said with a calmness he was far from feeling.

"It will be faster to walk," she suggested, and they hastened across the park and east on Eighth Street.

There were a few late shoppers left in Wanamaker's, but the huge doors had already been barred.

Mr. Fath pounded violently and an attendant appeared.

"It's half past five, sir. The store is officially closed."

"Well, my son is not officially home," roared Mr. Fath. "Let me see the manager immediately."

In a few minutes a gentleman in a cutaway showed himself in the doorway. He listened, then admitted the Faths.

Together they hurried to the toy department, but one by one the salesmen reported they did not remember seeing Henri or the tutor.

Now Mrs. Fath was swaying.

"Madame," the last of the salesmen said, "there were so many children, I could easily have missed him. He might have been here after all."

The Faths seemed incapable of moving.

The manager said, "Perhaps your little boy arrived

home while you were on your way here. You may be worrying yourself needlessly."

Mr. Fath took the arm of his wife, thanked the manager and the salesmen. "Come, my dear," he said gently. "Perhaps it is as the gentleman says. Probably Henri is already home."

She permitted herself to be led to the entrance.

Outside, she recovered. They started homeward slowly, but they were almost running as they neared the house.

Fraulein was waiting for them in the front hall; there had been no word of Henri.

Mrs. Fath sank onto the hatrack bench. "Oh God," she moaned. "What shall we do?"

Monsieur Fath suddenly was galvanized by an idea. "Of course! He has taken the child to church! Quick, Fraulein. Which church did Monsieur Dupier attend?"

"*Ich weiss nicht, Herr Fath,*" she whispered. "He never said."

"Someone must know. His family. His friends. What references did he give?"

"The agency," Mrs. Fath faltered.

"Yes, yes, I know. But what references?"

"Only from a Father Leclerc at St. Boniface. It's on East Twelfth Street, I think."

"Then that's where he must be." In a flash Fath was at the door. "You stay here in case he telephones. We must not miss any message."

Outside a tired cab horse limped into view. Mr. Fath got into the four-wheeler and banged his clenched hands on his knees in exasperation at the animal's slow gait. Finally the church loomed beside them.

"Wait here," he commanded the driver. "I will need you."

Inside the little church it was dark and silent. A few lonely worshippers were like dark shadows against the flickering light of the candles, and Mr. Fath experienced a strange feeling of unreality. As he approached the door beside the altar, a surpliced young priest appeared beside him.

"May I help you, my son?"

"Are you Father Leclerc? Do you know Monsieur Paul Dupier?"

"I am quite new here. Perhaps our priest —" He opened the door and ushered Fath into a small vestry. "Wait here a moment. Father is in the rectory." He disappeared behind another door, and returned a few minutes later with an elderly priest, who was introduced as Father Mahiere.

"Father Leclerc is no longer at St. Boniface," the old priest said. "I understand you are looking for a Monsieur Dupier?"

Mr. Fath told of his son's disappearance and, being essentially a fair-minded man, tried not to accuse Dupier falsely. After all, there might have been an accident. "But today was his last day," he concluded carefully, "and he has disappeared with my son."

"And you thought he might have brought him here?" The priest looked puzzled.

"Father," Fath spoke with difficulty, "I am not of your faith. Monsieur Dupier is a Catholic, extremely devout, perhaps too devout. He persisted in taking my children to Mass against my express instructions. I was obliged to dismiss him for that reason."

The priest began to show signs of agitation. "Have you been to his lodging house?"

"Not yet. There has been no time."

"I will go with you, Monsieur."

The young priest helped him on with his coat. Together Father Mahiere and Mr. Fath left the church and moved off in the waiting cab.

The brownstone lodging house at 201 East 14 Street was shabby, and the landlady slovenly. She knew nothing. Dupier had been paid up to the following Monday. Grudgingly she admitted them to Dupier's room. It had an untenanted look. Every vestige of an individual occupant had been removed; not even a scrap of paper had been left. The landlady unlocked the closet door. The closet had a toothless look, frightening in its emptiness.

Mr. Fath felt as if he were drowning.

"Come," the priest said. "We can do no good here."

They went down the front steps and re-entered the cab.

"Perhaps the boy is now home," the priest said.

Mr. Fath buried his face in his hands. "I'm frightened. For the first time in my life I'm frightened."

"You must have faith. We must pray for the safety of your son."

Fath saw him bow his head in prayer, and in his heart he joined him.

Mrs. Fath, pale and anxious, stood waiting at the door, flinched at the sight of them alone. But even in her distraught condition she remembered the rules of hospitality, led the way into the parlor, and presided at the tray of liqueurs.

The priest cleared his throat.

19

"What I am going to tell you about Paul Dupier was not told to me in confession. Nevertheless I would like your promise that you will not repeat it."

"Yes, yes," Mr. Fath said impatiently.

"Paul Dupier at one time studied to be a priest."

"A priest!" Mrs. Fath cried out.

"But he never became one. The seminary, for reasons of their own, did not allow him to finish his training."

"Why?" demanded Mr. Fath, all his worst suspicions compressed into the monosyllable.

The priest turned his palms up and shook his head.

"Henri," Mrs. Fath moaned, "my little boy—" She began to sob, deeply, spasmodically.

When her sobbing abated, the priest said softly, "Madame, rest assured. Your child is alive and well. Wherever he is, with Monsieur Dupier, he is being cared for as if he were his own. He will return home. You will see."

"But when?" Mrs. Fath cried. "And how? Do you know, Father, how frightened a little boy of seven can be?"

The priest bowed his head and made his own way to the front door.

The northbound train rolled steadily through the darkness, and Henri slept on in his deep sleep. At 7:10 a vendor came through with coffee and sandwiches. Dupier reached carefully into his left pocket, brought out some change, and bought a sandwich. He ate it with as little movement as possible. Then he settled back once more in his seat to stare out at the dark countryside.

CHAPTER
4

As soon as Father Mahiere had gone, Mr. Fath again
pulled on his coat.

"Where are you going, Auguste?"

"I am going to the police."

"Wait, I'm going with you." She held up a hand to
ward off his protests. "Do not tell me to wait at home.
That is far worse."

Fath helped her on with her coat. In the last few hours,
the face he loved had been turned to a grayish pallor
and marked by lines of strain.

The Tenth Precinct was at No. 24 MacDougal Street.
In a matter of minutes they were standing before a high
desk, behind which was perched a policeman with large
strawlike mustaches. He was writing in a huge ledger,
but when he saw them stand before him, he rose to his
feet.

"Someone has gone off with our boy." Mr. Fath's voice
rang in the barren room. "He has been kidnapped."

"Then you'll be wanting to see the lieutenant, sir. If

you'll come this way." He led them into a square dusty room. Behind a battle-scarred desk sat Lieutenant William O'Brien. He rose to greet them.

"Now," he seated himself, "please start from the very beginning." The brisk competence in his voice stirred the first faint glimmer of hope in Dolly Fath.

The lieutenant sat very still until Mr. Fath had finished. "Have you any idea of where he might have taken the boy, Mr. Fath? Think. Try to remember the very last thing that Frenchman said to you."

"He was with us less than a month. I barely spoke to him in the six days after I gave him notice."

"And you remember nothing significant in that last conversation?"

Something formless nagged at Mr. Fath's memory. He groped for it but without avail. "Nothing."

O'Brien persisted. "Try to remember every word . . . French or English."

Perhaps it was the word "French" that did it. What was that phrase that Dupier had murmured to himself? At last he blurted it out: *"Un arc du bois . . . en gopher."* But it still didn't make sense to him.

"What do the words mean?"

"An ark of gopher wood."

O'Brien frowned.

A terrified look came over Fath. He leaned forward and gripped the worn edges of the wooden desk in his fingers. "Lieutenant," his voice came out thin and strained, "did any boat leave New York today?"

"We'll check." He pressed on a bell and gave a brisk order. "What makes you think that, sir?"

"That phrase was God's admonition to Noah when He was about to destroy mankind. Only Noah had found

22

grace with God. The quotation is in the Old Testament, in the Book of Moses. God told Noah to build an ark to save himself, his family and two each of all the animals he might need." Fath ran his tongue over his dry lips. He did not look at his wife, but stared straight ahead at nothing. "Lieutenant, I am convinced now: Dupier has taken my son on a journey!"

"Excuse me sir." The straw mustached came in. "No boat left today, sir."

Fath felt himself slump.

"But one is due to leave tomorrow."

"Then there is time for a search!"

"Yes. There's time." The lieutenant leaned back on his old mahogany chair. "You say that Fraulein was the last person he spoke to in the household? What did he say to her?"

"That he was going to take Henri to see the trains at Wanamaker's."

"Would you mind repeating the exact words?"

Mr. Fath sighed. Mechanically he said: "You know what Henri likes to see the most!"

"Exactly! Fraulein jumped to the conclusion that the trains Henri wanted to see were in the store."

"Are you suggesting, lieutenant," Mrs. Fath's voice strained out of her taut throat, "that Dupier's ark of gopher wood may have been made of iron and steel?"

The lieutenant nodded, ran a finger under his collar. "Well, now," he said kindly, "let's start from the very beginning and go forward one step at a time. We will comb the city. Give me a description of the boy, and we'll warn all precincts to be on the lookout." He drew a piece of paper in front of him, and with pen poised, waited for Fath to begin.

23

"Heavy brown hair, fair complexion, dark blue eyes, he is seven years old and tall for his—"

Dolly Fath cried out, "Henri! my son, my son!"

After a moment, she lifted her head. "I'm sorry, lieutenant. He has a short nose slightly thick at the nostrils, and a tiny scar on the right side of his upper lip. The top second teeth were just coming in . . ." A shuddering sob shook her. "When he left he was wearing a gray Norfolk suit, knee pants, white shirt, blue striped bow tie, a cap, black stockings and black shoes."

"Thank you. By midnight this description will be in the hands of all the precincts. I'll assign a detective to the case immediately."

"I want a man who will let nothing stand in the way of finding my boy!"

"Detectives have many responsibilities. But you may rest assured he will do everything possible to find your son."

"That's not enough. I must have someone who will do nothing else."

"In that case, sir, I can only suggest you add a private detective."

"Who?"

"We are not supposed to recommend—however, Frank Mahoney. One of the best. He's out on a case, but I can get him to you first thing in the morning. Meanwhile we'll get started." O'Brien pressed a button and sent the deskman for Detective Thomas. Then he brought out a printed sheet of paper.

"Where do you propose to start?"

"With the hospitals. There is always the possibility . . ." His voice trailed off.

"Of course."

There was a knock on the door and a moon-faced man entered, his hat pushed back on his balding head. He removed it quickly when he saw the Faths, took the sheet of hospital information, and left.

Fath rose and extended his hand to O'Brien. "Thank you, lieutenant. I know we are in the best hands."

Mr. Fath took his wife outside and hailed a cab.

"Go home, Dolly. There may still be word. There are things I must do before I come home myself."

He returned to the police station and waited while Detective Thomas phoned the hospitals. Then he wandered back to the Square. He questioned shopkeepers and acquaintances who passed by, but the only ones he could find who had seen Henri were Mr. Dowling and Madame Liebling. And they could add nothing more than they had seen Dupier and Henri cross the Square diagonally in the general direction of Wanamaker's.

Twice during the night, Detective Thomas thought he found someone answering Henri's description; twice Mr. Fath went with him on fruitless journeys. At four o'clock in the morning, Thomas gave up for the night and advised Fath to do the same.

Mr. Fath stumbled across his threshold and up to his room. His wife lay on their bed, fully dressed, fast asleep. Mr. Fath lay down beside her. They both slept.

And a little past four o'clock, the train dragged into Rouse's Point. Two customs officials boarded the train and moved quietly down the aisles, asking questions, rustling papers.

Dupier's voice was steady as he answered their questions. As the one official spoke, the other raised his lantern to look more closely at Henri.

"You will wake him," cautioned Dupier.

The lantern was lowered.

"A beautiful child, Monsieur."

Dupier lowered his head and crossed himself. "The orphan of my brother and his sainted wife. They were destroyed in a fire. I could save only him."

"A terrible tragedy, Monsieur, but a miracle the boy was saved."

"Yes," Dupier nodded his head, "truly God's will."

Early the next morning, a lean red-haired man paused on the stoop of the Fath house. He had hesitated about coming at such an hour, but O'Brien had said it was urgent. He rang the bell.

An hour later Frank Mahoney was back on the stoop. He descended the steps, and stood there for a moment sorting out his thoughts.

He dismissed the possibility of boats. First of all, the police were checking them. Secondly, he felt that Dupier would have been a fool to stay in the city overnight; the risk of discovery was too great.

Would Dupier be holding the child for ransom in a nearby state?

Perhaps.

But he doubted it. From what he had heard, they were dealing with a man to whom money was unimportant: in the time he had been employed, Mr. Fath had said, Dupier had never once asked for his weekly salary. In fact he had never collected the last week's salary due him.

Then where had they gone?

Fraulein, having seen them cross the park in the middle of the Square, had assumed they were on their way to Wanamaker's. He would have to retrace those steps.

He did, asking questions along the way. Soon he found himself on Waverly Place.

Dupier had either entered there or gone straight up Eighth Street in order to continue east. Mahoney hesitated a moment and decided on Waverly. The next cross street running north and south was Greene Street. He turned left on it and approached Eighth Street.

A shoe shine boy said, "Shine, Mister?"

"You work this beat every day?"

The boy nodded.

"Were you here yesterday, say, about four o'clock?"

"I said I was here every day."

"Did you see a tall thin man and a small boy pass around that time?"

"Lots of fathers take their kids out on Saturday afternoon."

"Here." Mahoney fished in his pocket. "Ever see this particular little boy before?"

The boy wiped his hands on his trousers, took the picture, and studied it.

"Yeah, I saw him. They went right by here yesterday. The kid had some swell clothes on."

"Which direction did they go in?"

"They walked to Eighth Street and turned right."

"Thanks, son." Mahoney pressed a quarter into the boy's hand. "Thanks very much." He broke into a dog-trot.

Wʜᴇɴ Henri finally awakened the sun was shining. He sat up, rubbed his eyes, and looked about him in bewilderment. "Didn't the train stop during the night, Monsieur?"

"Yes, it did."

"Where are we now, Monsieur?"

"Almost home, Henri." Dupier smiled. "Hurry now. We must get off."

"Home!" The boy said the word softly to himself. Relief rose and swelled within him. That meant Mama, Papa, Charles, and Emilie. Fleetingly he thought of all the things he would have to tell them. He closed his eyes the better to see them, and for an instant could almost smell Mama's lilac perfume.

When the train stopped Monsieur Dupier jumped off the high step, swung Henri high into the air before setting him on the ground. Henri laughed a little, pulled Dupier eagerly by the hand. The conductor saw them and waved. They walked rapidly out into the station.

But it wasn't the same station at all! Where was the Grand Central Station?

There were signs all over with two kinds of writing on them. It took a few moments before Henri, recalling some words from his few French lessons, was able to identify the second language. What kind of a station was it where they had signs in French? In a frightened whisper he said, "Monsieur, where are we?" And his heart felt as if it would pound through his chest.

Monsieur Dupier hurried on as if he had not heard.

Henri tugged violently at his hand once more. "Monsieur, this is not the same station at all!" Panic overwhelmed him. "Monsieur, we are not back again. I want to go home!"

His despairing cry rang out in the station. A few people turned their heads.

"Sh-sh, Henri. Remember you are a little gentleman. We must catch another train." Monsieur Dupier was almost running now. "Hurry, Henri, or we shall miss it."

"No!" Henri screamed and stopped abruptly. "I don't want to go on another train. I want to go home. I want my Mama!

He braced his feet against the floor and held his body rigid, immovable. "Mama!" he cried out. "I want my Mama! I want to go home!"

Monsieur bent down, put an arm around the boy's shoulders as if to comfort him. "It isn't nice to make a scene in public," he whispered. And before Henri knew it, he was lifted into the air and deposited on the top step of a waiting train. This was a smaller one. Not nearly so grand or noisy as the one from the city.

Henri grasped the meaning of the strange train. He

was being taken farther away from his Mama, Papa, Charles, and Emilie. He grabbed the side of the door jamb and began to scream in terror.

A man in the station started towards him. Just then the train began to move. The man hesitated a moment, then shrugged his shoulders and turned away.

With Henri still screaming, slowly the train clinked out of the station and picked up speed until it was rolling rapidly through green fields.

Monsieur Dupier disengaged Henri's hand from the door and dragged him along. He pushed him, still sobbing and shaking, onto a seat alongside the window, then sat down beside him so that he could not get out.

"I want to go home!"

Heads turned in the aisle. Monsieur leaned out and said something. In a moment, no one heeded his cries. But Henri continued to hiccup and sob.

Monsieur put his arms around him, trying to quiet him. Henri slid right through them onto the floor, between their seat and the one in front. His throat aching, he kept on crying over and over again, "Take me back. Please Monsieur, take me back."

How long he sat there sobbing violently, he did not know. Finally he leaned back, the sobs dying away in exhaustion.

Monsieur Dupier reached down, lifted him back on the seat, and held him there. "You must stop crying this way, Henri. I do not understand what has happened to you. Always you've been such a perfect little gentleman." His voice, low and reasonable, purred on close to the boy's ear. "Have you not always said you wanted to see trains—real live trains?"

Now Henri, his cap awry, his clothes wrinkled, his

heavy brown hair mussed, and his eyes swollen with crying, ceased to struggle.

"We'll get home eventually, I promise you. I have
never broken a promise to you, Henri. I never will."

Then Dupier released him and Henri leaned back
against the seat.

Mahoney crossed Astor Place and went on to Third
Avenue. Time. Time was so important. He ran up the
steps to the elevated.

"I'm sorry, sir." The stationmaster pushed the picture
back under the wicket.

"Is it possible that such a man with this boy bought
tickets from you yesterday afternoon?"

"Oh, it's possible. But I wouldn't remember. What was
the boy wearing?"

"Gray Norfolk suit, white shirt, cap, striped bow tie,
black shoes and stockings."

"There was a boy. I didn't see his face, but he was
wearing something like you say. They missed a train."

And from the agent Mahoney learned that a conductor
named Higgins had been on duty aboard the train that
Dupier had probably taken. However, Higgins would not
be coming through for another hour. Mahoney glanced
at his watch. It was almost ten. There was no sense in
waiting; he might as well go on to Grand Central.

On the train clinking northward, Dupier was doing his
best to distract Henri.

"Do you know why this train is different from the
others?" He explained at length, but Henri only stared
straight ahead, tears sliding down his cheeks.

A vendor came lurching down the aisle with a tray

31

of milk and rolls. Monsieur took some coins from his pocket and bought two rolls and some milk. The man exchanged a few words with Monsieur Dupier, then said something else to Henri.

Henri shook his head. What was the man saying? Had he started by saying "*Bonjour*"?

Bonjour? Bonjour was French—Monsieur had taught them that almost the very first thing. What had happened? Had he overnight slept into another world? Henri held the milk and rolls in his hands.

"Eat, Henri," implored Monsieur Dupier. "You must eat so as not to get too tired from this long journey."

He lifted the roll to his mouth and bit a piece off, but it would not go down. Even a long drink of milk did not help.

"Please, Monsieur, must I eat?"

"Very well." Monsieur took the roll from him and wrapped it in a clean handkerchief. "Later, then. It is a sin to waste. Later on you will eat it. Now drink your milk!"

Obediently Henri lifted the cup to his mouth. The milk tasted strange to him, but he drank it.

Mahoney showed the picture around at Grand Central depot, but no one recognized the boy. Then he went straight to the stationmaster.

The man looked at the picture, shook his head.

"Well, tell me about the afternoon trains out of here."

"That's a tall order, mister, but we'll try." He busied himself with some time tables. "What time do you think they got here?"

"They left the house just before four o'clock. I figure it took them about twenty-five minutes and he probably had it timed to board a particular train soon after they arrived. I'd guess the train left after four-thirty but before five."

"About four forty-five, eh?" The stationmaster found the place on the time table. " Here's one." Mahoney followed the finger as it trailed down the line: Albany, Glens Falls, Plattsburg, Rouse's Point, Ste. John, Montreal.

Montreal!

Montreal was out of the country. In Canada. Of course! Precisely where Dupier would go. Back to where he came from!

"Can we check at the windows? Maybe someone can recall selling them tickets for one of these places."

"We could ask."

No one at the windows could identify Henri. The stationmaster led the way back to his office.

"Three conductors were on that train. One lives in Albany, the other in Glen Falls, the third I don't know about. Want me to get their addresses?"

Mahoney nodded.

"They should have left Montreal this morning, and they'll probably get off at their homes on the way back. I'll check their days off." He glanced up at the clock. "A train leaves here within the hour. Gets you to Albany around five o'clock. There's a half hour layover there. If you move fast, you can catch it again. The next stop on the line is Glens Falls. I wish you luck."

The small Canadian Pacific train dragged from one small station to another. The sun climbed higher and higher and then began to recede once more. Finally, when it seemed as if the train could not possibly go any farther, it ground its way to a stop before a large open shed, a long, empty platform, and a big sign that said TROIS RIVIERES. To Henri, weary and disheartened, the sign meant nothing.

Monsieur Dupier did not take Henri through the station at all, but led the way to the end of the platform and stepped down onto a vast meadow. They crossed it, and Henri found himself walking along a broad dirt road. For a while they seemed to be paralleling the train tracks. Then they came to another broad dirt road which forked to their left. Large black letters on an arrow pointed the way.

"Shawinigan Falls," Monsieur said. "Factories, foreigners, and infidels. That is where we do *not go*. For us, Henri, the path will always lie straight ahead."

The country was hilly, with masses of gneiss and polished boulders. Even the trees looked strange to Henri, a profusion of tamarac, sparse spruce, and slim white birch. An occasional bird cawed in the great silence against the flush of the late September sky. There was no trace of a human being. How lonely it was.

This must be the end of the world, thought Henri. He no longer felt like the same little boy, but someone else, cut off from everyone and everything he had ever known. He felt almost like the mechanical boy who walked when you wound him up, a German toy Fraulein had given him last Christmas. And the man who pulled him along by the hand seemed a total stranger, someone to be afraid of.

Finally they passed close to a river, where low bushes of dull orange, tiny patches of russet and gold glinting in the sun peeped above the oddly shaped rocks.

"Mark these gorges, Henri. See how the sides run

down to the river. These rock formations have been left by glaciers of long ago."

Henri made no reply. Dupier looked at him sharply, opened his mouth to speak further, then decided against it. They walked on in silence.

Was it for one hour, two, or three? Henri did not know, but it seemed forever. He knew only that he could not go on any farther, but he did go on until his legs were iron weights and his eyes could not see. Finally he stumbled and sprawled on the ground. He tried to will his body to get up, but it would not obey him.

"I can't, Monsieur. I cannot walk any farther." He was too frightened even to cry, and lay quivering in terror on the road.

Monsieur Dupier lifted Henri in his arms, walked a short way to a stream, and laid him on the grass. From his pocket he took the roll, and fed it to him a little at a time. In his cupped hands he brought fresh water to Henri. It was barely enough to wet his mouth, but it refreshed him.

The boy rested.

"Can you stand now?" Dupier asked at last.

Henri stood up on trembling legs; he did not fall.

Monsieur shaded his eyes with his hands and scanned the landscape.

"Do you think you could walk that far, Henri?" He pointed to the dim outline of a farmhouse. "Perhaps the farmer there will drive us the rest of the way."

The rest of the way where?

He was not really going home. Henri knew that now. He was going farther and farther away from all he knew. What could he do? He wanted his mother so much. Perhaps he might get the farmer alone for a moment, and tell him how worried his mother must be. And his father, and Fraulein.

Yes. He would have to tell the farmer, and maybe the farmer would take him. He did not want Monsieur to take him anywhere ever again. He would like to lose him here, in this big strange country. Yes, he would talk to the farmer. Farmers were always kind men—his story-book said so. And big and strong. The resolution seemed to revive him more than the roll and water.

"I could walk that far," he said.

"Good." Monsieur took his hand.

It was so far to the farmhouse, but he kept telling himself that soon, very soon now, he would find a nice, kind, happy man who would lift him in his big, strong arms and take him home to his mother.

But this farmer was not big and strong, and did not look happy at all, or kind. He was sullen and dried out, and the only thing large about him were his whiskers, which were long and bristly.

Monsieur spoke to him rapidly, in the unfamiliar language Henri now knew was French, though he did not understand it. Moments later the realization sank in: this farmer would not understand one word of English. Despair engulfed him.

The farmer gestured at Henri. Monsieur Dupier began to speak more rapidly. The farmer shook his head and made signs for Henri to go into the kitchen.

A small lady, with the same dried-up look as her husband, stood before the stove. Seeing Henri, she dropped her ladle, and wiped her hands on her apron. She smiled at the boy. In a moment she brought Henri a steaming bowl of soup, and some fresh white coarse bread. For the first time he was able to swallow despite the terrible ache in his throat.

Monsieur Dupier stepped outside with the farmer.

Now! Now was the time. Someone had to understand him. She had to!

"Please lady!" To his own consternation Henri burst into tears again. He slid off the chair and threw his arms around the little woman's knees. "Please lady, I want to go home to my Mama. I don't want to see any more trains. I want to go home. Take me home to my Mama!"

Puzzled, she put her hand to his head. At that moment Dupier returned. She spoke rapidly to him in French.

Dupier shook his head and began to speak sadly and reasonably to the woman. Henri saw her eyes cloud over, as she bent down to lean her cheek against his. She said something to him in a soothing voice.

They left almost immediately after that. Henri did not say anything more to the farmer or his wife; he knew it would be useless. He allowed himself to be lifted by Monsieur Dupier into the rude farm wagon, and they drove off.

Soon a few small square houses began appearing at the side of the road, some with only one window and a door. The houses were precariously perched on short round posts, and the wind swept in slow gusts beneath their bottoms. Then no more houses, only the open fields rolling endlessly on either side of them, and a few cattle or an emaciated horse wandering about.

"But someone will come for me soon, and take me home," he said to himself, over and over again.

There was no hint of a village, but suddenly there it was, around a bend in the road—a sprawling stretch of boxlike houses with a dirt road running through it, and no sidewalks.

Dupier scanned the length of the shabby street. "The

Capuchins have kept Ste. Anne of the Prairies secure," he said with satisfaction.

And that was how Henri learned where they were. "Ste. Anne of the Prairies." He had never heard of such a place before, and he wondered if his father, who knew everything, ever had. But of course a man like his father would know of Ste. Anne of the Prairies. And of course he would know where to look for his little boy.

The one- and two-story buildings, sagging and unsightly, had only an occasional porch to relieve their monotonous similarity. Henri could not have told what color they were; they had no color. And the village people seemed colorless, too, and blended dully with the background. Here and there stood a group of meager birches. A few shop signs swayed in the evening breeze. Henri could not find a single English word.

Suddenly they were in the middle of a square, and Henri rubbed his eyes in amazement.

Rising above the low gray buildings was the most beautiful building Henri had ever seen—dark, majestic as a castle in a fairy-book, with tall, thrilling spires.

"Is it a castle?"

Dupier did not answer at once. Henri could see that his face wore a strange look, and he gazed at the wonderful building as if he could never see it enough.

"It *is* a castle! And you know what, Henri?" There was a flush in the tutor's cheeks and his eyes glittered as he bent his face close to Henri's. "The King is waiting to welcome us."

Mahoney sat back in his seat and listened to the rhythmic clicking of the wheels. The sun slid lower in the sky.

Two other trains had left within fifteen minutes of this

39

one—one bound for Boston, and the other for the west. Had he been right in deciding that Dupier must have taken this one, and just because he was French Canadian? Would he dare to go back home with a child who did not belong to him? It seemed very risky.

From all reports, Henri was an unusually bright child. How could he have allowed himself to be brought aboard a Montreal-bound train away from his parents? That was a puzzler.

Perhaps, thought Mahoney, he'd been enticed aboard just to look. Still, once there, he could easily have called for help. Henri could have asked the conductor to take him back.

It didn't make sense. Mahoney shook his head tiredly, and looked out the window. Fall had taken complete possession of the land. Acres of apple trees, stripped of their fruit, with withering brown leaves, slid by the window in the gray twilight.

The train barely ground to a stop at Albany when Mahoney jumped off and took a cab. The conductor he sought had the consideration to live within a short distance of the station, but he had never seen Henri before. He was positive.

Mahoney sprinted for the station.

The train was moving as he arrived. He swung aboard the last car.

It was the same story with the Glen Falls conductor, the only difference being that he could not get back in time to catch the train and had hours to wait, hours to torture himself. One break, only one—

If only he had a picture of Dupier, it would help. Or would it? Though he had one of Henri, so far only the description of the gray Norfolk suit had proved helpful.

The next train for Montreal was the four forty-five

from New York. It finally arrived ten minutes late, and wearily Mahoney climbed aboard.

Monsieur Dupier directed the wagon around a corner and drew up before one of the small gray boxlike structures. The farmer lit a lantern while Dupier fumbled in his purse.

Henri wanted to cry out to the farmer not to leave him, to take him home. Desperately he summoned all his strength and, as loudly as he could, called out: "Good-bye, sir!"

Both the farmer and Dupier turned around, startled by the outburst.

"One says *au revoir,* not good-bye," Dupier said to Henri.

The farmer's dried face cracked into a smile. He touched his hand to his worn cap.

"*Au revoir, mon petit.*" With a wave of his hand, he lifted his reins and clucked to his horses.

Henri gazed after the farmer's wagon. His throat was taut and his eyes burning as he watched his last hope drive away. His eyes strained after the flickering lamp until it became small as a firefly in the distance, then disappeared entirely.

Dupier had opened the door. He motioned for Henri to enter, and busied himself raising the wick of a lamp.

Henri stood at the door while his eyes reluctantly crept over the room. Something cold ran through his veins; the house was waiting for someone.

For him?

But why?

It couldn't be. He wasn't staying here, he didn't belong here.

Then why were there two cots?

41

Dimly he was aware of an iron sink, shelves with a few tins of food, and a squat, pot-bellied stove.

Fright and weariness propelled Henri forward. He sank onto one of the four straight chairs grouped about the wooden table in the center of the bare floor.

"Quickly now, Henri, get undressed and into bed."

With stiff, trembling fingers Henri removed his tie and suit. He hung the garments over a chair and stood uncertainly in his underwear.

Dupier pulled back the covers on one of the cots. Henri sat down on it and removed his shoes and stockings.

"Tomorrow," Dupier nodded toward the valise, "there will be a nightshirt."

Henri pulled up the covers and lay rigid. The sheets were cold and damp. He kept on shivering even after Monsieur had tucked in the covers.

He closed his eyes, but his mind ran around like a squirrel in a cage, seeking desperately for a way out.

Why was he here? Why was he not at home with his darling Mama and Papa and Emilie and Charles?

Slowly the warm tears rolled down his cheeks. He did not dare cry aloud for fear that Monsieur Dupier would hear him.

Why was he now so afraid of Monsieur Dupier? He had never been unkind before, he had never been bad. Why had Monsieur taken him away? He must have known that Mama would cry. That in itself made him bad, someone to be afraid of.

Henri turned on his side and lay listening, wide-eyed, to the pounding of his heart. And he thought of Mama. He stretched his hands in the night and could almost touch her. But when he tried, she disappeared, and his arms dropped emptily to his sides.

Mahoney got off at Rouse's Point, home of the third conductor on what he hoped was the train Dupier and Henri had taken.

The custom officials checked all the passengers; then, as the train pulled out, they escorted Mahoney into the immigration office.

They exclaimed sympathetically as Mahoney told them the story. Then he showed them the picture.

"Last night!" the official with the lantern cried out. "I remember him. A most beautiful child. Fast asleep!"

At last, here was a lead! "Are you sure?"

"Let us check our records. Paul Dupier, you say? Yes, yes. He was returning to Montreal with his nephew, Henri Dupier."

"Couldn't you tell the child was an American?"

"He was asleep, Monsieur. In a deep, deep sleep."

In a deep sleep. Of course! How simple the answer was. Dupier had given Henri a drug.

"Is there any way of checking whether he really got off at Montreal? He may have gotten off at St. John."

"We would have no way of knowing that, Monsieur. Unless perhaps a conductor saw them."

One of the customs officials knew exactly where the conductor lived and drove Mahoney there in his own gig.

The conductor listened quietly and peered closely at the photograph. "That's him," he said positively. "Got off in Montreal."

"Was he awake? Did he seem all right?"

"He was a fine boy, very well dressed. That's why I remember him. The man lifted him high into the air, and the boy looked up at the sun and laughed. Then they hurried into the station. That was the last I saw of them."

43

They drove back to the border station in silence.

The other official at the station had more good news for Mahoney. He had located Dupier's Montreal address.

Mahoney had prayed for a miracle, and for a moment he thought the prayer had been answered.

Mahoney walked up the ramp into the Windsor station. He glanced up at the clock. It was seven forty-five. If Dupier were in Montreal, he must have arrived at this station at just about this time yesterday morning.

Outside he spied one cab in the line with a small sign in the windshield, ENGLISH SPOKEN. He gave the address to the cab driver and settled himself within.

About fifteen minutes later, his driver was translating the rapid-fire patois of the landlady: "Dupier has not lived here for two years. He left no forwarding address. She remembers no relatives, no one visiting him."

The driver paused to listen a moment more, and added, "She says he was *étrange*—an odd one, Monsieur. Not like the rest of us."

"Insane? Could he have been insane?"

The driver turned to the landlady. "*En fou?*" he asked. Mahoney gathered that was the French word for insane. The landlady hesitated, then shrugged her shoulders uncertainly.

Mahoney left his card, but without hope.

Then came the routine of the police and the newspapers. Henri's picture would go into the Montreal papers the next day. The police promised to get in touch with the conductors on all trains leaving Montreal. Any identification would be telegraphed to New York immediately.

Exhausted and depressed, Mahoney rode back to the

Windsor station, paid off the driver, and sought out the stationmaster.

The man was most cooperative. He went off with the picture and returned in a few minutes. "No. No one has seen this child, Monsieur."

"Where do I go from here?" Mahoney muttered to himself.

"You could go anywhere, Monsieur. On the Canadian Pacific."

Of course! Mahoney hadn't thought of that. He had been so sure of finding Dupier in Montreal that it never occurred to him they might have gone beyond. Now the search was extended through all of Canada. The realization made him ill.

The stationmaster went on, "We have trains as far west as Vancouver, and as far north as Quebec. At eight o'clock in the morning there is a local that goes through Three Rivers up to Quebec. Have you any idea of their destination?"

"I wish I knew."

"Well, the Quebec train stops at Montreal West, St. Martin, St. Vincent de Paul, St. Barthelmy, Pointe du Lac, Trois Rivieres, and then fourteen more stops to Quebec City."

Mahoney stood motionless.

"Then there is the train to the west, Monsieur, also with many, many stops."

"Thank you," Mahoney said humbly.

"It is a vast search, Monsieur," the stationmaster said sympathetically. "I wish you luck."

"I doubt if anyone has that kind of luck." Mahoney said his good-byes and bought a ticket for New York.

CHAPTER
7

HENRI woke up with a start. He heard none of the familiar sounds of Fraulein bustling about, of Charles or Emilie. Only silence greeted him. He sat up in bed. His eyes traveled about the ugly room.

Monsieur Dupier's bed was empty. He was gone! Where? And for how long?

Realizing he was alone and free at last, Henri jumped out of bed and ran to the window. The sun was high and bright, and the people looked as if they had been up for hours. He dressed quickly, opened the door, peered out, and ran out into the street and off in the direction of the square they had passed the night before.

Along the way he passed no one. In front of one house he heard the wail of a child, and a woman's voice call comfortingly. Then he heard a man laugh. Mothers, fathers and children—what nice sounds they made.

Then he was in the Square, tugging urgently at a woman's skirts. "Please, my name is Henri Fath. I live at

77 Washington Square West, New York City. I'm lost. Please take me home to my mother."

To his horror the woman shook her head.

Why? Why wouldn't she take him home to his Mama? The woman looked troubled, and said something he could not understand. Of course! She did not understand him either!

Then a man passed close by and Henri ran to him. "Please, sir, my name in Henri Fath. I live at 77 Washington Square West—" The man shook his head, too, and moved on.

Henri could not believe it. Surely someone must understand English!

He ran about the square crying, "Please, sir, please, ma'am!" Yes, he had to remember his manners so Mama would be proud of him. "Please, please, my name is Henri Fath!" He ran from one to the other, tugging frenziedly for attention, but no one could understand, not a single one.

A policeman strode into sight, and Henri's spirits soared. Here at last was help. Didn't Mama always say a policeman would take him home if he were ever lost? He ran headlong into the man and clutched at his legs.

"My name is Henri Fath," he gasped and burst into tears. "I want my Mama," he sobbed. "Please take me home!"

The policeman gently disengaged the boy from his trouser leg and spoke to him in the language Henri had learned to dread.

Suddenly Henri stiffened. Monsieur Dupier, his arms full of bundles, was coming toward him!

Swiftly Monsieur put down his bundles, and lifted Henri in his arms.

"*Mon pauvre petit,*" he patted the tousled head. He turned to the crowd and spoke to the policeman, and Henri did not understand a word that was said. He knew only that the people shook their heads and looked sad and went away. He struggled, beat his fists at Monsieur's shoulder.

"No, no!" he cried after the people. "Don't go. Please. Please take me home to my mother." But he knew now it was no use.

"You have distressed me," Monsieur Dupier said, putting Henri back on his feet and picking up his bundles.

The policeman patted Henri's head, said something, and turned away. In complete disbelief Henri watched him go on down the street. If a policeman wouldn't help him, then maybe no one would.

Fearful and confused, he followed along after Monsieur.

They passed many of the boxlike houses. In one yard a woman was hanging out her wash; in another a woman was putting her baby out in a battered carriage; a third woman was walking down the steps with a market bag in her hand. This was what mothers did. Then why didn't they help him, even if they didn't understand his language? Didn't they see he was alone? That he didn't belong to Monsieur Dupier? That he must have a mama and a papa somewhere?

Together he and Monsieur Dupier entered the house. Trembling, he sat down on the edge of the cot, and gripped the side with his hands. What would Monsieur Dupier do to him now—now that he'd tried to leave him and go home to Mother? Monsieur might become angry, very angry.

Monsieur took his time. He put the groceries away.

Then he tidied his bed. Finally he spoke, but it was only to tell Henri to make his bed. With shaking fingers Henri fumbled with the covers. In the end Monsieur had to help him.

"But no more," he cautioned. "You are old enough to do it for yourself." Then he went and busied himself at the stove. "It is almost lunch time and we have yet to eat our breakfast."

The thick gruel was not very good, but Henri was afraid not to eat it. At last he was allowed to push the half-finished bowl aside, but he refused the thick slice of bread and molasses that Dupier offered him.

Monsieur rose and opened a small paper bag. He pushed his hand in and came out with a few colorless store cookies.

"Biscuit Village," Dupier announced with satisfaction. "I was able to eat these all through my childhood." He placed two in front of Henri. Then he poured some milk from a can into a thick tumbler. "Milk is a luxury in Ste. Anne. Usually we save it for special occasions. Why, do you know that in many homes, even the white sauce does not contain milk! It is made with water."

Henri watched Monsieur as he briskly worked the pump handle, rinsed the dishes and left them on the wooden drain board alongside the tin sink.

"*Bien*, Henri." Monsieur beamed unexpectedly. "Now we will talk about going to school."

Henri looked at him blankly. School! School was where Miss Brown was. Pretty, gentle Miss Brown. The thought of her suddenly gave him courage. "Please, Monsieur, Miss Brown will be quite angry with me if I am not in school. May we please go home now?"

"You *are* home, Henri." Monsieur's voice held conviction. His dark eyes, with their heavy lids, glittered at the boy.

Henri's eyes widened as he looked around the bare room. Home! This ugly place home? Here even the sun looked different.

This could *never* be his home. Mama and Papa weren't here. He began to tremble again. "I want my Mama."

"The Mother of God," Monsieur whispered, "is the Mother of us all, Henri. And She is here."

Monsieur rose and took a blue china statue from the shelf where it had been resting under the picture of a man on a cross. Henri had glanced at the man once, but not again: he had found him strangely upsetting.

"This is Mary, Mother of God, Mother of us all, Henri."

"It is only a doll," Henri blurted out. "Like Emilie's, almost." Then he added miserably, "Only this one's hands and arms don't even move."

"Oh, yes, they move!" Monsieur's dark eyes bored into Henri's. "They move, Henri, in mysterious ways. When you learn to believe in Her, you will find out how your prayers can be answered. But first you must prove yourself worthy."

How could a china doll get him back those many miles? There was no one to help him. He sat quiet and hopeless.

Then something stirred in his memory. The lady looked familiar because he had seen her before, in Monsieur's church at home. She was much bigger there. He had seen many people kneel before her. Monsieur had told him that they came to her for help and guidance.

But what did Henri have to do with her? She didn't belong in a place like B'nai Peyser any more than Henri belonged to St. Boniface. She concerned people like Dupier. There was no relationship between him and Dupier. There never would be. So far as Henri was concerned, the only mother who could help him was his own. And she would find him. Very soon now. He would write her a letter.

That was it! He would write her a letter. He could write his name and address, and enough to make his mother know where he was, so she could come for him.

But where could he get some paper and an envelope? What had Dupier been talking about before he spoke of the blue china lady? A school. He had better get there as soon as possible, so that he could get hold of a paper and pencil without Dupier knowing.

Dupier was on his knees before the figure. Henri glanced up at her face. She seemed to be smiling a little in a sad kind of way. Well, he didn't dislike her.

But his concern now was to write a letter. How could he get Dupier to take him to the school as quickly as possible?

"How soon can I start learning?"

At the question Dupier had turned pale. His thin neck jerked. Henri could see the big bump in the middle of it move up and down.

"My son," he whispered huskily, "it is never too soon. Today we shall finish preparations. Tomorrow we shall begin."

Mahoney's train from Montreal was a slow one. It brought him into the Grand Central Station about six-thirty Tuesday morning. He had breakfast and at seven-thirty he rang the bell of the Fath house.

51

He reported to Mr. Fath briefly, offering no false hope, concluding only that Henri was alive and well when last seen in Montreal. After that, nothing.

"Alive and well." Mr. Fath ran a hand over his unshaven chin. "How alive and well can a child—?" His voice broke.

"The police were very cooperative, sir. They promised to canvass the country and wire us immediately."

"They were most cooperative, most kind," Fath said dully. He pushed several telegrams forward. "From all reports, Henri was seen as far west as Vancouver, and as far north as Quebec. At least six tall, thin, dark men with French accents were traveling with young boys in gray Norfolk suits this past week-end."

"They all have to be checked out."

Mr. Fath brought out a map. "Would you like to see this, Mr. Mahoney? When the wires came, I checked the area of Canada. It is 3,684,723 square miles." He traced the boundaries with his finger. "Taken altogether it is approximately three per cent larger than the United States and Alaska combined."

Mahoney nodded.

"But somewhere in there is my son, Mahoney. I want him back if it costs me every penny I have in this world."

"Of course you know, sir, that at best it is only a remote chance."

"Yes."

"In that case," Mahoney said, rising, "I'll get help, and we'll give it the best we've got."

Mr. Fath saw him to the door. Only when he returned to his study did his composure break. He lifted his face, swayed back and forth. "My God, my God, why hast thou forsaken me?"

After a while he listened. Dolly—had she heard him? He must not upset her any further. Quietly he tiptoed up the stairs.

There she lay, wide awake and staring. He sat down beside her and smoothed back her hair.

"Would you like some breakfast, my love?"

"I would like to die."

Shocked, he sat speechless. Finally: "Mahoney has gone to hire more help. We will comb Canada."

"And you will not find him."

Her certainty chilled him and angered him at the same time. Of course she was wrong, but it would not do to argue with her now.

Suddenly she rose, put on her robe and went to the door.

"Where are you going, Dolly?"

"I am going to Henri's room." She moved swiftly down the hall.

Slowly Mr. Fath got up and followed his wife. He was in time to hear her lock the door of Henri's room and throw herself on her son's bed. He waited for the sound of weeping but none came.

"Dolly!" He rattled the knob. "Open the door. Let me stay with you."

"Please leave me now. Please go away. Please."

Mr. Fath hesitated, then turned and walked down the steps and out of the house.

Go? Where should he go?

He walked. His lips were moving, and he was barely conscious of the words. "Deliver me, O my God, out of the hand of the wicked, out of the hand of the unrighteous and cruel man. For thou art my hope, O Lord God, thou art my trust from my youth . . . ."

Suddenly he focused on the building before him.

It was the synagogue to which he contributed generously from his purse, but little from his heart.

B'nai Peyser, his synagogue. His? Had he any claim anymore?

He entered. A man in the back handed him a Tallith and a Tephillin.

"Blessed art thou, O Lord, our God, King of the universe, who hath sanctified us by his commandments . . . ." His lips murmured the long unused prayer as he wrapped the Tallith, the praying shawl, around him.

"How precious is thy loving kindness, O God . . . ."

Moving forward to join the meager congregation, he readied himself to coil the Tephillin, the leather strap, around his arm. To lay the Tehpillin meant dedicating his strength to God.

Strength? He had none left for himself. What did he have left for God? When he had finished coiling the leather thong around his middle finger, he began the prayer which traditionally followed: "Sanctify to me every firstborn, whatsoever openeth the womb, among the children of Israel, both of men and of beast: to me it belongeth . . . ."

"Forgive me, O Lord." Fath bent his head in anguish. "Even to you could I not bear to deliver my firstborn. Is that why I have been punished? Is that why he has been taken from me?" He wept into his open palms. "Take me. Take everything I own, but deliver back to me my son . . . my son . . . my son . . . ." He sobbed silently.

The half-hour service ended with the Twenty-third Psalm.

The Lord is my shepherd: I shall not want.
He maketh me to lie down in green pastures . . . .

Yea, though I walk through the valley of the shadow of death, I will fear no evil: for thou art with me: thy rod and thy staff they comfort me . . . .

"But I can find no comfort, oh Lord," Fath whispered brokenly. "Forgive me. I am alone and lost."

When Henri awoke early the next morning, Dupier had returned from Mass and was making breakfast. Henri was able to eat little of it. Dupier talked incessantly during and after the meal. When he had cleared away the dishes he said, "Come now, Henri. Take your cap. We must go and see what Our Lady, the Blessed Virgin has ordained for you." He took Henri's hand and they started out.

It was a long walk. They left the village behind and climbed a narrow path winding up a hill. Dry leaves crackled underfoot. Henri was grateful for the sound: everywhere else there seemed to be an unearthly stillness. Sawed-off tree trunks raised their dead humps amidst uncut weeds; and through the branches of the trees the sun slanted in long uneven slices.

Monsieur finally stopped and looked around. He spied a log. "It does not matter if we rest a bit."

Henri sat silent beside him. A bird screeched into a patch of sun, then darted upward and disappeared. He stared after it.

That seemed to be the only way to get out of here, thought Henri. Only by flying above the treetops. His eyes aching from looking into the high glare, he looked down. His shoes, he noticed, were quite dirty and covered with a fine layer of dust; his stockings were crooked and his knickerbockers wrinkled from the long journey.

Mama would be sad if she saw him this way.

His eyes filled with tears, and fearful lest they fall, he looked steadily down at the ground. He was barely conscious of Monsieur's voice running evenly alongside of him.

"Remember I am your family now. You must call me Uncle Paul. And Henri," Monsieur's eyes burned in his pale face, "if you wish to place yourself in Her care, you must not mention those others." He jerked his head to the south. "If the friars knew about them, you would not be permitted to enter, and the Blessed Mother of us all could not intercede for you."

He kept his head bent.

"Say Uncle Paul, now, Henri."

Henri's lips moved but no words came.

"Try again!" Monsieur's voice was sharp.

"Uncle Paul." It came out a small whisper.

"No matter." Monsieur was satisfied. "It will come with practice. It is time to go on now."

It was not much farther after that. They came out into a broad clearing; beyond a low brick wall, thick evergreens huddled together like a group of frightened children. On the left, lonely against the hill, stood a long sparse line of larches. Before them rose a small slim structure of gray stone with a tall spire in front, and a smaller one in the rear. They walked past the stained glass windows, and beyond lay a huge, three-story pile of dull red brick, with two wings jutting forward. The windows were small and narrow. Henri shivered. Surely she did not need so much room. And if she did, why did she have such small windows? Didn't she want to look out on the whole world?

They walked up a cobbled path. Grass hugged the sides like discolored carpets. The bell was in the form of a huge ring. Monsieur lifted it once. The bell sang a gentle tune. It was only two notes, but it made a song.

There was no sound as they waited. For a moment the world seemed to stand still. Then the door opened and a bearded young man appeared before them.

The first thing Henri noticed were the leather-thonged sandals on his feet. Then his eyes traveled up the long brown robe to the white cord around his waist. There were three heavy knots in it about eight inches apart. A heavy string of dark beads with a huge cross swung across his thigh as he moved.

The man listened to Monsieur and then motioned for them to follow. As he turned, Henri noticed a small round circle shaved close to the scalp at the back of his head.

For an instant they stood at the threshold of a long dark hall. Henri strained his eyes to see. At the very end of it he made a faint glimmer of light. With his hand still firmly held by Monsieur, he walked forward into the dark.

AT THE end of the hall Henri and Dupier were ushered into a small office. It was empty but for an old desk and four straight-backed chairs. On the bare walls were a figure of the man on the cross and a picture of the blue china lady. The bearded young man left them.

Through an open window Henri saw two men standing just outside. The one in a brown robe had his back turned, but Henri could see quite clearly the face of the other, a priest in a long black robe.

The priest laughed a little as he turned and sprang into a buggy. He clucked to his horse. Apparently he was very happy today. As his horse started to trot, he began whistling a song that sounded like "Sweet Genevieve."

Henri's lips silently formed the words:

> Genevieve, sweet Genevieve,
> The days may come, the days may go—

Henri stood stock still. That was the song his mother

sang! He could almost hear her at the piano right now. Anyone who knew that song would help him!

He broke away from Dupier, dashed out the door and into voluminous folds of cloth. He fought wildly.

Strong arms caught him, held him firmly at a distance, drew him back into the room.

"He's going away," Henri cried frantically, as he twisted to get free. "Please let me go or I will never catch him." And when he looked out the window again the buggy was disappearing from view.

Henri became aware that the man was talking to him, talking gently, but he did not understand his words nor did he care. He could only stand staring at the bend in the road where hope had once again disappeared.

Dupier said, "This is the Father Guardian, Henri. He is head of the friars in the monastery here."

Henri remained frozen in silence.

Dupier spoke rapidly to the friar in French.

Henri was aware only of the friar's pitying eyes. Unexpectedly he knelt beside Henri and put his arms around him. He had brown eyes as soft as velvet.

"No French?" Father Guardian asked in painful English.

Henri shook his head.

The friar pointed to himself with one hand: "No English." He pointed to Henri with the other hand: "No French." Then he put one hand across the other and smiled.

It took a moment for Henri to understand. The friar was trying to say he would teach him French, and in turn Henri would teach him English! Looking up, he caught the tight smile on Dupier's face, and knew he was right.

Henri's heart began to beat so loudly he was afraid

59

Dupier would hear it. Of course! He had to learn French! He had to learn French, or teach the Father Guardian English, so he could tell him how Dupier had taken him away from his Mama. And he would see to it that Henri got home. How long would it take before they could understand each other?

Then Henri remembered the letter he was going to write. No, he wouldn't have to learn French or teach the Father Guardian English. His mother would get his letter very soon. And the minute she got it, she would come for him. He knew she would.

The Father Guardian smiled and reseated himself behind his desk. Henri felt comforted for the first time in all those desperate hours, for he knew he had found a friend.

"It is settled, then," Dupier said. "You see, Henri, the good Capuchins keep an eye on the parochial school, which is a half mile to the west of here." He waved his hand in the direction of the plateau, in the center of which lay Ste. Anne. "But the seminary within these walls, ah, that is a goal to work for. Just a few are fortunate enough to be admitted here."

His eyes were fixed on Henri. After a moment, he continued: "There are so many applying from all the neighboring villages that the Capuchins take only the best. Only the *very* best. You would have to prove yourself a good student. And worthy."

The boy remained silent. He only half understood all that Monsieur Dupier was saying, and he did not care. He knew he would leave Ste. Anne and be at home again long before he was ready for any seminary.

Monsieur Dupier was waiting for him to speak. Henri raised his eyes to the friar's. Father Guardian did not need words. His smile seemed to understand.

"*Au revoir, mon petit,*" he said.

60

That meant good-bye. "*Au revoir*" was one of the words Monsieur had taught them when he had learned "*Bonjour*."

"*Au revoir*," Henri said.

The friar looked startled, then he laughed aloud. "*Ca va bien!*"

Ça va bien. Henri repeated it silently. *Ça va bien.* That must mean something is good. Then he repeated it out loud, and all three of them laughed.

Monsieur Dupier was in high spirits all the way home.

"You are not the only one who is going to school, Henri," he announced. "I am going also."

Henri looked at him in amazement. Whoever heard of a grownup going to school?

Monsieur seemed to read his mind. "Yes. It is the truth. We must eat, and in order to buy the salt pork, bread, sausages, and potatoes, one must work. What kind of work shall I do?" He cocked his head and waited for the boy to say something, but he continued to walk with his eyes glued to the ground. "I will teach," he announced triumphantly. "Is it not fortunate that my uncle left me a house near a village that needs a schoolmaster?"

In another moment they reached a dirt road, and the village lay before them. They had come down from a slightly rolling hill, but Ste. Anne itself was on very level ground, giving an impression of flatness.

For the first time, Henri was aware of a small cluster of houses that looked a little more like the homes he was used to. They had wooden verandas painted white, with larger plots around them and a trace of rough grass.

Dupier nodded his head toward the largest of the group. "Monsieur la Roache, the banker, lives there. And it is fitting. He is a devout man."

Henri decided the house wasn't pretty after all. Nothing was pretty in this village, neither the land, nor the houses, nor the few people he had seen. With one exception, Father Guardian. When he smiled, to Henri he looked beautiful.

As they neared the first house on the road, a woman appeared with a huge clothes basket. She wore a long gray skirt, a waist and a sweater which might have belonged to her husband. Her dull golden hair was coiled in a knot at the back of her head. She did not look nearly so beautiful as his Mama. He could not imagine ever wanting to rest his head against her shoulder as he did with his Mama.

When the woman caught sight of them, she removed the clothes pin from her mouth, jabbed it firmly to a sheet on the line, and called, "*Bonjour,* Monsieur Dupier."

At that moment, Henri caught sight of a small golden-haired girl in a black pinafore who peered around a corner of the building.

Monsieur Dupier hesitated, then said stiffly, "*Bonjour,* Madame Laurent."

The girl peered around the corner of the house again. This time her mother caught sight of her, called her out, and said something to Henri. He could only shake his head.

"Madame Laurent is introducing you to her daughter, Jeanne Marie." Dupier sounded none too pleased. "Say *bonjour,* Henri."

"*Bonjour,* Jeanne Marie," he said repeating her name as his mother had taught him to do when introduced. "How are you?"

"*C'est bien!*" Madame laughed a little. She spoke urgently to Jeanne Marie. The little girl answered hesitantly, and somewhat stiffly.

"Bonjour, Henri. How—are—you?"

Father Guardian's phrase came to him: *"Ça va bien."*

They all laughed except Monsieur Dupier. Suddenly he seemed angry and in a hurry to leave. Henri continued to look back at Jeanne Marie. Just before they disappeared from sight, she lifted her hand and waved, and he waved back.

There was just the suggestion of daybreak when Monsieur called Henri. As long as he could he resisted the awakening.

"Come now," Monsieur's voice was quite sharp. "Father Antoine will expect you to attend the Mass before you start your day's work. It is a sin to be late for Mass. Hurry."

Father Antoine. Who was he?

Henri struggled into his clothes. Holding his hand firmly, Monsieur hurried him across the square to the beautiful church Henri had thought was a castle.

Along the way Henri stared about him at the people. They seemed so drab and poor, like their houses. He wondered where this beautiful building had come from.

It was still early when they arrived. A boy was lighting candles, one on either side of the altar. His mother lit candles in their home every Friday night to usher in the Sabbath. She covered her head and said a prayer as she did it. His father had translated it for him. Henri remembered how it began.

"Father of Mercy, keep thou far from us all manner of shame and grief and care—"

God was supposed to be listening to her. Surely then He would return Henri to her.

Inside the church people were rapidly gathering.

Henri felt quite cold. He moved instinctively toward Monsieur to keep warm, then stopped. Many children were there with their fathers and mothers, each family keeping close together. Inside the synagogue, he had sat close to his father. His mother had worshipped with the women in a space set apart for them. His eyes filled with tears, and he kept his head bent.

Suddenly a sharp awareness struck him. He wasn't supposed to be here. He wasn't supposed to be in any church at all. His father had forbidden it. He had explained it all very clearly: God loved everyone but people were born into different faiths. And if Henri wanted to worship, his place was in the synagogue. He felt set apart, unhappy and alone.

He looked around. He had not gone to the synagogue very often, but he remembered it clearly; and the inside of it was much like the inside of the church. There were the same kind of pews and stained glass windows except that these had people in them. Then why was he so uncomfortable being here?

Could he get out of here? No. The wooden separation in the center of the pews hemmed him in on his right, and Monsieur Dupier blocked his way on the left.

Henri focused his attention on the altar. There was a large cross on it and a small kind of house beneath it. On either side were two tall candles.

In the synagogue, people said Ark, not altar. The Torah lay behind the sliding doors. He wondered why they didn't have the same thing in the small house here.

Soon Father Antoine entered. Henri noticed the stole he wore. It looked not unlike the shawl worn by their rabbi at B'nai Peyser. The priest was carrying something covered with a piece of silk. Henri had seen what was underneath it at Monsieur's other church. And it looked like the goblet of wine that was placed on the Fath table at the first and second Passover meals.

Everyone in the congregation rose.

Father Antoine paused at the steps for a few minutes, and placed the goblet on the altar. His lips were moving, but Henri could not hear him. Then he came back down the stairs, crossed himself, and the congregation sank to their knees. He then ascended the steps once more.

It seemed to Henri that he was on his knees for a long time before he was allowed to rise again. In the synagogue everyone had chanted the prayers together aloud. The people here kept silent throughout the service that went on and on. He felt lonely and uncomfortable in the unaccustomed silence. Finally the priest came down the steps and made the sign of the cross then turned and knelt with his back to the congregation. They all knelt with him, and for the first time came the subdued murmering of audible prayer. The Mass was over. Dupier went forward with several others. He threw back his head, opened his mouth and the priest put something that looked like a tiny piece of matzoh on his tongue. Dupier swallowed it.

The candles, the goblet of wine, the matzoh—they all reminded Henri of Passover.

The people poured out of the church, scattering rapidly in all directions.

Monsieur took Henri by the hand and walked him to the path they had climbed the day before. A boy with black hair and a running nose stood there, hands dug deep in the pocket of his overalls.

"Ah, Louis!" Monsieur greeted him. He spoke rapidly to him.

"Louis will wait for you every morning," Dupier seemed pleased. "He will take you to school."

Every morning! The pain shot across Henri's chest. How many more mornings would there be before he was back where he belonged? Silently he turned and followed Louis up the path.

THE NEXT day, Henri's first at school, he received his books and supplies, including a pencil and tablet of lined paper. He was excited.

Two hours went by. The pictures and numbers on the board made sense but little else. He tried to pay attention.

Recess time came, and Henri walked slowly after the rest of the children. He passed the open drawer of Father Lawrence's desk. Among yellow pads, rulers, colored pencils, and erasers lay a packet of white envelopes. The priest followed his gaze, then looked into his face and spoke gently to him. But Henri did not understand; so Father Lawrence offered him a colored pencil, then an eraser. Hesitantly, Henri pointed to the envelopes.

Father Lawrence withdrew an envelope from the pack and handed it to Henri.

"Thank you very much, Monsieur." Henri carefully placed the envelope between the pages of his book. Then he went out. He stood alone in the schoolyard while the other children played.

After supper, Monsieur settled himself to correct papers under the light of the kerosene lamp. Henri opened his book, slipped a piece of paper into it and began to write furtively:

Dear Mama
    Come and get me. I am here.
                                        Henri.

He had just finished when a hand reached down and snatched it from his grasp. Monsieur was bending over him. Henri was frightened.

"This is wrong, Henri." Slowly he tore up the letter. "I shall pray for your forgiveness."

Dupier got on his knees before the Virgin, crossed himself, and began murmuring under his breath.

Henri did not cry. He tried to tell himself that he was dreaming, that he would wake up soon in his own comfortable bed on Washington Square. But as his hand felt the rough coverlet, he knew that he was not, that he was far from home.

But he still had the envelope! He would try again tomorrow.

The next day during recess he stayed in and wrote his letter. After school he walked into town with Louis. Louis chattered along the way, and pointed out the various shops.

On the main street they caught a glimpse of a man sewing in the front room of his house which had been made into a shop. The top of his head looked like a shaggy mop. He wore steel-rimmed glasses, and as he lifted his head to thread a needle, Henri caught a glimpse of bright blue eyes. This, Louis said, was Maurice Claveaux, *le tailleur*. Why, that meant tailor!

Across the street, a wisp of a man walked out of his house onto the street holding a shoe in his hand. He examined it critically in the sunlight.

"*Bonjour*, Monsieur Pillon!" Louis waved.

Pillon looked up and waved. His small waxed mustache rose as he smiled a greeting.

After a few more gray wooden houses they came to one with a worn porch and a sign over it. Henri saw a woman come out with a market basket; this was the grocery.

Then Louis pointed to a clothing store. "*Mon pere*," said Louis, and ran up the porch into the shop.

At the end of the street, Henri found a big red brick building. Golden letters said *Banque* on the large plate glass window. It was the only brick building in Ste. Anne. The inside of it looked like a bank. Henri guessed that was what *Banque* meant — a bank.

Alongside it, Henri found a tired looking house with a large sign over the doorway: *Poste*. A man came out the door carrying a sack of letters, and threw it in the wagon.

Henri ran across the dirt road.

"Here," he said, holding his letter up, "please take mine, too."

The man examined it, smiled, and returned it to Henri. Then he pointed indoors, swung up on his wagon, and clucked to his horse.

Henri walked slowly up the steps into the bare room. A man stood behind a little wicker window. Henri gave him the letter. There, it was done!

But the man shoved the letter back under the window. He said something Henri could not understand. Finally

69

the man showed Henri a stamp and held up three fingers. Henri guessed it must mean the stamp cost three pennies. He shook his head. He had no money. Not even one cent. His eyes filled with tears.

"Please take it," he cried, pushing the letter back. "My mother will pay you back."

The man continued to shake his head.

"Please, please take it! You must!"

But the man pushed the letter back again. Finally Henri lifted a listless hand and took back the letter. Desperately he looked about the room, located a small slot with the word *Lettres* above it. When the postmaster turned away, he ran to the slot and dropped his letter in. Then he left quickly.

B EDTIME was always the worst.

Every night Henri lay rigid, waiting for the warmth of sleep to overcome him. The ache in his chest made breathing difficult. With the pain tears slid slowly down his cheeks. Fearful lest they be discovered, he would turn his face away. After a while the figure of Monsieur Dupier, hunched over his missal at the flickering lamp, would become blurred. It was then, worn out by the long day and his silent weeping, that he would finally drowse off.

One night, it was his seventh or eighth night in Ste. Anne, sleep seemed further away than ever. As Monsieur removed his shoes and socks, Henri's eyes fell on Dupier's feet. The joints at either side were red and badly swollen. "Yes," Monsieur said with satisfaction, "there is pain. Much pain. From shoes that are better than a size too small."

Henri began to tremble.

"Each day," Dupier continued, "there will be more and more, until one day," he sucked in his breath, "one day, the body will be purified, making it truly acceptable to His Grace!"

Day after day Henri waited for Mama to come; but she didn't come and he began to believe the postman had not sent his letter. Night after night he tried to retrace the journey that had brought him to Ste. Anne of the Prairies. Then one night he *knew* that Mama wasn't coming for him, and tomorrow became the day on which he had to go back to her by himself. Some way, somehow, he had to reach the station that had signs in English as well as French. He had no clear idea of how he would get there, only a hope that it was possible.

In the morning he made his way slowly to the path where as usual Louis Ferragne was waiting patiently for him.

Louis grunted a greeting and turned to start the trip to school.

Henri held him by the arm and pointed to himself. "*J'ai mal*," he said. Then he pointed from himself in the direction of his house. "*Chez moi*," he said.

Louis pointed toward the school and grinned. "*J'ai mal aussi*." He bent over as if he were violently ill. Then he winked conspiratorially, wiped his nose with the back of his hand, gave a brief salute, turned and walked alone up the path to the school.

Henri stood transfixed by his success. He made himself walk slowly down the hill, though his inclination was to run as fast as possible. Carefully he skirted the Square and the main street.

The woods were wet with the mist of early morning, but he went through the trees in order to stay on the outskirts of the town. Finally the broad dirt road to the South lay before him. A fallen log invited him to rest, but he dared not stop. He glanced up at the sun. It was to his left, in the east, just as his father had taught him; and he was going south.

Stacks of hay, like misshapen old women, hunched against the sky. The slightly rolling wheat-colored land stretched endlessly away on all sides of him.

Soon Henri spied a wagon coming toward him, heading in the direction of Ste. Anne of the Prairies. A huge bearded driver rolled back and forth on the seat, and chickens cackled in the crates behind him. As he passed the man bellowed a greeting. Henri jumped and the man laughed heartily. Suddenly Henri was worried. Would the farmer tell anyone he had seen him? He would have to hide in case anyone else passed.

Henri plodded on. Here and there along the road, lines of clothes flapped in the breeze—sturdy, worn clothes made for work. Each of the few times he saw a farmer in the field or a woman by her house he hid until they were out of sight; it was still too near Ste. Anne's.

Just before noon, the hunger growing inside of him became impossible to ignore. He found a hidden place off the road to sit down. There he opened his lunch packet, considered it carefully, then divided the bread and cheese into halves. He tried to eat the first half slowly, but it seemed to disappear within the instant. He took up the rest, but put it back and rewrapped it.

After that, it seemed to Henri that he had to stop more and more often to rest. The sun had passed over to his other side; the afternoon wore on. He had no idea of how far he had come. He knew only that the horizon to the south looked as far away as ever, and that he could no longer ignore the persistent demands of his stomach. Reluctantly, he left the road and ate the rest of the bread and cheese.

Soon a chill wind came up, moving the branches of the trees. Henri shivered a little and hugged himself to keep warm. In a minute his eyes closed, and he imagined his arms were his mother's arms instead. He tried to picture her face.

Suddenly a man's voice bellowed at him from a distance. It sounded like the farmer he had passed, but Henri did not stop to make sure. He turned and ran wildly for the woods.

He heard the wagon roll up and the man get down and thrash his way toward him. Branches scratched Henri's face, and thorns snatched and tore his trousers, but he kept going.

Finally, trembling and out of breath, Henri hid behind some sumac bushes. He could hear the scuffing of dead leaves, and the crackling of dried twigs underfoot as his pursuer tried to find him. Then the man stopped and called out. Henri remained motionless, hardly daring to breathe, for a long time. Only the sound of small animals in the brush disturbed the stillness.

Again and again the man called out and waited. Finally he turned and, muttering to himself, made his way back to the road.

Henri waited until the horse's hoofs faded away, then ran headlong toward what seemed to be a clearing up ahead. The trees grew sparse before him. Then his toe caught on the rough ground and he flew into space, falling, rolling over and over. He heard the crack as of a pistol and felt a shooting pain. Terrified, he caught a glimpse of the water below. He grabbed at a bush, and then he knew nothing more.

How long he lay there, Henri did not know. As he opened his eyes, the sun was sinking, the wind stinging his cheeks. He made a movement to rise. The pain darted through him and he felt himself falling into blackness. Desperately he struggled to rise above it; his body became drenched with perspiration. He forced himself to lie still.

Slowly the blackness subsided. Henri turned his head from side to side, slowly, very slowly. He was lying on worn rocks near the bank of the river. He must get out of here; there was no time to lose. Gathering all his strength, he tried once more to lift himself. This time the pain mercifully brought him unconsciousness.

When he came to again, he fell asleep. He dreamed a lady dressed in blue was standing, watching over him. It was the blue china lady! And in that moment the picture changed and he saw it was his mother. He tried to tell her he was on the way home but he could not seem to form the words.

Something woke him. He opened his eyes to complete darkness. There was calling in the distance, and some pinpoints of yellow light. The calling grew nearer, and suddenly he had to close his eyes against the flickering light which shone in his face. When he opened them again, he found himself staring into Monsieur Dupier's eyes. There was a stranger with him.

From then on he remained conscious for only brief lapses on the painful journey back to Ste. Anne of the Prairies.

"The Blessed Virgin has saved him," Dupier cried.

"She had not a little help from that farmer. If he hadn't wondered where the strange little boy came from, we would never have found him."

Henri lost consciousness once more.

He awoke back in Dupier's house. There was a stirring within him and he felt warmer now. Even the cot did not seem as hard as usual. Doctor Senntiere's hands were snipping away at Henri's overalls.

"You have broken your leg, Henri," Dupier explained. "The doctor here will set it for you." His eyes glittered strangely as he added, "You will suffer some pain, but it is punishment for disobeying me, and you are brave. You will bear it."

Henri stayed quiet. He did not cry. He felt instead as if he were choking.

For Henri realized then that he was never going to get home. Never.

He had tried to tell them what happened, but no one understood him: no one seemed to want to.

He had written a letter and Monsieur had taken it from him. He had written another and didn't even have three pennies to send it.

He had tried to go to his mother and had failed.

Now he couldn't even walk—much less run away. He was lost and he would never be found!

He turned his head and deep convulsive sobs shook his body. How could anyone expect a boy of seven to be brave when he knew now he would never see his mother again!

Several days later Henri was lying on his cot, his leg rigid in its cast, when Brother Armand, the lay monk from the Capuchin monastery, knocked on the door and entered, carrying a small pot.

"*Comment allez-vous, mon fils?*" asked the friar.

Henri looked at him, then stared at his curly black beard.

"*Il est après-midi. Avez-vous mangé?*"

Mangé. The word had something to do with eating.

The friar moved to the stove and stirred up the fire. The soup plopped thickly into a pan.

Just then Madame Laurent burst in with a covered pot in her hand.

The friar smiled when he saw it. "*Entrez*, Madame."

Then followed a rapid exchange in French of which Henri understood nothing.

And then there was a third knock on the door, and the Father Guardian entered. There were kindly conspiratorial smiles on the faces of the three as they stood around the cot. Henri peered up at them, and slowly he understood they were concerned about him. They wanted to be sure he was cared for. A little warmth stirred within him.

Brother Armand pointed to the two portions of soup and made motions of eating one after the other. Then he pointed to Henri's stomach, patted his own.

Henri's smile crept up like a sun rising through a haze; Madame Laurent's eyes filled with tears, and the two men withdrew to a corner of the room while she served Henri his soup at the table.

"The little one, he sits there so pale, so sad," Brother Armand sighed. "It's enough to make one weep."

"Dupier says it hasn't been long since he lost his parents. The wound is still fresh."

Brother Armand shook his head. "Dupier. I do not understand that one."

"He is a dedicated son of God," Father Guardian said slowly. The silence became weighted with things that could not be said. Brother Armand bowed and departed.

As he ate Henri kept his eyes on Madame Laurent, and longing flooded him. Then, rising from the table, he lost his balance and made no effort to break his fall. The cast on his leg made a dull thud as he went down. Madame Laurent helped him quickly to his feet. He waited for her to put her arms around him and comfort him as his mother used to when he hurt himself. But she only helped him to the cot and went back to work. Then, her chores finished, Madame Laurent bade them good-bye.

Father Guardian sat down beside Henri. Smiling with mock sadness, he pointed to himself: *"Encore pas de—*English."

Henri frowned. What was the friar trying to tell him?

That he still did not understand English? Yes. That must be it. He pointed to himself: "*Encore pas de*—French."

Father Guardian laughed and drew nearer Henri. "*Je veux apprendre l'Anglais*, Henri."

"I don't understand," Henri said.

"*Attend.*" Then he shook Henri's hand gravely and said, "*Bonjour*, Henri."

"*Bonjour*, Monsieur," Henri answered.

"*Je suis Pere* Joseph."

"You are Father Joseph."

"*You* are Henri Dupier."

"*Je suis* Henri *Fath!*"

Father Guardian looked puzzled. "You are Henri *Dupier*."

"*Non, non, Monsieur, ma mere et mon pere suis*—"

"*Sont*," interrupted the friar.

"*Ma mere et mon pere sont . . . .*" How did one say *alive*—alive, not dead? "*Ma mere et mon pere sont chez moi!*"

The Father Guardian shook his head sadly. "*Non, non, mon enfant, ta mere et ton pere sont morts.*"

Mort. So that was the word for dead! "*Non, non Monsieur, ma mere et mon pere . . . ils ne sont pas morts!*" He clutched the friar's hand. "*Ils* ne sont pas *morts!*"

"*Pauvre petit.*"

"It is true, Monsieur," Henri cried. Then: "*Ma mere et mon pere, ils ne sont pas morts!*" As the friar continued to shake his head, Henri burst into tears. "He took me away on a train! Oh Monsieur, I want my Mama! Please take me home to my mother."

The friar lifted him to his lap and put his arms around him, rocked him gently in his arms and whispered to him in French.

Finally, pointing to Henri's cast, the friar made a motion as if to split it with an axe. Then he stood up and walked around the room like a soldier on parade. But he could not coax a smile out of the boy. With a sigh he bade him farewell and left.

English or French, Henri thought, it was no use. He had found a way to tell them, but no one would believe him. He sat in the bed, staring wide-eyed into nowhere.

The Father Guardian was well along the road to the monastery when he stopped, looked down the hill at the church, hesitated, and finally turned back. Soon he was knocking on the door of the rectory.

Father Antoine tried unsuccessfully to conceal his surprise. Knowing that the monastery was one affair and the parish another, Father Guardian spoke of several things before he ventured to speak of the subject that brought him here.

"This Paul Dupier. What do you know of him, Father Antoine?"

"All there is to know, Father Guardian," the priest said stiffly. "He is an honest, godly man. For me that is quite enough."

"True," the friar murmured. "It is just that I find it so odd that he should have such a child."

"Henri is his brother's child. Who would have a better right?"

Father Guardian took a deep breath. "I knew Dupier's uncle. I never heard him mention two nephews."

"He might have had ample reason not to mention the other one."

Father Guardian sighed. "The child seems so alone—surely there was someone else left who must have loved him dearly."

Father Antoine thought for a moment before he spoke. "Henri's parents were not good Catholics. Henri practically never went to church. The family were destroyed in a terrible fire. Henri was saved. Dupier feels God must have saved him so that Henri could serve Him. He decided to remove the child from all his former influences. He brought him here to grow up a true son of God."

The Father Guardian nodded. "And yet it is so strange—"

"What is?"

"The child insists his parents are not dead."

"Not dead! Are you suggesting that Dupier, a devout Catholic who never misses a Mass, would lie about his brother's death?"

"Forgive me."

"Can't you understand a small boy's unwillingness to accept the loss of his parents?"

"Of course, Father Antoine, of course." And the Father Guardian took his leave, apologetic but unconvinced.

The next day, Father Antoine detained Dupier after Mass. "Henri has told a strange tale. He says his parents are not dead, and you are not his uncle."

Dupier stiffened. "Henri's parents exist no longer, and the child belongs to me. You have my word, Father."

"But why does the child insist his parents are not dead?"

"He still grieves for the past, Father. He does not yet know how joyous the future will be."

Father Antoine made as if to go, hesitated and turned back. He said slowly, "Care for him, then."

"I shall, Father, I shall."

Dupier hurried home, prepared breakfast, and sat down opposite Henri. They ate in silence. Each time he looked up, Henri found Dupier staring fixedly at him. Finally he could bear it no longer. "Is anything wrong, Monsieur?"

"Uncle Paul!"

"Uncle Paul."

"You know very well what's wrong. Breaking your leg was no lesson for you. Now you go around telling that story. You have no right to tell that story."

"But, Monsieur—"

Dupier rose, banged his hand so hard against the table that all the dishes on it clattered. "They are dead! I forbid you to mention their name again."

Something cold began to seep through Henri. He began to tremble. His hands gripped the arms of the chair so that the skin had white spots. He sat rigidly unable to move.

Only Jeanne Marie was glad to see Henri when the cast came off and he returned to school. As he entered the classroom, she came up and spoke to him. And at recess time, she walked with him to the yard.

The commotion began when someone knocked a ball out of Louis' hands. As he bent to pick it up, Jerome Giradot, the butcher's son, kicked him in the buttocks. Louis went sprawling. Everybody laughed. Henri laughed with them.

Louis picked himself up and stalked off to the swing. Before he had a chance to grip the rope properly, Jerome, followed by several of the other boys, ran behind him, and gave the swing a big push. Louis almost fell off. He began to yell. But Jerome only shouted *"Plus haut,"* and pushed Louis higher than ever. Louis's face began to turn gray with fear.

Henri limped to Jerome's side, leaped into the air, caught the swing and hung on to it, dragging it to a stop.

By the time Jerome recovered from his surprise, Louis had jumped off the swing and was running into the building. Jerome yelled hoarsely to the others. Before Henri knew what was happening he was lifted on to the swing and was flying out into the air.

Like Louis, he almost fell off, but he too gripped the ropes just in time. He wanted to yell stop, but he didn't want to let them know he was afraid. He closed his eyes, clenched his teeth as he swung madly higher into space. He tightened his grip on the ropes and let his head sink between his hunched shoulders. For one instant he tasted the thought of letting go.

At that moment Father Lawrence, their teacher, called out sharply. The boys dispersed. The priest strode up, caught at the wooden crosspiece, and slowed the swing down. Henri climbed off. For a brief second he and the teacher faced each other. Henri walked slowly back into the classroom.

After school that afternoon, Louis was waiting outside for him. He said nothing, only swung in step with Henri and walked until they came to Dupier's door. Then Louis thrust out his hand awkwardly, pumped Henri's up and down twice. He grinned and turned away.

Louis was on his side! Henri knew he had found a second friend in Ste. Anne of the Prairies. As he went indoors, his heart was lighter than it had been for a long time.

M<small>R. FATH</small> paced the hall outside his wife's bedroom. The wind whistled as it broke against the house. It straightened its ranks and rode on to strike again.

Outside, the world lay under a frozen comforter of white. It was the middle of February, almost five months since Henri had disappeared. It seemed like five years, and all of it winter.

Mr. Fath shivered and pulled his dressing gown tighter.

Now the sound of the wind came from inside the house, and Mr. Fath caught a glimpse of Charles in his nightshirt peering around the corner of the hall.

"Whoo," Charles peeked around again.

"I'm the wind now," Emilie cried. "It's my turn!" She tried to make the "whoo" sound, but failed.

"You can't be the wind," said Charles loftily. "You're a girl."

"I can so be the wind!" She puckered her lips but still no sound came out, and she burst into tears.

Mr. Fath picked her up in his arms. "You can be something better than the wind," he whispered. "You can be the sun."

She stopped crying. "How, Papa? What shall I do?"

"Just smile, darling."

"Like this, Papa?" The tears dried on her cheeks as she parted her lips happily.

"Just like that." He extended his hand to her. "Come on, Sun. It's time for bed."

He took Charles's hand, too, and led them back to their rooms. He was tucking Emilie in when the door bell rang. That would be Mahoney. He went to meet him.

Mahoney had barely taken his finger from the doorbell when Fraulein admitted him. He met Mr. Fath at the second floor landing. They shook hands in silence. Fath, his shoulders sagging, led the way to the study. Mahoney winced at the change in the man; since the kidnaping Fath had lost twenty pounds; there were deep lines around his mouth, and his dark hair was graying fast.

In the five months neither of them had faltered in the search. Time and again Mahoney had returned to Canada. He had combed the area between Quebec and Montreal. He had tracd a Pierre Duchesne and his nephew Hubert Duchesne from Quebec to England, and Mr. Fath's detectives had finally located them in France. In the end it had all come to nothing.

Meanwhile, Mr. Fath had neglected the business he had so proudly built, and had spent well over ten thousand dollars trying to find Henri. Perhaps it was nearer twenty thousand. He didn't care, except that he had suddenly found himself in a dangerous financial position. He would have to liquidate his business to satisfy his creditors and continue the search. With what was left he could enter a partnership with a friend who had started a new business in Philadelphia.

And there was another reason for moving: the doctor had said Mrs. Fath was approaching a nervous breakdown. She had to get out of the house, away from the scene of the tragedy and the reminders of Henri.

Still in silence, Mahoney and Mr. Fath sat close to the fire and stared into it for a long time.

Finally Mahoney said, "There's nothing new, Mr. Fath. The conductor saw them last at Three Rivers, but I haven't been able to find a single person in the town who saw them get off that train. Perhaps we'd better pull in our horns, sir, until we get a more definite lead from somewhere."

"I will never give up, Mahoney," he said clenching his fist. "Never, do you understand? So long as I live I will search for my boy. And you must help me."

Mahoney nodded.

Fath saw him to the door, then went to his study. He sat down at his desk and dropped his head onto his arms.

"Oh God," he whispered, "what do you want with one small frightened boy? And we need him so." He opened his clenched fists in a gesture of pleading. "Take everything I own, O Lord, but give me back my son." His voice cracked, but he did not cry. He sat there dry-eyed, while slowly inside of him something solidified like stone.

As time went by, Henri and Dupier remained strangers in a cold house. If anything, Dupier became more and more withdrawn. Henri was grateful for his silence. He was grateful, too, for the chores that kept him busy throughout the day. He thought as much about his mother, but now the weeping came less frequently. The sharp pain subsided into a dull ache.

Early each morning, Dupier would take Henri's hand in his and walk to the church. In storm or snow or bitter cold they never missed a Mass. Each time they entered, Henri looked for familiar faces. One was always there— the blue china lady. She was smiling a little, as if she were waiting specially for him.

The heavy candelabra on either side of the altar looked exactly like the Menorrah at B'nai Peyser except when he counted the candles in them, there were fewer. He guessed that one of the missing ones was the "shamus" candle—the one you used to light the others with. He wondered why.

And Madame Laurent, with Jeanne Marie at her side, was usually there. As the winter days became colder, Jeanne Marie looked more pale, more fragile. She shivered from time to time, and Henri wished there was some way in which he could help keep her warm. She always seemed to know when he was looking at her, for she would turn and smile at him.

During Mass, Dupier's devotions often became so intense that Henri would stir uneasily. And when the Mass was over Dupier would talk about the liturgy, the priest, the robes, and the Mass itself. But his favorite topic was the most disturbing one to Henri.

"There is a place in Heaven for every Catholic. It was for them the Blessed Virgin intervened, and through her Son she brought the Catholics truly within God's loving grace. But for the non-believers, there is only Hell. Hell and Damnation!"

And Dupier would strike his fist into his palm. "Only Hell and Damnation. I am saving you, Henri. I am bringing you to Him. But you must believe, and you must learn, and above all you must obey."

Henri was not sure he understood all this, and he was not very interested in it. The man on the cross continued to seem far away to Henri, but he liked the blue lady. She always smiled. He never lost the feeling that some day she would hear him and help him. And so he began to learn the catechism.

The third Sunday in February, Henri attended a Mass at which some children were receiving their first Holy Communion. But it wasn't until ten o'clock, when the service was over, that he realized its meaning for him.

"I am going to receive Holy Communion next year," Jeanne Marie said outside.

"So am I," boasted Louis Ferragne.

"Are you, Henri?" she asked.

Was he? Was this what would happen next? He remembered his first visit to Church with Dupier; how he had known people were born into different faiths; how he had felt strange and unhappy and alone. But he didn't feel that way any more. The church had become a familiar place, a friendly place, somehow it was part of his new life, no stranger than the strange school he was attending and the strange language he was learning to speak. It was something he had accepted, something he was used to, like the gruel, bread and molasses he now ate for breakfast.

But Holy Communion? It seemed too important to accept just because the other children were accepting it. And suddenly, painfully, he saw his mother again. He was back in the familiar room. He could almost smell her perfume, feel her gentle touch. The pain swelled within him, almost cutting off his breath. His eyes filled. Turning from Jeanne Marie and Louis, he ran away.

Henri did not stop until he found himself at the walls of the monastery. Aimlessly he wandered around in the snow. He made some snowballs and dashed them against the wall. Then he turned and leaned against the stone, with his face toward the cold sun.

It did not seem possible that a journey which had taken only a few days—he did not know how many—should have carried him so far away. It seemed as if he were at the other end of the world. He wished he had someone he could really talk to. He had tried the Father Guardian but it was difficult. Perhaps one day, when he could speak the friar's language better, things would be different. Meanwhile, he could speak only to the blue lady. But did she hear him?

It was almost noon before he finally came back to the house.

"I have looked everywhere for you." Monsieur's voice was sharp. "I was afraid something had happened to you."

"Were you, Monsieur?"

"But of course. You should know, Henri, that you are my first concern. Haven't I sacrificed everything for you?"

"You work very hard, Monsieur."

"Well, I knew I had no need to worry. God will always bring you back to me."

89

Henri wanted to say he was hungry, and that was what had brought him back, but instead he blurted, "Am I going to receive Holy Communion?"

Dupier stood looking at him for a long time. Then, his voice trembling, he said," "Communion, Henri, is only the beginning."

The beginning of what? As Henri sat down to his simple meal he wished he knew.

That Sunday night it was Dupier who did not sleep. Henri had to be received into the Church, but how?

Through the night, and in the days that followed, he asked the question of himself over and over again.

Henri's story would have to be told. But to whom and where?

Finally he realized it could be told safely only to the priest in the confessional. But having found the answer, Dupier could not persuade himself to go, he could not bear to part with his secret. Time and again, he would enter the booth, make his confession, and leave with Henri's story still untold. But each time he looked at the calendar May twenty-second, Henri's birthday, moved closer.

Then on May 18 Dupier could endure it no longer. He jammed on his hat and ran all the way to the Rectory.

"Father Antoine," he muttered, staring at the old lady who answered his knock. "I, I must see him. The confessional—"

The old lady nodded toward the church. "The Father will be there soon."

Dupier entered the church, crossed himself, knelt, and said his prayer. Then he entered the confessional. Kneeling on the small bench, he rested his head against his clasped hands near the opening through which the priest would soon hear him.

The door to the confessional opened. Robes rustled, then there was silence.

Frantically Dupier began to speak, but stopped in dismay. This was not what he had meant to say. He started again. Then he felt the blessed relief of unburdening himself, and raced on.

"Night after night," he cried, "Our Lord visited me in my room. Night after night, He pointed to the evils of Henri's father, and commanded me to take the boy from the house of Sin. Finally I could no longer disobey Him, and I brought Henri here to Him." Then he began to babble incoherently again.

"And now Henri must be received into the Church. But in order to be received into the Church he must be baptized. And in order to be baptized he must have his baptismal certificate. What shall I do, Father!" He buried his face in his hands and waited.

For a long time there was silence, a shocked silence. Then the priest said, "My son, you have sinned. For this you must do penance."

Dupier bowed his head: he had expected penance.

"But first you must write and return the child to his parents."

"No."

"You must. It is true that God wishes us to save souls, but not in this way."

"You cannot tell!" Dupier cried. "You will betray your own oath!"

"I will not betray you. You will betray yourself. God will not receive you until you have righted this wrong. You must return the child to his parents."

"He would burn in Hell. It was a godless home. I tell you they knew no God!"

"Then we must pray that one day they will find Him. But you must return the child."

"How?"

"The same way in which you took him."

"But that took everything I had. I swear I have nothing left!"

"You must find a way."

"I have only my little house. And if I sold it and was unable to find the family, what would Henri and I come back to? Where could we go? Who would care for us!"

"You must rectify your sin. Go to the police. They will help you return him."

Dupier's sallow skin turned a sickly green. His mouth twitched violently and his normally hooded eyes widened. They had an insane stare. "You cannot mean that, Father. You know what might happen to me. Then what would become of Henri? Will he be doomed to perdition? Will he never be permitted to serve God?

Father Antoine sat in silence. "You must do everything possible to return this child. The burden lies with you."

There was a soft movement, and Dupier knew the priest had left the confessional. He rose and stumbled out into the Church. A few figures were bent in prayer, but no one took notice of him as he dropped to his knees and buried his face in his hands and wept.

For several nights, Dupier had the same dream. A house was burning and a voice kept crying out to be saved. Sometimes it was the house on Washington Square, other times the house on Fourteenth Street where he himself had lived. Soon the two houses became intermingled with each other so that he was unsure of which one was burning. But always it was the same voice which cried out. And in the end, it was the house on Fourteenth Street which kept burning . . .

The broad face of Rouen, the postmaster, intruded itself on Dupier's consciousness. The words rearranged themselves and swarmed over the envelope. For a moment, Dupier felt dizzy. Then a fit of trembling seized him.

"Are you ill, Monsieur?"

Dupier shook his head.

"Not bad news I hope?"

"Bad news!" Dupier threw back his head and laughed. Then he slipped the letter into his pocket, leaned furtively toward the postmaster. "Good news, Monsieur. The best."

Dupier started for the rectory. Alone on the street now, his fingers shaking, he took the envelope out again. In fascination he stared at the letters stamped across the front of the envelope.

UNKNOWN AT THIS ADDRESS. RETURN TO SENDER.

Clearly this was a sign from the Almighty. God knew what he had done. Had He not told him what to do visiting him night after night? And this was the way He had taken to show that He approved.

Father Antoine received him almost immediately, and eagerly Dupier began his recital. He had sent the letter to the Fath family as the priest had instructed him to do. The letter had been returned. He took it out. Father Antoine looked at it. Yes, it had been addressed to a Mr. Fath at 201 E. 14th Street, N.Y.C. Wherein lay the truth?

93

Were the parents missing, alive, dead? Alive would they not have left a forwarding address—It was barely nine months since Henri had arrived in Ste. Anne. Had the family given up searching for him, or was there no longer a family?

Dupier was still speaking. Was this not God's way of showing them what had to be done? Surely the priest would not deny the right of baptism to the boy. Without the baptism Henri could not be received into the Church —the Church he attended as regularly as anyone in Ste. Anne. He sat back in his chair and waited.

Father Antoine's hands were folded, his head sunk forward. Never before, he was sure, had such a large problem been placed in the lap of a humble village priest. Dupier's confession was sacred. Father Antoine had taken the vows of the Church to keep it so. He knew that even if he had to lie, he had to keep the confession inviolate. He was powerless to do more than urge Dupier to right his sin.

"Monsieur, I beg you. Go to the police."

The muscles in Dupier's throat worked violently. One could see he was making a tremendous effort to control himself. His voice trembled. "And if the police took me away? Henri would surely be lost then. No, Father." Dupier held the letter in his left hand and tapped it with his right. His voice became shrill and dangerous sounding. "This is a sign from God to show His wish that Henri remain here."

"I implore you to reconsider."

"I will obey God."

Father Antoine sighed heavily. "I will pray for you, Monsieur Dupier. You must give me your word that you will continue your search. I don't know how but you

94

must find a way to return this boy home." He waited. Dupier remained silent. Finally he spoke . . .

"I promise, Father Antoine, that I will obey God's will and lead Henri to his true home."

For a while nothing further was said. Then Father Antoine spoke unhappily. "In the interim, Henri is to be baptized so that he may receive Holy Communion. That is your wish?"

"Yes. Yes."

"But there are the necessary papers. There must be proof the parents were legally married."

"They were, they were, I swear it!"

"Can you also swear the parents are no longer living? That it is their wish for the boy to be a Catholic?"

"I can swear it is the parents' wish for Henri to be received into the Kingdom of Heaven."

The priest stood up. "Go, my son. I cannot resolve this. There is much to think about, a great deal to be done. I must seek guidance. I shall have to consult with the Bishop of Quebec to see if a conditional baptism is possible."

"How long will it take, Father?"

"When I am ready I will send for you."

That night, Father Antoine knelt by the side of his bed and prayed. "Blessed Virgin, help me. What shall I do? I cannot go to the police and I dare not even hint to anyone at what has happened without betraying the most sacred vow of the Church. If the child is lost, surely a provisional baptism would do no harm. Help me, Mother of God, help me."

He knelt for a long time, and when he finally climbed into bed, it was to sleep only intermittently for the rest of the night.

Early that summer Henri spent a week helping Dupier build a small hen house. And behind the small gray box of a house they, like everyone else in Ste. Anne, planted a vegetable garden. Without a garden, they could not last out the winter, Dupier told him. Each bean and potato would count.

Every morning after Mass, Henri fed the hens and weeded the garden. He wondered what Ste. Anne would look like if the houses were built in rows like the plants, all colored green.

Oft-times he found himself shading his eyes with his hands and straining to see as far to the south as possible, hoping in some vague way for a sign—something, anything—to help him get back home. But only the flat fields stared back at him. He was sorely tempted to run away again but the memory of the last attempt held him back.

Sometimes, Jeanne Marie would come and keep him company. She was frail, and her father did not want her to weed too long in the sun; but while she was there she would chatter gaily to him. Some of it Henri still did not understand, but daily his ear was becoming better attuned to the French. Speaking was more difficult. Many times he could not find the words for what he wanted to say. However, he would try, and both he and Jeanne Marie would laugh at his mistakes. He grew fonder and fonder of her.

After lunch, Dupier would insist he study the catechism. Only after that was he free to go off swimming with Louis and on long walks with Jeanne Marie.

And then one day, summer was over, and they went back to school again. Henri studied long and hard, and time passed.

It was after Mass on the first Monday in November that Dupier told Henri he was to be baptized. Though Henri was used to the church now he had not forgotten the synagogue of his father. The baptism seemed wrong for him. Wouldn't something happen to him if he were baptized?

He made up his mind: he was going to disobey Monsieur and tell. This time he was going to make the Father Guardian believe him. As soon as school was out he'd go straight to the monastery and talk to the Father Guardian.

That day the catechism class seemed to go on forever.

"Who is the Mother of Jesus?"

Henri felt a poke in his side.

"That one," Louis Ferragne whispered, pointing to Madeleine Rouen, "will never be the mother of anything."

Henri couldn't help but smile. Poor Madeleine! God had staked her eyes out in a broad plain. As if that were not enough, he had directed one straight ahead, and the other to the side.

Suddenly he heard a sharp crack, and he jumped in his seat.

The priest was leaning over Louis, with a pointer in his hand. Louis was rubbing his knuckles, on which the wooden stick had left its mark.

"Stand up, Louis Ferragne!"

Louis rose slowly.

"You were talking during class!"

Louis remained silent.

"Now Louis, possibly you can tell the class what great pearls of wisdom could not await the end of the day."

"I—I was speaking of the possibilities of becoming a mother."

Someone tittered nervously.

"Surely," the priest said, "you were not entertaining such a possibility for yourself?"

In the ensuing roar of the class, the priest's face showed an involuntary flush of pleasure at the success of his own wit. Louis thought at that point it was safe to sit down. He was wrong.

"Stand up!" The pointer smacked sharply against his knuckles once more.

This time Louis's face became sullen. He rose again.

"You will stay after school and write ten Hail Marys before you go home." The priest looked around the class. "One more sound in this room," he thundered, "and Louis will have the company of the whole class at his literary exercise." Twenty heads dropped obediently. The priest strode to the front of the room. "How does the bread and wine become the body and blood of Christ?"

No hand was raised.

Henri raised his hand, then at the priest's nod rose and recited:

"Through the words of the priest saying, 'This is my body, This is my blood.' Thus the change is effected."

Father Lawrence's face softened. "May I remind the rest of the class that Henri cannot receive Holy Communion for anyone but himself! Each of you must know every answer perfectly. Together now: when will Jesus come back to judge us?"

Twenty singsong voices answered, "No one but God knows . . . ."

Now the day was nearing a close and the pot-bellied stove had lost its heat. Henri shivered a little. All through the day the thought of the baptism remained heavy with him. Time and again he had closed his eyes, desperately sought to bring his mother into focus. Always the familiar surge of longing welled up in him.

Darkness was slowly descending when Henri finally came to the Father Guardian. The friar roused himself and lit the lamp on his desk.

The light flickered. The friar smiled. "The French has gone very well, one hears," he beamed. "It is well that you have learned the French. For me the English—"

Henri knelt and clasped the friar's knees. "Oh, Monsieur," he cried, his hands clutching the folds of the Capuchin robe, "I am to be baptized, so that I may receive Communion."

Baptized! Now that is strange. A child of eight to be baptized! "Is it that your parents were not church-goers and made no provision for your being received into the Church?" he asked softly.

"Mama used to take me to the synagogue. It is true

Papa seldom went. But Papa said a good Jewish man worshipped God in his heart, and was free to worship Him anywhere."

"Jewish!" The friar leaned forward and gripped Henri's arms. "What are you saying, child! Your parents were Catholics."

"Oh no, Monsieur! That is why Papa was so angry when Monsieur took me to the Mass."

"But your parents are dead!"

"No! Not dead at all. They were only resting—as always on Saturday afternoon. Emilie and Charles were getting ready to go to the park. Monsieur did not tell anyone he meant to take me away on a train. He only said he wanted to show me the trains."

"Hush, Henri. A moment. Give me time to think. Then we will start from the very beginning."

Henri watched the Father Guardian's lips move in prayer as he fingered his beads. Finally he dropped them, and straightened.

"My child"—his voice was still rough and strained—"what place did Dupier have in your family?"

"He was my tutor. My name is Henri Fath, not Dupier. I tried to tell you. And then there was no one to tell it to for so long. I tried to learn the French quickly. I knew you would help me find my mother." Then he began to cry. "Oh, Monsieur, I don't want to wait for the baptism. I only want to go home to my mother."

The friar held up his hand. "Henri, I can't help you until I know the whole story. You must go slowly from the very beginning."

It was 7:30 when Father Guardian heard the last of Henri's story. For a long time he sat unmoving. Henri could be telling him a tale fashioned out of desperation at the loss of his parents. But the blue eyes blurred with tears, fastened so hopefully on him, convinced him against his will. He wished despairingly that he could doubt him. Finally he roused himself, and glanced out the window.

"It is way past time to go home, Henri. Monsieur Dupier will be more than a little concerned." He did not miss the expression on the boy's face, and realized with a start that Henri was the cause of his ready belief. From the very first moment he had noticed how rigidly Henri had held himself away from Dupier. He remembered that first time so clearly.

And Henri's mother! How could he be baptized without her consent? He felt perplexed, cold with doubt.

"Yes, you must go home now, Henri. I will speak to Father Antoine. We will see what can be done." He looked down on Henri, and smiled the smile which Henri had learned to love. "And, Henri, do not worry about the baptism. One should fear sin, but not having it washed away."

Father Antoine's head was bowed as he walked along. Now what did the Father Guardian want with him at this time? Unconsciously, he girded himself for battle. He and the friar were both men of God, but they were also men and, as such, subject to their frailties.

Father Antoine accepted his orders as a priest should, but there were many things he did not understand. Why, for instance, had the parochial school been built so close to the monastery? The Capuchins had the seminary. Was that not enough? He and the friars worked toward the same end, but still there were many differences of opinion. The Father Guardian's rank gave him a superiority in so many questions.

The priest sighed deeply as he lifted the bell.

"Ah, Father Antoine," the Father Guardian greeted him warmly. "It is good of you to humor an old man on such a day."

Father Antoine knew that the friar was forty, exactly two years older than he, and considered himself anything but an old man; but he took the safest course and said nothing.

"A glass of port?" The Father Guardian picked up a decanter. "Many men make wine with their hands, but this," he shook his head in appreciation, "this was made with the heart as well."

Father Antoine nodded. He was very familiar with the wines of the monks.

"Yes," sighed the friar, "we do many deeds with the hands and the mind, but when they are also done with the heart—"

Father Antoine stiffened.

"And how are things in our little town?" the Father Guardian continued.

Father Antoine enumerated some of the problems. One of the greatest was the poverty of the people. They gave what they could. But what they could give was not enough.

Father Guardian nodded sympathetically. He knew the story all too well.

Father Antoine said, "It is as if the people drained themselves to build this beautiful church, and having built it exhausted themselves of all means to support it. If it were not for the Archdiocese, who knows what might happen? And such a beautiful church—"

"Perhaps Ste. Anne also needs a beautiful factory with plenty of work for our poor people."

Father Antoine shook his head. "If you fill the factory,

you might well empty the church. There is nothing like worldly goods to make them forget their need of God."

Father Guardian shrugged. He wanted to say that no religious body should live removed from the realities of the present world and its needs—that James, brother of Jesus said "What does it profit my brethren, if a man says he has faith but not works?" Faith, by itself, if it has no works, is dead. But this was no time for dialectics. He felt that conditions of the body did little to affect the soul. The need of spiritual salvation would always fill a church if the house of God could continue to provide such a comfort and salvation.

"And so, Father Antoine, you are working hard with the little ones for the Holy Communion."

"Yes. Each year they appear slower, less eager to learn. Now with this new decree, I cannot delay any longer. Next year they must receive Communion by the age of seven. How I will do it, I do not know."

"How fortunate," the friar's voice was a bare murmur, "there is need of no such training for baptism."

Father Antoine flinched. "We have much to be thankful for," he said simply.

"Father," the friar began, "Henri Dupier has come to me with a strange story. I tried to believe it was all in the child's imagination. When one is deprived of his parents so young, sometimes he reverts to the world of fancy."

Father Antoine said nothing.

"But one thing puzzles me. Is it true that, at the age of eight, Henri is about to be baptized?"

"People have been known to be baptized at the age of seventy."

"True. But why with this child?"

103

"Perhaps his parents were not true Catholics."

"Father Antoine, the story Henri tells me is that his parents were not Catholics at all! Is this true?"

In the eyes of the Church it was not considered lying in order to protect confession. Father Antoine said, "That may or may not be."

"Is it also true that this child was removed forcibly from his natural home by Monsieur Dupier."

"I wouldn't know."

"Perhaps you can tell me why no effort is being made to return this boy to his mother."

"I can tell you nothing other than that a child has not been baptized. A request has been made. The Bishop of Quebec, whose authority in this Diocese one does not question, is satisfied that Henri is in need and has seen fit to receive him and save his soul."

"The Bishop of Quebec!" The friar's voice broke. "I can hardly believe it."

Father Antoine rose. "The papers are all in order. There is nothing more to be done."

Father Guardian rose with him.

"One thing can be done, Father Antoine," his voice was passionate, "and I hope you will join me in it. I shall pray—for Dupier, for you, and for myself."

Father Antoine bowed, turned, and departed.

A week later Father Guardian called Dupier to his study. At the appointed time Dupier arrived anxious and out of breath, his nose red with cold and his lips turned blue in the walk up to the monastery.

"Monsieur Dupier, I have two favors to ask of you."

"Anything." Dupier looked around the room, thinking this was where he should be. "Anything at all, Father Guardian."

"First I ask that you delay the baptism of Henri."

"But we have the permission, Father!" Dupier cried.

"Of that I am well aware. I ask the delay for another reason. I wish," he bowed somewhat ironically, "with your permission, of course, to serve as Henri's godfather."

Dupier's face went slack.

"Unless," continued the friar, "you have someone else whom you deem more worthy."

"Assuredly not. Such an honor!" He was almost incoherent. "But begging your forgiveness, Father Guardian, is it not most irregular?"

"Most," agreed the friar. "But there is some precedent. That is why I ask you to wait for my answer from the Capuchin Diocese."

"Then they will have to know!"

"They have to know only that an innocent child is lost in the Canadian backwoods. That I wish to assure myself always of his well being. Perhaps this small thing will help God in His Mercy to expiate this awful sin."

"Sin! Sin, you call it!" Dupier shouted. "A sin to save a soul that was doomed to hell and damnation! In a house that knew no God!"

"That house contained the child's mother. Her child was born to her through God's grace. Surely He felt He could trust her with his soul. You are not God, Monsieur Dupier!" he thundered. "It is evil to think you are. Take care that you yourself are not damned for this presumptuousness!"

The friar stopped and finally succeeded in regaining his self control. "I shall pray for you, Monsieur Dupier. I suggest also that you pray for yourself."

Dupier turned to go.

"Wait. Do I have your promise, Monsieur, to wait until I hear from my Diocese?"

"You have my promise, Father Guardian," Dupier said sullenly as he shuffled out of the room.

It was not until the end of February that word came from the Capuchin Archdiocese. The Father Guardian sent for Henri.

"How would you like me for a godfather, Henri?"

"I do not understand." Henri shook his head, bewildered.

"It is all very simple." The friar's eyes twinkled. "One day I awoke, and said, 'If I had a godson, what would he be like?' I looked around, and there you were!" He smiled at Henri.

"Come here, my child." He drew Henri to his knee. "I have received permission to be your godfather when you are baptized. That means I shall watch over you always." He paused and added slowly, "I shall have no worldly goods to give you, my child. But I will give you something more enduring—my help and my love."

Henri felt warm and comforted against the coarse wool robe with the friar's strong arms around him. Timidly he laid his head against his shoulder. A curious peace stole over him.

"And that means you will help me find my Mama?" he asked.

"I can only promise"—his voice was rough with emotion—"that no matter how strange the way, my son, I shall try to lead you home."

BUT THE baptism continued to weigh heavily on Henri. A few days after the Father Guardian told him he was to be his godfather, Henri appeared before Brother Armand at the monastery.

"I wish to see the Father Guardian, I mean Father Joseph."

Within the Capuchin order, no friar could hold the position of Father Guardian for more than a three-year period. Then someone else had to serve at least one year before the preceding Father Guardian could be re-elected. But while the Capuchins here adhered to the letter of the law, no matter who took Father Joseph's place in that fourth year, in everyone's mind he remained the real Father Guardian.

Henri stood before him now. He spoke wistfully.

"Father, couldn't you arrange to have me put on a train at Three Rivers? I could find my way home from there. I know I could.

The friar shook his head. "I have found out, Henri, that we tried to find your parents and failed. They are no longer in the house where you left them."

"But they couldn't have moved away without me!"

"I'm afraid they did, Henri."

"Why don't you help me find them?"

"But where would we start? Who could go with you to look? It would take so long and so much money, and we might never find them. Ah, Henri, I thought you had begun to be happy here. What has happened to change that?"

"It's the baptism, Father. It still seems wrong for me to be baptized!"

"You have learned to speak so well in French, Henri. I am pleased that you have learned to speak to me from the heart as well."

"It's because I trust you, Father."

"Thank you, Henri. And I shall try to reward that trust." He looked into Henri's eyes. "What does the baptism mean to you?"

"It is the washing away of sin."

"Do you know what sin is?"

"I think it's doing something bad."

"Have you sinned?"

Henri stood in silence for a while. "The only *really* bad thing I can think of is I can't love Monsieur Dupier."

"Can you learn to forgive him?"

"Yes."

"Can you learn to love him?"

"You want me to speak the truth, Father?"

"Only the truth."

"No. I don't think I ever could."

"But you don't hate him."

"No, no I don't hate him."

"Then how do you feel about him?"

"I think I feel sorry for him."

"Do you know why Dupier took you away?"

"No."

"Because he loved you and he wanted you to love God as he does. And he wants above all for God to love you."

"Doesn't He love me?"

"Of course."

"Then why doesn't He listen to me?"

"He is listening."

"How can I be sure?"

"You must believe to be sure."

"Then I want to believe."

"You will. And God will reward you. As for the other, have faith, my child. The way is not always as we see it."

That spring the people of Ste. Anne said they must have displeased God in some way. The rains came and persisted; the village wallowed in endless lanes of mud. The water rose above the river and spilled over its banks. Cellars became flooded, and food, carefully stored to last until the summer, rotted away. Illness was rampant, and Doctor Senntiere's buggy rode from early dawn till late into the night.

And so Henri's strongest impression of the baptism was of wetness, though he barely felt the light scattering of the holy water. The request from the Provincial had been granted: Father Guardian became Henri's godfather. During the ceremony, Henri thought of his parents. He remembered his father's anger when Dupier took him to Mass. Surely a baptism was far worse. His forehead and upper lip became blistered with perspiration, his hands wet. He began to tremble, then he looked up and found the Father Guardian's eyes upon him. It seemed as if he were saying, "Have no fear, Henri. Once your father understands how it is, he will not be angry. He would trust me, as you may, to take care of you." The church seemed warmer then, and he felt comforted. He had someone to look after him now, someone who had promsied to bring him home some day. And then the baptism was over.

They parted at the Church door. The friar smiled at him. "And now, my little one, go with God."

Henri watched him pick his way up the road, the skirts of his brown robe growing heavy with wetness, the white knotted cord swinging heavily against his side, the crown and cross held in his hands. His figure grew blurred. Henri rubbed his hand across his eyes. Then he put on his cap and walked home alongside of Monsieur Dupier.

After lunch, Louis came over to visit.

"Someone is sick on the next street," he announced importantly. "I just saw the doctor's buggy slow down there."

"Who is it?"

"I don't know. I didn't wait to see."

"I wonder if it could be at the Laurents'," Henri frowned. "Let's go see."

They walked up one block and turned left. Sure enough, there stood the buggy, right in front of the Laurent house.

His voice trembling, Henri said, "Maybe it's Jeanne Marie. Maybe she's dying."

Louis was torn between the dread and the excitement of disaster: "Maybe she died already."

Henri knocked him down.

Louis sat there stunned. "Now why did you do that?"

"Because you're a stupid boy. What would God want with Jeanne Marie? She's only a girl! She can't even— she can't even fish!"

He left Louis, turned, and ran down the street to the Laurent house. The doctor was just leaving.

Henri came to a stop before him. "Doctor, she's not going to die?"

The doctor was startled. "Who?"

"Jeanne Marie."

"Jeanne Marie isn't ill; it's Madame Laurent."

Henri's eyes filled with tears. The doctor patted Henri awkwardly on the shoulder. "No need to worry. Perhaps by tomorrow, Jeanne Marie will be able to tell you her mother is better. Run along now."

Henri went. Madame Laurent was sick. How cold he felt. He had never been cold in his own home. If he could only get back. But he couldn't run away again. Now he knew it was too long and hard for a boy to find by himself. If he were older he'd be able to do it by himself. Why couldn't he fall asleep that night and wake up old enough to find the right way home?

Madame Laurent was ill for a long time. Finally, Jeanne Marie came back to school, but each day she had to hurry home to help care for her three younger brothers. She asked Henri to promise he wouldn't go fishing till she could come along. He promised.

And Henri remained true to his word. On Saturday afternoons well into the summer he wandered the main street; joined the crowd that gathered at three o'clock around the Post Office to wait for the mail wagon; and sat in the shops, watching and listening to the townspeople, saying a few words to the shopkeepers in the moments when they were alone.

His favorite tradesman was the shoemaker, Achille Pillon. Sometimes Henri would go about his shop, straightening old piles of shoes. Other times, Pillon would tell him wonderful stories from the history and folklore of the country. Henri would sit and listen by the hour. And he'd watch and listen with a different kind of interest when Monsieur la Roache, the banker, came in. Monsieur would blow himself up like a balloon and berate Pillon for talking against the clergy, and then they'd argue long and loud, as if they both enjoyed it. Their arguments were always the same, and each time after la Roache went off in a huff, Henri and Pillon would laugh together.

It wasn't until the first Saturday in August that Madame Laurent was strong enough to free Jeanne Marie for fishing. That was a beautiful, warm day; and arm in arm Henri, Louis and Jeanne Marie left for the river early and returned home late. With the next few Saturdays to look forward to, Henri found that the week's chores passed swiftly, that the summer was gone.

The last Saturday before school began Jeanne Marie caught three big pike, and Henri stayed to help the Laurents eat them. After dinner, as Henri sat drawing, Madame Laurent remarked, "Classes start Monday, Jeanne Marie. This spring comes the Holy Communion, but only if you know your catechism. When I was ill, you missed so much."

Madame Laurent looked down with interest at the house that was taking shape under Henri's pencil.

"How clever you are."

"Thank you, Madame." Henri flushed with pleasure.

"Are you as clever with your school work as well?"

"Oh yes, Mama," Jeanne Marie cried. "He is the brightest in school."

"I don't care who is the brightest in school, but, Henri, if you will help Jeanne Marie with her catechism, I would take it as a favor. A great favor indeed."

Jeanne Marie clapped her hands. "When shall we start?"

"Why not today? And your salary, Henri, will be to stay for supper with us."

Henri would never forget those long fall and winter evenings: the soap-scrubbed oilcloth, the smell of wet boots steaming and drying in the corner, the haze of smoke near the ceiling, the ever-present odor of onions, the logs spitting and crackling in the fireplace. He felt warm and safe.

Each night, after the boys were put to bed, Madame Laurent finally sat down near her husband at the stove. Not to be idle, but to darn and sew. Henri never knew anyone else who had quite such busy hands.

And Monsieur Laurent read incessantly. This was a mark of distinction among grown-ups in Ste. Anne: schools were few in their childhood, and few could afford the time to attend them regularly. In fact—and Madame was very proud of it—Monsieur Laurent had taught himself to read, write, and calculate.

One evening in February, after Henri had been studying with Jeanne Marie for about an hour, her attention began to wander. He pressed his questions; her answers were slower and slower in coming. To call her back, he raised his voice and asked:

"Is the Catholic Church, then, the only true Church?"

"Henri, how big is the world out there?"

Henri looked up. Jeanne Marie was staring out into the falling snow, and beyond. "I don't know, Jeanne Marie. I do know that you can travel for miles and miles and there is still more to go."

"How do you know? Did you travel for miles and miles before you came to Ste. Anne's?"

Yes, he wanted to cry out. But instead he said, "You haven't answered the question, Jeanne Marie."

"Oh." She tossed her head. "Everyone knows that one. The Catholic Church is the only true Church established by Jesus Christ, while the two hundred or so Protestant Churches are false or man-made Churches."

"Protestants," Madame said softly. "In all the village there is not one of those people."

"And what if there were?" Monsieur Laurent retorted.

Now it was Henri whose attention wandered.

"What if there were!" Madame cried. "Suppose their children played with yours? Think what might happen!"

"What?"

"They might learn all sorts of terrible things!"

"Such as, that other people worship God in their own way? Who says," he lowered his paper and looked straight at his wife, "that Heaven is reserved only for Catholics?"

"Sh! It is blasphemy to joke about the Church!"

"I was *not* joking."

Madame caught sight of the children staring at them. "Go back to your catechism," she said sharply. "Children should not listen to the conversation of adults!"

Henri bowed his head guiltily. After a moment, Jeanne Marie did the same.

"I'm glad," she whispered to Henri, "that there aren't any Protestants in Ste. Anne's."

Henri looked down at the next question: Could the Catholic Church ever teach error? He could not bring himself to read the word. "Would you play with someone who isn't Catholic?" he asked.

"Would you?"

"It wouldn't make any difference to me," he answered slowly.

"Well, it would to me. I know that good Catholics are assured of a place in Heaven. No matter what Papa says, I am not at all sure of the others."

Henri stood up. "I'm going home. I'm tired, Jeanne Marie."

"But it's before our usual time!"

Henri bowed politely to the Laurents, put on his boots and coat, and let himself out.

"There," Madame Laurent said. "You've upset the boy, you and your blasphemies."

"If I have upset him enough to think for himself, then that's all to the good." Monsieur Laurent settled into his leather chair and went back to his paper.

Madame Laurent shook her head.

Somehow, Jeanne Marie felt it was not her father who had disturbed Henri. She was the one.

CHAPTER
15

ON HIS next Friday visit to Father Guardian Henri found it hard to talk. For a long time he sat listening to the faint drip, drip outside the window, broken occasionally by a faint crash as an icicle fell. Finally he said, "Catholics must be born Catholics. The others don't belong!"

The Father Guardian studied Henri. "What's troubling you, my son?"

Henri moved the toe of his foot across a crack in the floor. "It's Jeanne Marie," he said in a thick voice. "She wouldn't play with me if she knew I wasn't a Catholic. If she wouldn't, then the others wouldn't either."

"Henri, we are all sons of the same Heavenly Father. Among us there must be only the brightness of love and its practice. I am very disappointed in Jeanne Marie. But there's no need to worry. You *are* a Catholic. You were baptized as such. I know of no one in the village who is better prepared to be received into the church. I'm so proud. First in your communion class!"

"But if the others knew I wasn't born a Catholic, maybe they wouldn't let me take communion."

"No one can stop you except yourself. If you have faith, the Church will receive you with great joy."

"I try to have faith, Father Guardian." Henri raised his eyes.

"My child, try to understand what I have to say. There is no need to mention that far off place you came from."

It took Henri a moment to focus. "You mean not even Mama, Papa, Charles, or Emilie?"

The Father Guardian nodded gravely. "If you keep them sacred in your heart, no one will be able to take them from you. It's enough that you know they are there. You don't need to share them with the others."

"I promised Monsieur Dupier I wouldn't mention them."

"Perhaps he was right, Henri, to ask for your promise. After all, we have tried to find them and have failed. It will do you no good to speak of them. If they are alive, perhaps they will find you. With God's help you will find them one day. If not, surely you will meet them in a Kingdom more everlasting than this one, Henri."

"But I know they're alive, Father."

"I pray they are. But for now, Henri, try to think of those around you. Look at Mathew Chaumière, who wants so desperately to go to school, but must stay home and work on the looms to make a few extra pennies for his family; and Robert Rousselein, whose mother just died. There is so much you can do. You could help them all, Henri, those who have also known much sorrow. You are not the only one who has suffered."

Henri closed his eyes, squeezed them tight to keep back the tears. He was all by himself. He knew that he

117

had to remain here for some time; and knowing it, he wanted so much to belong here. If only they'd let him!

He opened his eyes and found the Father Guardian watching him.

"I will try to do as you say. Some day I'll explain it all to Mama. She'll understand."

"I am sure she will, Henri." He nodded his head. "I am sure of it."

Now Henri studied the catechism harder than ever. Almost always his answers were letter-perfect. Torn between pride and jealousy, Louis would say, "You don't have to kill yourself. We're going to receive communion anyway." Yet Henri felt he could afford to leave no room for doubt.

Monsieur Dupier was delighted with Henri's progress, but not so much as to buy him a new suit for the occasion.

"We will press this one," he declared, holding up a shabby suit the boy had worn over a year, "and it will look quite presentable."

Henri stared at him in disappointment.

Catching the look, Dupier said angrily, "We do not have money to throw out. This is an occasion of the soul. What the body wears is inconsequential."

Henri sat with bowed head. He did not mind the old suit in itself: it was the effect on the other children. Jeanne Marie had shown him the lovely white dress, shoes and veil she would wear. And Louis had bragged about the suit his father had bought him from the very store in which he worked. What would they say when they saw him in his old suit? No matter how he tried, he always seemed set apart from the others.

Next Friday afternoon Henri, ashamed of his reaction, tried to hide it from the Father Guardian, but he could hide nothing from him. Saturday afternoon, Dupier answered a summons to the monastery.

Without preliminaries, Father Guardian asked about the suit.

"I do not have the means for a new suit," Dupier said sullenly. "In the eyes of the Lord, it makes no difference."

"I'm afraid that at the age of ten a boy is also concerned with the eyes of the villagers. I should like time to think of it."

"You propose something, Father Guardian?"

"I have already done something: I have prayed. I am sure the Lord will not fail to answer me."

Dupier was not long gone when the friar finished a letter to his sister in Montreal and summoned a lay brother to take it out with the rest of the mail. In no time at all, the Father Guardian's prayer was on its way to Montreal in a thin white envelope.

The land thawed out, and there was a breathlessness in the air as the day of the Holy Communion drew near. Poor as they were, somehow all of the parents managed to provide their children with new outfits for the occasion. And somehow Henri got a new suit, too.

"I do not understand it," Louis's father muttered over and over again. "That Dupier. I always said he was a strange one. Cries poverty, and then for the Communion suddenly a new suit appears. And such a suit! It would take many days of work to purchase such a suit."

He was wrong in one respect. Dupier had worked for none of it. When the Father Guardian's prayer had been answered, he had summoned Dupier to him, and given him the suit for Henri.

When the boy tried to thank him, Dupier's bitterness

spilled over. "I could find better ways to spend my poor amount of money! Thank your precious Father Guardian."

And to do just that Henri hurried to the monastery. "Just a secret between us, eh, my son?" The Father Guardian smiled down on Henri.

For answer, Henri grabbed his hand and pressed it against his cheek, while his eyes showed the love that consumed him for the man in the Capuchin robe.

It was a clear, sunny May day when the children gathered for first communion; but to Henri everything was blurred by a strange feeling. As he passed down in the procession, he did not know whether this strange wonderful feeling came from being part of the village group, or from the solemnity of the mass. But he was glad. Briefly he thought of Dupier, and was surprised that for the first time he seemed to think almost kindly of him. When thoughts of his family crept into mind, he brushed them quickly aside. He did not want to think of them now; he had no desire to dwell on his past. It was almost as if he had accepted the fact that his life started with the moment he had arrived in Ste. Anne of the Prairies.

Then it was over. The families spilled over the steps and onto the road. Their chattering made happy sounds in the sun.

Madame Laurent stopped Dupier, smiled at Henri. "It would please us so much if you and Henri would dine with us."

Dupier stood there uncertain, embarrassed.

"Oh please say yes," Jeanne Marie cried.

Finally Dupier bowed and said, "We would be honored."

Waiting for them at the steps of the Laurent house was a sparrow of a man, loaded with photograph equipment. "Hurry," he called. "Madame is late. There are so many others."

"Yes, of course," Madame Laurent said. "Accept my apologies, Monsieur. Come on. Perhaps a glass of wine—"

The little man fussily began to set up his equipment. "I'm afraid I'm much too busy to take time for trifles."

"One can see that," Madame Laurent agreed, as she moved swiftly. "Here. I've poured it for you to save time. It will fortify you for the day."

She had barely finished the sentence when he snatched the glass, swallowed the wine, and thrust the glass back in her hand.

"Now where is our little angel?" He wiped his mouth with the back of his hand and turned to Jeanne Marie. "Ah! An angel indeed."

When Jeanne Marie's pictures had been taken the photographer turned to Henri. "Perhaps the young man," he suggested.

"No," Monsieur Dupier cried. Then, modifying his tone, "I'm afraid that's impossible."

"Perhaps the two children together," Madame Laurent said.

Quickly he posed them like a small bride and groom.

"No!" Dupier leaped forward and dragged Henri away from Jeanne Marie.

"Time enough for that, eh, Monsieur?" Laurent grinned.

"Yes, yes," the photographer said. Then he collected his belongings and departed.

Soon they sat down to the table.

The meal was a strange, uneasy one, with Bernard,

Martin, and Pierre Laurent stirring restlessly, Madame Laurent reprimanding them from time to time, Monsieur Dupier barely looking up from his plate. Henri himself had eyes only for Jeanne Marie. Her white communion dress, with the lace ruching around the neck, made a perfect frame for her flushed, happy face. Her eyes seemed bluer than ever; her long hair, held back with a ribbon on school days, was now spread into a golden fan about her shoulders. Henri thought she was the prettiest girl in all of Ste. Anne. Toward the end of the visit, Dupier caught him looking at her, and for some reason he quickly dropped his eyes.

Then they had finished. At once Dupier made their adieus and hurried him out. As they reached the rutted road Dupier said, "Jeanne Marie knows her catechism now. She should also have caught up with her lessons. You are not to go there to work with her any more!"

Henri was bewildered.

"Promise, Henri!" Dupier's voice rose shrilly. "Promise!"

His mind racing, Henri said in a low voice, "I promise not to work with Jeanne Marie on her lessons any more."

"Good!"

For the rest of the way home Dupier was silent. Once inside the door, he made Henri sit on a straight chair opposite him.

"I find I must speak of this sooner than I thought," he began, "but you are never too young to know the meaning of evil." His eyes had a look that Henri dreaded.

"Women are evil! Remember that. If Eve had not given in to temptation all the world would not be committed to everlasting sorrow, and the burden of trying to find favor again in the sight of God!"

As Dupier went on, quoting more and more from the Bible, Henri recognized much of it but understood little of what Dupier was trying to tell him.

"Soon there will come a time when the girls will smile at you. They will beckon and call. But you must hold yourself above the temptations of the flesh. Remain chaste. Have nothing to do with them. Now or ever. Serve woman only through Mary, the Holy Mother of us all. It is the only way, Henri, the only true way to live."

"But Monsieur—"

"It is for the others to marry and sin with women. It is not for such as we. You will mind what I say." He smiled, showing his poor teeth, chucked Henri awkwardly under the chin, and went to his prayers.

That night it took Henri a long time to go to sleep.

What was Dupier trying to tell him? That he was not to be like other people? And who had singled him out to be different?

Often when he fashioned houses in his play, the thought had taken shape that one day he would live in just such a house. Jeanne Marie would be the mama, he the papa, and there would be children, of course.

Now Monsieur said that was wicked; that he would always have to live alone.

What was wicked about getting married? What did Monsieur Dupier want? Did he want him to become a priest? The thought made him feel cold and lonely.

Then Henri remembered the Father Guardian. He would talk it over with him. *He* would tell him what to do.

The future began to retreat; growing up took many years.

With that comforting thought, Henri fell asleep.

CHAPTER
16

MAY 22, 1910, was just like any other day for Henri. In fact it was not until he arrived at the Father Guardian's study late in the afternoon that he realized it was a special day.

"Happy birthday, Henri," the friar greeted him.

"That's right. Today is my birthday. I had forgotten."

"Isn't it unusual for a boy of thirteen to forget such an event?"

"I don't think of birthdays any more. I only think of my life in Ste. Anne."

"Well, I hope, Henri, that this next year will be a happy one for you." The friar seated himself opposite Henri. "Now, haven't I always said I chose well? The good priests say that you have learned all they can teach you. Secure in the arms of the Church, you are ready to go forward now."

Henri felt warm: he had pleased his beloved Father Guardian. But was that where he wanted to be forever, in the arms of the Church? The Father Guardian was so sure it was the best possible place to be that Henri felt guilty for not feeling equally as certain.

"Well, my son, where do you wish to go?"

"Monsieur Dupier wishes me to become a priest," he said in a low voice.

"And you, my son? Do you wish to serve God?"

There was a small silence.

"I, I don't know." Henri raised his eyes to the man. "To be a priest like you must be a wonderful thing."

Deeply touched the friar looked away.

"Then sometimes, when I see Monsieur Laurent with his family about him, I think that's what I'd like, too. A family I belonged to and that belonged to me."

The friar nodded.

"Then, too, I've never given up hope of finding my family. Is it wicked to long so for my mother? Am I too old now to need her?"

The friar shook his head.

"If I could only see her once—" he sighed—"perhaps I wouldn't even care to stay with her. Perhaps, after all, I'd find I am happiest here. But how will I know if I never find her?"

Now the friar sighed.

"If I become a priest," Henri continued slowly, "I should never be free to go back. So you see, I do not know what to do."

The friar took a deep breath. "To minimize something that means a great deal would be foolish indeed. However, if you decide to enter the seminary here, it doesn't mean you must become a priest or a monk. You need not enter your novitiate at the end of the six years, or at the end of three more, or at all."

Henri's eyes widened with surprise.

"That is so," nodded the friar. "Sometimes during the advanced learning period a boy discovers that he is not meant to devote his life to God in that way. It is then that the career of teacher, lawyer or doctor seems more desirable."

"I don't have to decide now?"

"Not now. Or for some years to come."

"In that case, if you'll have me, I'd like very much to come."

"There is no one we would rather have. I am convinced Henri, that you will serve God no matter what you do; but if you decide to serve Him as a priest, don't think you would be forsaking your family. If it is God's will, you will find them. The surrender that goes with rest in God will bring you a sureness of shelter, delivering your soul from dread and solitude."

"There is one thing. I would like your word that you'll not leave us rashly during your studies. You are still too young to go off and look for your family. You are to stay with us until your education is completed. If you are still of a mind to look for them then, I give you my word I will do all in my power to help you."

"Six years," Henri said. Six years was a long time. In six years he would be nineteen. He was certain he could work and earn money long before then. But how long before? And what would he do in the interim. He loved learning. Young as he was, he knew with certainty that for him an education was as important as life itself. At nineteen he could go look for his family. Yes, the moment he finished his schooling, he would leave and find them. "Yes, Father, you have my word. And thank you."

Henri left the Father Guardian and walked slowly

home. Every so often he would pick up a rock in his path and throw it so far that he'd have to stand an instant and wait for the sound of its falling.

Spring was everywhere. Here the white blossoms of a wild apple tree were peeping through their hoods of pink, there stood a clump of mountain laurel. How blessed was their sparse shade in the warm sun. There was so much to be thankful for today, he thought, continuing down the path.

The friar was like a father to him. In his patient wisdom he knew the answers to all uncertainties. No problem was so complex that it did not become simpler in the telling to this gentle man. Henri felt as if he belonged more to him than to anyone on earth; and Father Guardian should know better than anyone else where he really belonged.

Then he saw Jeanne Marie, hanging up the wash in front of her house. Straightening out a large white sheet to hang it properly, she held it to her chest, and her long blonde hair fell over it. She looked up and caught sight of Henri.

"Well, look who we have here," she called. "It is a long time since school was dismissed. Where were you? Flirting with Madeleine Rouen, no doubt."

He laughed and Jeanne Marie laughed with him.

"What do you say we play mama and papa," she suggested.

"Don't be foolish," Henri said. "We're too old for that."

"My Papa helps Mama all the time. And you can help me hang up this wash."

"That's not playing papa and mama," he said ruefully. "That's working at it." Nevertheless, he picked up the pins and began to hang the opposite end of the sheet.

"You are a darling! I love you, Henri!"

"Because I am helping you hang up the clothes," he grinned. "What would have happened if I didn't play your game with you?"

"Oh, I would love you anyway," Jeanne Marie said airily.

"Well, if I'm to be worthy of such love, we had better hurry. Monsieur Dupier will not appreciate your devotion if I don't have the supper ready on time."

Dupier chose that day to arrive home early.

"Surely you were not in school all this time. Classes were over a long time ago. Where did you go?"

"To see the Father Guardian," said Henri.

"Always with the friar! One would think he was responsible for you." Dupier moved about the room picking up his books. "And what did Monsieur Friar have to say at such length?"

"He asked me if I wished to enter the Capuchin seminary this fall. I said yes."

"So you said yes," Dupier muttered. "And what about your poor Uncle Paul? He'll have to shift for himself, and work extra hard to put clothes on your back while you stay comfortably shut away for the winter!"

Henri knew that Dupier wanted him with the Capuchins more than he wanted anything else on earth, so he made no reply.

They sat down to their simple supper. As soon as they had said grace Dupier began again.

"Let me tell you, young man," Dupier waved his fork in the air, "it's a rare privilege to study for the priesthood. Not many get such an opportunity. But if you think it's coming to you, if I must sacrifice myself for you, you

must start doing some work to help yourself through!"
He glared at Henri.

"I'll be glad to work, . . . Uncle Paul." Odd, six years
had passed and the words Uncle Paul still stuck in his
throat. "I'll see Monsieur Laurent first thing in the morning. Perhaps he can find some work for me at the mill."

"Are you sure it's Monsieur you wish to see, or is it
his daughter?"

Henri continued eating in silence.

"And when is my wood to be cut for the winter? Or
am I supposed to freeze while the friar's pet remains
good and warm!"

"I'll cut enough to last until next summer."

"Well, see that you do it then!"

With which gracious remark, they continued the meal
in silence.

Late that same afternoon Mrs. Fath sat in the parlor
of her home in Philadelphia. Outside, the white spirea
moved gently. In the breeze, the sweetnss of the lilies
of the valley mingled with the scent of new-mown grass.
From where she sat, she caught a glimpse of Emilie and
Charles leaping from the pony cart. They ran laughing
up the walk, and halted abruptly.

Dimly Mrs. Fath was aware of Fraulein shushing
them, explaining with a glance toward the parlor.

That was not right, she thought distantly. Emilie and
Charles should not be made to suffer because of her unhappiness.

Then her eyes returned to the picture of Henri. His
blue eyes continued to smile down at her. He cannot be
dead, she kept thinking. Not her beautiful boy. It cannot
be.

129

In the distance, wheels crunched on the gravel, and then heavy steps approached her door. Mr. Fath appeared in the doorway.

"How are you, my dear?"

"Today"—his wife seemed not to have heard his greeting—"he would have been wearing your prayer shawl." Her eyes dropped to her hands lying idle in her lap. "It would have been a blue suit. Remember how blue brought out the color of his eyes—blue lamps they were, surrounded by circles of darker blue. Any color is permissible for the suit, you know, but I thought navy would be the best." Her voice became suddenly anxious. "You do not mind the navy?"

Mr. Fath shook his head silently.

She nodded her head as if in relief. "How firmly he would hold the Torah! And how Henri could sing. You remember, do you not? His voice would fill the synagogue with the prayers that make music."

Mr. Fath sat down, pressed the heels of his hands into his knees.

"We were too proud," his wife whispered, "too proud. That is why God has left us only a picture for his thirteenth birthday. Oh God, why?" Her voice cried out despairingly. "Henri was so good. He didn't harm anyone!"

Fath said, "We must always remember that. Henri did harm to no one! God would not forsake him. He is in his hands. Somewhere God is watching over him."

The first week of the summer dragged by with Henri working hard at the lumber mill, gathering the wood shavings to be sold for kindling, a job Monsieur Laurent had secured for him.

Saturday evening, with his first week's pay of four dollars and fifty cents in his pocket, he stopped by to visit Louis.

"It is harder to work in the store," sighed Louis.

"You think so?" Henri rubbed his sore muscles.

"Maybe not," admitted Louis. "But I would rather work outdoors with you. Think of the fun when the girls come to bring their fathers' lunches. No one ever comes into this place who likes to laugh! And I never get out at all."

"You're closed on Sunday," said Henri. "Why don't we go fishing tomorrow? Surely if we go to early Mass, God will forgive our getting cooled off a bit at the river."

"It is not God's forgiveness that worries me," said Louis. "It is my father's." He made a droll face and Henri could not help laughing with him.

Sunday Jeanne Marie came along with them. It was a beautiful day, made for drowsing and resting. The sunlight poured down through the trees, baking the patches of ground beneath. The only relief was under a large tree, whose branches overhung the river. The three of them sat there, their lines trailing lazily in the water.

"Henri," Jeanne Marie broke the stillness, "would you like some cold buttermilk and cookies?"

Just then Louis's line bobbed and he pulled it in. It was empty.

"What a time to choose to speak! Just when I had a fish on the line! 'Henri, would you like some buttermilk?' " he mimicked. "Never 'Louis, you must be dying of thirst.' Or 'would you like a cookie?' Even a dog deserves a drink on a hot day. But no, never Louis. Only Henri. Now my fish is gone!"

"You're being silly, Louis," she said.

"So only Louis is silly—"

"Sh-h," Henri whispered. "I think I have something."
He worked his line. Soon a silver fish danced in the
sun.

"You certainly have something. Why can't I be that
lucky?"

Henri worked hard through the summer. He rose early
and cared for the vegetable garden before going off to
work in the mill all day. At night, he helped gather and
preserve the vegetables as they became ready, gradually
filling the cellar shelves in preparation for Dupier's long
winter.

And he cut wood. The men employed at the mill and
their sons were permitted to cut a certain amount of
wood for their own use with the Company's tools, and
on the lumber mill's property. It was an important con-
cession. Those not employed by the mill had to pay for
the privilege, or pay for the lumber in cash in the winter,
when money was scare.

Henri cut and stacked wood until his arms and legs
felt like dead weights. The only relaxation he had was
the occasional fishing on Sunday afternoons.

One Sunday, as Henri and Louis ambled leisurely
down the dirt road to the river, they met Edward Rousselin, Jerome Giradot, François le Clerc, Gaston Fouchette, and someone who was rarely able to get away for
any fun, Matthew Chaumeire.

How thin Matthew was, Henri thought. The Chaumiere family worked so hard. From the first streak of
light to the onrush of darkness, they worked the shuttle
of the handmade looms back and forth. Laboriously they
turned out blankets for some agent in Shawinigen Falls.

So many children with no father. So many mouths to feed.

"Matthew, how is the history book I lent you?" Henri asked.

"It's taking me so long," sighed Matthew. "I never have time. And there are so many wars to read about. I don't understand all those people. Why did all of them make wars, Henri? Our country doesn't make wars."

Henri patted him awkwardly on the shoulder. "There's plenty of time. And people are really the same all over. They are either good or bad."

"You think so? Well, you should have seen my father's great aunt. She came to visit us all the way from Neuilly in France. And you should have seen the way she acted!"

"I guess the only real difference is the way people think."

"If good is good, and bad is bad, how can they think differently?"

"I don't know," admitted Henri.

But Matthew was no longer paying any attention. He was watching a train of wagons unloading on the road up ahead.

A major event had just taken place in Ste. Anne: eight Protestant families had just moved in. They had rented some homes south of the town, several of which had long been empty.

A tall, sturdy woman shielded her eyes against the sun. She turned to a boy, who Henri judged to be a year or two older than himself.

"Oh, Harry, tell them where to go. They *would* have to deliver our things on a Sunday!"

Harry walked up to the lead driver and gave the wagoners directions. Then he returned and continued un-

133

loading the wagon that held their own possessions.

The boys watched the unloading for a few minutes and walked on. François le Clerc said, "I wonder what will happen now that we have Protestant families in the village?"

"Probably nothing," Louis said casually. "What do you think, Henri?"

"They aren't any different from us. They'll probably see things as we do."

Matthew said, "They'd better see things the way Father Antoine sees them."

"They shouldn't have come," Gaston said. "There isn't enough work for the Catholics."

When they reached the river, Jerome stretched out under a tree. Louis looked at him in surprise.

"Aren't you going to fish?"

"Yes, but not here."

The boys looked at him. He seemed to enjoy their curiosity.

"In a little while they'll be swimming at Marin's landing. I'll fish there."

"You can't go there," objected Louis. "That's the girls' place."

"Who's going to stop me?" Jerome looked around the circle and grinned.

Edward Rousselin grinned back. "How do you know for sure they will be there?"

"I heard Madeleine Rouen tell Marise Claveaux. She is going with Toni, Rita and Jeanne Marie."

"Then what are we waiting for?"

Louis whirled on Edward. "You are not going to Marin's landing!"

"How are you going to stop me?"

"By using one of your tricks. I'll go and tell Father Antoine!"

Edward came up short and swallowed hard. "I was only fooling," he muttered. Then, spitefully: "I thought Jeanne Marie was Henri's girl, not yours!"

Henri looked up, and Louis got very red.

"Jeanne Marie can do what she wants," Louis said hotly, "with anybody she pleases!"

Jerome said, "And if she pleases to go with you, so much the better, eh, Louis?"

Louis turned away.

"You're disgusting, Jerome," Henri said. "All you have on your mind is girls."

"And you? You haven't, I suppose."

"All right!" Louis cried. "But at least we think of something else once in a while."

By the middle of August the children had tired of teasing Louis, Henri, and Jeanne Marie and left them alone to fish, walk, loll about under the trees and talk. They spoke of their plans and chores, of the coming school year, and particularly the hardships of winter. For Jeanne Marie, just now recovering from the work she did during her mother's illness, Louis had some stern advice.

"Don't do it again, Jeanne Marie," he said one Sunday. "If it's not your mother, it's somebody else, and you're not strong enough. Why do you have to stay up half your nights taking care of sick people? Why does it have to be you?"

"Father Antoine says charity brings joy."

"Charity," Louis retorted with asperity, "begins at home. Every winter you're sick for weeks on end. There are others stronger than you who can help. It's silly for you to make yourself sick over other people."

"I'm happy when I'm helping. Can you understand that, Henri?"

"Yes. Yes, I can."

"Not me," declared Louis. "I find the greatest happiness when I take good care of myself."

"I don't believe you," Henri said.

"Neither do I," Jeanne Marie said. "I think you like chasing the girls best of all."

"That's not true, either," Henri grinned.

"And why not?" Louis said. "You think I'm like you? The minute you're alone with a girl, you run. What are you afraid of, anyway?"

"I'm not afraid. I just don't seem to have anything to talk about."

"You do plenty of talking to Jeanne Marie. Or don't you think of her as a girl?"

Henri stared at him without answering. How could he explain to Louis how he felt about Jeanne Marie? She was such a dear part of his life. She'd been so very close to him from the day he had come to Ste. Anne. She was like a member of his family—someone to be taken care of and cherished.

Jeanne Marie saved him the trouble of answering.

"Now you're getting silly again, Louis. Let's decide what we are going to do for Father Antoine's picnic. Wouldn't it be nice if the three of us could think of a new way to raise money?"

It turned out they couldn't think of a new way to raise money, but in the next week the three of them worked hard making preparations.

When the big day finally dawned, Henri and Louis

arrived early with several others to help. Jeanne Marie was already there with her table decorations.

"I thought you'd never get here," she said. "You have to knock the tables together, so that I can set these down."

Louis looked around him in mock surprise. "I see Henri's friend Harry has not arrived yet. Can it be that he overslept?"

"Henri," Jeanne Marie said, "why must you be so friendly with a Protestant?"

"I'm not being friendly with a Protestant," he said easily. "I'm being friendly with a boy I like."

"Ah," groaned Louis, "I should know better than to start up with St. Henri of the Prairies."

"That's not fair," Jeanne Marie said. "But, honestly, Henri, I can't understand why you're always sticking up for the Protestants. Aren't you glad to be a Catholic? Look what our Church does for us. They help feed and clothe the people, visit the sick, and bury the dead. Where would we be without the Church!"

"There are other churches, Jeanne Marie, and maybe they do as much for their people."

Louis said, "It's a good thing there's no Protestant church in Ste. Anne. If there was, I bet you'd go there, too, just because Harry's your friend."

"No, I wouldn't," Henri said. "It's forbidden. But I wish the Protestants had their own church in town."

After that they finished their work in silence; and because he had other work to do Henri stayed for only a little of the picnic. All summer Dupier who was getting more crotchety than ever, had been saying, "I feel it in my bones that this will be a worse winter than usual. Put in plenty of wood, my boy. Plenty of wood." Henri had

137

cut wood until he thought his back would break, and now he went out and cut some more. He didn't mind missing the picnic: it was a small price to pay for a year of school.

Then it was the last Saturday of the summer, and Henri left work a little earlier than usual to say good-bye to his friends in the village. He mixed with the crowd at the post office. Everyone seemed proud that a boy from Ste. Anne would be attending the Capuchin Seminary, and there was a round of handshaking and good wishes.

Then, saving Monsieur Pillon for last, Henri went up and down the main street shaking hands with the shop-keepers.

As Henri stepped into Claveaux's shop, he wished he had not chosen this moment to come. Madame Giradot was there haggling with Claveaux over the price of a winter dress. Haggling was a vital part of business in Ste. Anne and of all the merchants only Claveaux, who set honest prices and held to them, had no patience for it. Now Henri stood there suffering with him.

"It has not turned out well," Madame Giradot announced, watching Claveaux and fingering the garment. "The cut is poor; the sewing, it is not what I expected. I can't accept it."

"I refuse to discuss it," Claveaux said.

"Of course if you would take something off the full price—"

"I refuse to discuss it."

"I'll have to speak to my husband. Imagine! Full payment for something so unsatisfactory!" Even as she spoke, her eyes caressed the suit hanging on the wall.

138

"Good-bye!" The bell tinkled; she slammed the door behind her.

Claveaux threw up his hands, but then his face lit up with an idea. "Excuse me a moment, Henri." He went to the back of his shop, rummaged about for several moments, then came out with a musty funeral wreath in his hands. To Henri's astonishment he hung up the wreath on the door. And he sat down with an air of deep satisfaction.

In a moment, Madame Giradot burst into the shop. "Who was it? Who died, Monsieur?"

Claveaux did not raise his eyes from his sewing. "I did," he answered evenly.

"You!" She turned to Henri and pointed a quaking finger at Monsieur Claveaux. "You can see him there as plainly as I can, Henri. He is not dead. He's not dead at all." She turned back to Monsieur Claveaux. "You're alive!"

Claveaux raised his eyes, looked dolefully at her for a long time. Then he said, "You call this living, Madame?"

Without another word Madame Giradot counted out the full amount, took her suit, and left the shop.

Henri said good-bye to Claveaux, spent a short time with Pillon, and then his summer was over.

O N SEPTEMBER 3, Henri packed his cardboard suit-
case and climbed on the wagon alongside Monsieur
Dupier.

He would not be coming home that day, or for many
days to come. But he felt no sadness at the thought,
rather a secret joy. Being with his beloved Father Guardian every day would be more like home than the small
gray house had ever been.

Henri's farewell to Dupier was short. He took his suit-
case, walked to the gate, and entered the Capuchin walls.

The routine at the Seminary was rigorous, but Henri
adapted himself to it quickly. He liked the mass at five-
fifteen, and the prayers that followed. They sat down to
breakfast at seven o'clock, but Henri felt more than
fortified for the long day of studies, chores, prayers, and
meditation. Then came a simple supper at six, more
prayers and study, and bed at nine.

The monastery at Ste. Anne was occupied by sixteen

friars. Of these, four were Henri's teachers: Fathers Thomas, Martin, Anthony and Georges. It was Father Thomas who bore the brunt of Henri's growing curiosity.

An intimation came the third day of the first week, as Father Thomas related the Miracle of Lourdes. Henri raised his hand and asked, "Why doesn't a miracle happen to everyone who needs one?"

"St. Augustine described a miracle as something difficult, which seldom occurs, surpassing the faculty of nature, and going so far beyond our hopes as to compel astonishment. Do you understand that?"

"But Father, I still don't know why miracles don't work for everyone."

The friar closed the subject: "It is not for us to question God's will."

On his weekly visit to Father Guardian, Henri said, "I think I upset Father Thomas with my questions."

"What kind of questions, Henri?"

"Well, first I asked him why there are miracles for some and not for others."

"And you were not satisfied with the answer Father Thomas gave you?"

"No, Father, I was not. Do *you* know why there were miracles for some and not for others?"

"No, Henri, I do not. I can surmise that miracles are granted only to those who are wholly at one with God." The Father Guardian smiled. "One should not regard experience as the only source of knowledge."

Henri wandered about the room. "Why can't I believe everything that is taught to me here, Father? I want to so much."

"Faith is a habit, Henri. You will form it in time. And when you have, it will sharpen your reason and intellect." He smiled at Henri. "A questioning mind is an alert mind, but you must also learn to accept certain facts which the Church gives you as incontrovertible."

But Henri's doubts left him restless. There were so many things the Church had no answer for; so many things he was forbidden to think about; so many deeds he could not question—that he was afraid to question.

Then came the day they discussed the Spanish Inquisition in class. Father Thomas was disposed to pass over it lightly. Henri raised his hand timidly.

"Wasn't it wrong to persecute people just because they chose to believe in a different God?"

"Where did you get such an idea, Henri? The Inquisition judged only two groups of persons as heretics. They were Marranos, converted Jews, and Moriscos, the Moors. These people committed crimes of treason against the State as well as heresy against the Church. They had become Catholics for personal profit and social gain. They used their advantages to undermine the faith and the nation.

"They were given a fair trial. Those who repented were given a penance and reconciled with the Church. Those who did not, were condemned and put to death, just as they would have been in any court in Europe."

Henri opened his mouth to speak, to ask how anyone could call *fair* the burning alive at the stake of so many people who wanted only to practice the faith of their fathers. But Father Thomas with a lift of his hand stopped him.

"The Church doesn't favor too much time wasted on such a subject. I do not wish to hear any more about it."

But Father Thomas was as upset as Henri. Finally he took up the matter with the Father Guardian.

"The boy seems unable to accept certain things on faith. I do not know what will become of him!"

Father Guardian smiled. "Henri searches only for the truth. Do not forget, that is what Jesus promised His disciples in His teaching. 'You shall know the truth, and the truth shall make you free.' Faith based on truth, Father, shall endure."

And so it went. Finally the Father Guardian felt he had to bring up the subject again. "Henri, it seems you're making so little progress. Father Thomas grows more concerned. And so do I."

"I'm sorry, Father. But the questions. There are so many questions."

"But you can't always find an answer. It is possible some of them will remain unsolved."

"You mean like the Spanish Inquisition?"

The Father Guardian sighed. "There is nothing unsolved there. It's merely a matter of interpreting facts. Don't forget that the Church's interpretation is based on historical research."

"Are you satisfied with that interpretation, Father?"

"Henri, I do know this: the Inquisition at its worst was not as bad as its critics would have us believe. At its best, it left a great deal to be desired."

"What can I say, Father? I'll try to stop asking questions. I'll try even harder. But there are so many things that one is asked to accept beyond the realm of reason. I find it difficult."

"I don't want you to stop questioning, Henri. Ethics is the fruit of faith. I understand that man's intellect discerns the credibility of the truth to be believed and calls for faith. Faith is a kind of knowing. Faith transcends the power and leaps the frontier of reason. You must begin to believe. You must accept and remember that in the act of Faith, the activity is with God revealing and addressing His word to man."

"I suppose so," Henri said slowly.

"But you're still not sure?"

"I think you're angry with me, Father."

Unexpectedly the Friar laughed. "No, Henri, I'm not angry. When you are sure, you will believe."

"Will the day ever come?"

"The day will come, Henri. It will come."

But that, too, Henri could not accept on faith, and the Father Guardian was forced to admit to himself he had done little to relieve the situation.

Winter rode in early and entrenched itself. Dupier had been right in his prediction of the weather. The snow was deep and temperature thirty degrees below zero when Henri came home for his Christmas vacation. He found that the season's crops had been unusually poor, and hardship had settled over the village.

And the shortage of firewood was acute. Many in the village had not been hired by the lumber mill that summer. Consequently, they had had no chance to cut the free wood vouchsafed employees by the company; and there was less money than ever with which to buy wood.

To meet the crisis Father Antoine called his people together. "Unless we help the needy," he said, "they will suffer cold and privation at this most holy time of the year. I have no right to ask you to share what you have worked so hard for, but the warmth you will lend someone else's hearth may give you such comfort as never came from fuel. Surely that is the greatest warmth of all."

A low murmuring arose.

"I shall leave you to decide," said the priest. "I know you will try to do God's will." He stepped down.

The voices grew louder.

Monsieur Laurent urged by several around him, arose and came forward.

"I have been asked to speak. Are there any objections? Is there someone who would prefer to take my place?"

There was no one.

"I suggest, if I may, that we write down how much each of us can spare, and bring the wood here. Someone will be here to receive and store it. Then let the others write down what they need and come to the church, and they will be cared for as far as the wood goes."

"You speak of the needy," Rousselin called out. "Does that include the Protestants?"

There was a startled silence. Then a voice called out, "Let their church take care of them, just as ours takes care of us."

"But they haven't any church here," said someone from the back.

"That's right," Roget le Clerc cried. "So let them go back where they came from."

And there was a rough laugh.

Achille Pillon rose. "All men, regardless of creed, are entitled to respect, fair dealings and charity. In the Old Testament the rabbis taught that we should support the poor among the heathen along with the poor of Israel, and bury their dead along with the dead of Israel in the interest of peace. Shall we as Catholics do less for a people who are not heathens, who believe in God? For if there is a God, he is God to us all and He teaches you to love your neighbor."

"The Protestants aren't our neighbors! They're intruders."

"Let Achille Pillon speak!" The elder Giradot stood up, his eyes flashing.

The congregation was dumbfounded. Of all people, Giradot! He rarely had a pleasant word for anyone.

But Pillon waved a weary hand, murmered in disgust, "I have nothing more to say."

"Well, I have something more to say!" Monsieur Claveaux stood up. "Perhaps some of us do not realize that our Church believes the gates of Heaven are open to everyone. One does not have to be a good Catholic. One has only to be good. And I say, do unto others as you would have others do unto you."

Madame Giradot was carefully not looking at Monsieur Claveaux.

La Roache rose. "I say we've done enough for them already. We've allowed them to settle in our village and follow their own beliefs, and we've traded with them fairly. What else can they expect? We didn't ask them to come."

As the banker sat down the opposition was silenced, at least momentarily. La Roache's opinion could carry the eventual decision.

Monsieur Laurent thought for a moment, and held up his hand. "Before we decide, perhaps we should hear from the young people. A great deal of this store of wood is the result of their hard labors. They should have a say in disposing of it."

And before anyone could object, Laurent called, "Louis Ferragne!"

Louis stood up, bewildered. His father's eyes were fixed on him. "My father is older and wiser than I." He knew instantly that was what his father wanted to hear. "Whatever he decides will be right with me." He sat down.

"That's a good boy."

"A truly devoted son."

Monsieur Ferragne was delighted.

Monsieur Laurent did not give up.

"Jean la Roache."

"Let charity begin at home. That's all."

Down the line. Jerome Giradot refused to speak. Jacques Claveaux opened his mouth to say something, hesitated, and muttered that he would do what the others wished.

"Henri Dupier."

Henri stood up slowly.

The people watched him, waited with interest. After all he was a student at the Seminary with the Capuchin Fathers. Not many from Ste. Anne's had that distinction. He was a boy being raised well in the sight of God. In all likelihood, some day he would speak for Him.

Henri knew that la Roache had already spoken for the congregation. His voice trembled as he began to speak. "I want to tell you about a family I know. You know the family, too, but I don't think you know what happened to it last winter.

"There was a little boy in the family. He caught scarlet fever, and the people stayed away from his house, and no one helped the family.

"One day, a neighbor found the mother of the family wandering around in the cold, trying to gather wood to keep the dying child warm. This neighbor told his friends, and each gave part of their wood every day. The boy died anyway. Then the neighbor and his friends

147

got together and somehow collected enough money for a funeral."

"What I want to tell you is this: the family whose little boy died is Catholic, and none of us helped them. But the neighbor and his friends, the only people who helped the Catholic family, were Protestants."

There was the sound of sobbing, and Madame Daumier stood up. "It's true!" she cried. "It's true. My poor Robert. And they were so good to us."

Henri was still standing when Madame Daumier sat down. Monsieur Laurent looked at him with shining eyes, then cleared his throat.

"I take it you vote to help all who are in need?"

Henri nodded.

"We will take the vote now," Monsieur Laurent announced. "All those opposed to helping our Protestant neighbors, raise their hands."

Not a hand went up.

Outside in a small circle stood the vanquished.

Edward Rousselin muttered, "That Pillon! Love thy neighbor. I chose my own neighbors."

Just then Henri came out.

"Yah!" snarled Jerome Giradot, "here comes the big one who gives away our wood."

"I think Monsieur Claveaux is right," Henri said. "We must do unto others as we would have them do unto us."

"Yes, that's all we can expect," François le Clerc said bitterly, "from one of those amateur monks." François's father was mayor as well as grocer, but this had not helped his son pass the examinations to enter the Seminary.

"Let's take him down a peg!" Giradot shoved through the group toward Henri.

148

Henri was tall, but Jerome was twice his bulk.

"You leave him alone!" Jeanne Marie sprang in his path.

"Out of my way!" Giradot brushed Jeanne Marie aside.

Louis Ferragne's fist flew out and landed squarely on Jerome's jaw, knocking him down. Louis was more surprised than Jerome.

As Giradot rose, François lunged at Louis. Henri dove in between them, fists flying.

Jeanne Marie's screams brought her father running, and with several others he succeeded in separating the boys.

"What is it? Have you gone mad?" He held Henri and Jerome by the scruffs of their necks. "Will someone tell me what this is about?"

The boys stared down at the snow.

Then for the first time Laurent became aware of his daughter's presence. "And what are you doing here? In a street brawl!"

"Boys," Monsieur Laurent went on, "this is even stupider than I imagined. Why, you don't even know what you're fighting for. Now go on home, all of you, before Father Antoine hears of such behavior!"

As the little crowd broke up, Monsieur Dupier came up to Henri. "Now that you've done your level best to insure my greatest discomfort this winter, let's hurry home."

"Madame Laurent has plenty left of a good soup," said Monsieur Laurent kindly. "Won't you stop by and enjoy it with us?"

In a brief struggle between pride and hunger, Dupier's keen appetite won. "If you insist." He bowed formally.

They were all scraping the last of the soup from their bowls when Dupier suddenly clapped his hand to his forehead. "Mon Dieu! I've forgotten to correct the papers for the holiday exhibit. They're due the first thing in the morning."

He slapped on his cap, struggled into his coat and overshoes and opened the door. The cold seemed to remind him of proper behavior.

"Madame," he bobbed his head, "Monsieur, I thank you for the soup." He glared at Henri. "It helped eradicate a bitter day. You, Henri, are to follow me, but immediately!" And he strode through the door.

The Laurents sighed audibly as Henri reached for his things. Jeanne Marie stood by as he dressed. He smiled: just standing near her gave him a warm glow.

"You don't really believe," she whispered, "that Protestants are permitted to enter Heaven?"

He straightened up, startled. "Not only Protestants, but others as well—Jews, Mohammedans . . ."

Horrified, Jeanne Marie cried, "Not Jews! Not the people from Hebrew Land."

"They're not from Hebrew Land," he explained patiently. "They come from countries all over the world, just as Catholics do. And they're no different from you, Jeanne Marie. They eat, walk, and talk just as you."

The girl kept shaking her head.

"Oh no, not the Jews!" She rolled her eyes for emphasis. "Never."

"Do you think Heaven would be denied to me?" he asked slowly.

"You! Of course not. But then you're a Catholic."

"I was born Jewish."

"No!" She put a clenched fist to her mouth and, looking at Henri as if she had been suddenly confronted with the devil, began to back away from him.

"You're joking!" And then she began to cough.

Henri made a hopeless gesture with his hands. Suddenly he was alone again. Of the two people he loved the most in Ste. Anne, one despised him, and he was a trial to the other.

He longed to comfort Jeanne Marie, but what could he say? That he had been joking? That he had always been a Catholic? These were things he could not say.

A shudder ran through him, and he opened the door. "Good night, Jeanne Marie."

She had stopped coughing now, but continued to stare at him in disbelief.

Henri trudged slowly down the snow-packed path.

Henri returned to the Seminary in a deep depression. For a while he had no questions, and his work suffered; but within a month he was himself again. It was with reserved optimism that he prepared to leave for the Easter vacation.

The first night home Dupier announced, "The Laurents have invited us to dinner Easter Sunday."

"I'd rather not go," Henri said quietly.

"What did you say!" Dupier exclaimed.

"I said that I'd rather not go."

Dupier tried to hide his astonishment, then took a viewpoint which was in opposition to his usual one in relation to the Laurents. "Kindly people offer you the bread from their mouths, and you choose to refuse it. Possibly you think you are now too good for the likes of us since you have entered the Capuchin walls. You will go to the Laurents', my fine young man. If your precious friar does not teach you manners, I will!" Dupier stood over him with an upraised hand.

151

Henri stood up. Nearing his fourteenth birthday, he was as tall as most men in the village.

"You think I can't force you to go to the Laurents?" Dupier shouted. "I'm still your legal guardian."

"You needn't scream at me," Henri said. "*You* were the one who didn't want me to go there. Haven't you told me to stay away from Jeanne Marie?"

"Don't try to confuse me! You know perfectly well I don't want you to be seduced by a temptress."

"I'd hardly call a devout girl of thirteen a temptress. But don't worry. I know Jeanne Marie isn't for me."

"That's more than I gave you credit for!"

An awkward silence fell between them.

On Easter Sunday they started for the Laurent house directly from Church. Henri walked along deep in thought. Since the night he told her he had been born Jewish, many times he had seen in his imagination that incredulous look on Jeanne Marie's face. In a way he feared this meeting. What would she say to him now? Had she told her family? No, she hadn't done that or they'd never have invited him. Madame Laurent was a good woman and devout, but her mind had been closed many years ago, leaving her rigid and uncompromising. As for Monsieur Laurent, while he was of liberal mind, he had learned long since not to argue with his wife.

Jeanne Marie greeted them gaily at the door, but her eyes did not meet Henri's.

There was a coarse white cloth on the table for this important occasion. The smells of spices mingled with the aroma of freshly baked cake.

Easter time. Henri closed his eyes for a moment, and the Passover came back to him. The faces were blurred, but the snowy white tablecloth and sparkling silver were suddenly quite clear, and the murmering of voices, and a feeling of being fondled by unseen hands. His face grew warm, and he turned it away lest it betray him.

To calm himself he sat down in a corner, and silently began to pray: "Oh my God, I love Thee above all things. . . ."

The gentle face of the Father Guardian floated before him, the silent worshiping, and his own small room. All this and more eased his heart, and he felt comforted. These were the things no one could take away. Back there at the monastery his life knew no fears or doubts. There he belonged, and wanted to stay.

"Why so quiet, Henri?" Madame Laurent smiled at him. Then she saw the rosary hanging from his hand. Her eyes widened with pleasure. He knew in that instant there was no one Madame Laurent would rather have in her house.

Night came on with a sudden rush. Dupier and Henri made their adieus.

At the door, Jeanne Marie placed a hand on Henri's arm.

"You're not angry with me any longer?" she whispered.

"I am not angry."

"Then we will be friends just as before." She stood very close to him.

Suddenly, before he knew what happened he bent over and kissed Jeanne Marie's cheek. Then he ran after Dupier.

CHAPTER 18

In JUNE of 1914, five weeks after Henri's seventeenth birthday, the Archduke Ferdinand of Austria was assassinated. The Great War began and slowly spread, reaching out far beyond the Old World shores.

But for Ste. Anne of the Prairies, almost a hundred miles from Montreal, it all had little meaning. The village might have been an island, detached spiritually as well as physically from the sounds and meanings of the spreading disaster. Only rumors of an impending draft and the enlistment of Henri's friend Harry reminded him of the terrible events far away.

As summer began, Henri went back to work at the lumber mill. He worked hard and continued to turn his earnings over to Dupier. His sole relaxation was fishing. Louis was his constant companion. Jeanne Marie spent most of the summer tending a sick aunt in St. Marc, but when she was home, she went with them. Without intending to, Henri kept at a distance from her.

Whatever free time Henri had, he spent in reading. His friend, Monsieur Pillon, owned a veritable mountain of books not available at the Seminary, and as Henri later found out forbidden to those entering the priesthood. Pillon lent them to Henri and he read far into each night.

Henri pondered what he read. One day, near the end of the summer, he walked up the long hill to the Seminary and presented himself to the Father Guardian.

"Father, I am troubled."

The Father Guardian smiled his own special smile. "More questions, Henri?"

Henri had not intended to begin so abruptly. "Father, Jesus was a practising Jew. He attended the synagogue three times a day until he died. He practised no other religion all his life other than Judaism."

The Father Guardian nodded.

"Why then, in the entire Mass is there only one reference made to the faith of our Lord, 'oremus pro perfidis Judaeis'—we pray for the traitorous Jews. Judaism is a religion of righteousness and justice. Why do people try to obliterate it and treat it with contempt?"

"First of all, Henri, the true and literal meaning of perfidis is not traitorous, it is unbelieving, so we say we pray for the unbelieving Jews."

"What's the difference what it really means if people interpret it as traitorous, and so far as I know there has been no attempt to correct that impression!"

The Father Guardian nodded. "You are partly justified, Henri. I can only say that I pray one day the Holy Father in Rome will remove a phrase from the Mass which has been so misconstrued. I think one day he will."

"Why does the Church try so hard to forget Judaism? Why is it never mentioned by name?"

The Father Guardian rose and stood at the open window. He turned back to Henri and said softly. "My son, often do men neither speak nor mention that which lies closest to their hearts. Have you ever heard the question, 'Why is this night different from all other nights?' "

Henri hesitated. "Yes, yes I remember. It is one of the questions asked by the youngest son the first seder night of the Jewish Passover."

"Do you not realize, Henri, that many questions like it are included in the singing of the Exalted on the Holy Saturday of the Catholic Easter?"

"No, I didn't."

"Henri, there are so many things." The friar's voice was gentle. "On the Day of Atonement, Yom Kippur, the holiest of all Jewish days, the high priest in Jerusalem entered the inner sanctuary of the temple and all alone stood before God to intercede for himself, his household and the whole people of Israel. As he stood there, he burned incense that its clouds might veil his eyes, a token of the mysterious solitude of his prayer. During our Benediction service that same kind of incense is used in the Thurible. No, Henri, we have not cast off Judaism. We have fulfilled it as Jesus himself wished it to be."

That winter Henri read more than ever before: the lives of the Saints, the history of the Church, science and mathematics. He became enthralled by the glories of ancient Greece—its art, literature, poetry, drama, and philosophy. Greek architecture fascinated him. He studied the town planning and building techniques of the Greek; he could reproduce the Parthenon from memory; and in his spare moments he amused himself by redesigning

Ste. Anne as a model Greek community. His blueprints were rough but practical.

The night before his eighteenth birthday, Henri lay on his narrow cot, hands clasped beneath his head. He made a conscious effort to sum up his eleven years in Ste. Anne.

How familiar this little world had become to him. He knew everyone in it, everything about it. And he could predict what would become of his classmates almost as surely as he'd predicted what they were doing now.

Louis was now working in his father's shop; François, Jacques, Jerome, and the rest were doing the same. They would live and die in Ste. Anne.

Somehow the butcher shop was a fitting place for Jerome. He was not unlike a fresh, raw side of beef: red, improperly dressed, waiting to be seasoned.

Henri's heart warmed at the thought of Louis. How he had grown. Standing behind the counter taller and bulkier than his father, he had a solidity which went far beyond his bulk. Whenever Henri teased him about how the girls were running after him, he had a standard reply: "You know, Henri, every little girl wants to tend store at least once in her life."

Little girls had become big girls. They did not interest Henri especially, except for Jeanne Marie. And he thought of Jeanne Marie not primarily as a girl, but as something a part of him. He could never be separated from her. She was as dear to him as his family had been.

His family. He remembered the desperation with which he had sought to get back to them. Somehow the urgency was no longer there. In another year he would be free to go and look for them. There was no hesitancy in his mind about that: he would go to New York and search for them because he would never be at peace with himself until he did. He would go, but he would come back.

What would happen to Dupier when he left? Henri found that he still felt nothing for Dupier. The old fear and the anger were gone. If there was anything left, it was pity—the same pity he had spoken of to the Father Guardian years ago.

Henri's thoughts of the future stopped with his finding his family. What would happen afterward? When he came back to Ste. Anne what could he do here?

Would he enter the Church after all? He didn't know. There were so many unresolved questions in his mind, so many differences he could not reconcile. How could such a union be a happy one? Yet there were differences between everyone in the world, and marriages based on trust and love were happy ones. And so it might be for him.

There was trust and love between him and the Church.

And there was a growing faith.

On his eighteenth birthday he stood before his beloved Father Guardian—towered over him, in fact, for he was now six feet tall. The friar held two books in his hand. "I have been sent two American classics in English. I thought you might enjoy them."

"Thank you, Father, for thinking of me."

The friar sat and looked up at Henri. "Well, my son, how does it feel to be so grown up? Another year and you will be in our College." He sighed happily. "A wonderful dream come true."

"But Father Guardian—"

The friar held up his hand. "No. Don't say it, Henri.

I know you have not decided yet. It is just as well. No one knows better than I the weight of the decision you must make. Take your time."

"You must think me ungrateful," Henri said.

"My son, you've given me some of the happiest years of my life. It's I who would be ungrateful if I urged you to make a decision you were unprepared for." He clapped the boy's shoulder. "Go now. Take your holiday in the village. Your examinations have earned you that privilege."

On his way to Dupier's house, Henri stopped and examined a tree which had burst into bloom.

A month ago each leaf had been like a small bird grown too large for the nest, and the furry edges had been crowding through the bud, eager to come alive and share the sun. And then the staminate flowers had appeared, like colored feather dusters. Today they were spread out like green fans glistening in the sun.

As Henri stood in awe of their beauty, he wondered why, as St. Thomas Aquinas said, every day presented moment-to-moment choices of Heaven or Hell. Why Heaven or Hell? Why not just peace on earth? What in heaven could be more beautiful than this budding tree? What could be more perfect?

A squirrel scampered through the woods, and, spying Henri, darted up a tree trunk and disappeared from view.

Henri felt a brief moment of sadness. Just so did the people of Ste. Anne have to scurry around in the summer, getting what little work there was available on the farms, the roads or the mill, in order to buy food and store it up against the long hard winters. He wondered if there were not an easier way for these poor people.

Henri looked around. Everywhere, green was creeping

159

around rocks, crevices, and trees. The air was alive with the excitement of growing things. He gazed back at the monastery, and wished the Father Guardian could share this holiday with him. Each time he left, he felt a sense of betrayal.

But how foolish. The friar had urged him to go, and he would be returning soon. He shrugged his shoulders, began to whistle "*Sur le pont d'Avignon,*" and walked leisurely down the familiar path to Dupier's house.

Dupier did not look well. Now he too had the persistent cough that plagued so many people in Ste. Anne. Henri mentioned it casually, but one could never talk to Dupier. The morning seemed dull and endless.

Finally Henri was free to leave. Jeanne Marie was waiting for him on the steps of her house, her chin in her hands, looking off into the distance.

"I would hate to die and leave such a beautiful day," she sighed.

She was wearing a cotton dress of blue that matched the blue of her eyes. She had never looked more lovely.

"By the time you're ready to leave it," Henri replied, "you'll be so old you won't care any longer what kind of day it is." Then his smile faded. "But you *are* too thin. You do not eat enough!"

Jeanne Marie did not answer.

They called for Louis but he was not ready. He stood distraught outside the store. "It's the inventory. Papa's suddenly decided to count all his worldly goods. You'd think he was going to be called to account by God tomorrow. There's no reasoning with him."

"There will be other times," Henri said.

Louis sighed wistfully. "It's never quite the same."

Henri carried the tackle and Jeanne Marie's little food

basket. As they walked along the road, she stopped and picked up a daisy. It came up root and all.

Henri looked at it a moment, and quoted softly from Tennyson:

> I hold you here, root and all, in my hand,
> Little Flower—but if I could understand
> What you are, root and all, and all in all,
> I should know what God and man is.

"Does the flower tell you nothing, Henri?"

"Oh yes. I see many things. Perhaps I see what Tennyson thought he didn't: Heaven on earth in a wild flower."

"Do you? Perhaps I'll find Heaven in it, too." She began to pull the petals.

"He loves me, he loves me not," she chanted. "He loves me!"

"Who? Do I know him?" Henri smiled.

"You can't know everyone, cloistered so long behind those walls!"

"Ah," he laughed, "it is a secret."

"Yes." Jeanne Marie was suddenly sober. "It is a secret."

They took out their tackle and sat under a tree. The fish were lively and elusive, and exhibited not the slightest interest in being caught. After an hour, Jeanne Marie pulled in her line.

"Let's walk to the end of that road," Jeanne Marie said. "Up to the top of that small hill." She pointed off in the distance.

"Are you sure?" Henri was doubtful. "I have never known you to be such a walker. It's very far—almost to the edge of nowhere."

"Oh, you are always so cautious." She shook her head

impatiently. "For once in your life do something mad. What if it is too far? What if we do perish along the way? Isn't it enough to die doing the thing that was most pleasing and exciting?"

"I have never known anyone to die walking up the Restigouche road," he answered drily. "I have known only of people whose feet hurt them along the way."

Jeanne Marie laughed with him. "If they hurt too much, I will pretend to faint and you can carry me."

Henri stood still.

What was the matter with him? Why did the thought of touching Jeanne Marie set his blood racing? He took a deep breath and started walking along.

The heat was unusual for that time of the year. It was gathered in a thick haze. The tall grass and the new leaves were motionless in the stillness. But for the chirping of the birds and the occasional stir of a jackrabbit and the rustling of the field mice amidst last year's leaves, they walked in silence, alone as if they had reached the edge of nowhere.

It was as long a walk as Henri had predicted. Jeanne Marie had to stop frequently to rest. Finally, fatigued by the heat as well as the miles, they reached the top of the distant hill.

Henri dropped down on the grass.

"I am absolutely dead," he announced. "I don't even care if I have to leave such a beautiful day."

Jeanne Marie laughed. She dropped down on the grass also, and the tilt of the ground urged her close to Henri. He did not know how she came into his arms but it seemed the most natural place in the world for her to be, near his heart. His arms tightened around her, and he buried his face in her long, heavy blonde hair.

"Jeanne Marie," he whispered, "my darling."

Her arms were clasped firmly around him and she did not answer. Instead she lifted her head, and he found himself kissing her warm lips. He strained his body to hers.

At last he pulled away. "Jeanne Marie! What have I done!"

The hand he passed over his forehead came away wet. He was trembling as if he were ill. Somehow he got to his feet, looked away, stammered, "Can you ever forgive me?"

Jeanne Marie sat up. Her arms locked around her knees, she looked at him fixedly. Then, instead of answering, she began to cough.

"It's damp." He caught at her hands and drew her to her feet. They faced each other then at the top of her hill. "The ground isn't good for you."

"I love you, Henri."

"No. No, you can't. I'm not worthy. It could never be!"

"So you have not forgotten after all," she declared passionately. "Do you think I'm a stupid girl who has not grown up enough to know better?" She gave a little sob. "Do you think what you were born would make any difference to me?"

"You see, my darling Jeanne Marie," his voice was low, "there it all is. You look down upon it as a difference. I regard it with honor and respect."

"Henri, try to understand. As a child, my mother was all things to me. That night you told me you were not born a Catholic, I began for the first time to understand my father. 'Only an open mind can create a truly understanding heart,' he always said." She looked toward Ste. Anne, then back to Henri. "You think I see only the village. But it's been a long time since I learned to look far beyond its boundaries. Henri, beloved, my mind will never be closed again."

Finally Henri said, "Come here, Jeanne Marie." Gently he eased her onto a fallen log. "I want you to listen to a story that the Father Guardian asked me to forget. But at this time, it is only right that I should remember. When it is told, you will know why our love would be an impossible thing."

He seated himself on the grass alongside of her, and it was his turn to clasp his arms around his knees. He looked out into the distance.

"I was born many miles from here." He pointed to the south. "I don't think my parents were poor, for I remember a house full of warmth and color." He closed his eyes as if to capture it once more within his memory. "There was Fraulein to care for Charles, Emilie, and me. I think my mother was Viennese and my Father was Belgian. He had spoken French as a child, and my mother decided we should know it also. Monsieur Dupier was our tutor."

"Then he isn't related to you at all!"

"No."

"Then what business did he have with you?"

"Religious. He decided we were not being properly brought up, so he took Charles and me to his church. My father found out and discharged him. So, when he left, he took me with him."

"But how could he?" she cried.

"So very easily. You see, Dupier had promised to show me some trains. How was I, a child of seven, to know that was to be the longest journey of my life? How he got me across the border I still don't understand. I'm sure he drugged me for a good portion of the journey."

"But when you got here! Why didn't you tell someone? Surely there was someone who would have helped you."

"How many people in this village speak English?"

She caressed his hand and held it to her face. "My poor Henri. I remember now. The story about the little boy who ran all over the village looking for his mother. How he refused to believe she was dead. How horrible!" She began to cry.

"Please, Jeanne Marie." He sat up and took a handkerchief from his pocket. "It's been many years since I cried for my mother. I've learned to accept another life, possibly a more worthy one, in its place."

"But your mother, your family—"

"A dream now, Jeanne Marie."

"Have you no wish to find them?"

He was slow in answering. "It is the thing I have prayed for the most of my life."

"Then why haven't you tried? Why do you just sit here in Ste. Anne of the Prairies praying? Why haven't you done something?"

"What would you have me do?" His voice was gentle. "There was an attempt made to find them years ago. The Father Guardian told me they had moved. Probably to another city. Years ago, I tried running away and ended up lost in the woods with a broken leg. Now, where would I begin my search? What would I use for money? To run away from the friars—for what? To spend my life in a search that might yield only pain in the end?"

"I can't understand how you can just give up."

"Oh, no. I have never given up. I know now that I will find them again some day. I am as sure of that as I am that the sun is setting. And I am also sure I've found the way, though I told the Father Guardian I was not sure. In my heart I knew a long time ago. The only thing that kept me from binding myself to the religious life was you."

"So you were in love with me all along! The flower was right."

"I must have been," admitted Henri.

"I've always loved you, Henri. Everything I do, every book I read, is with the thought of pleasing you. Didn't you feel the same way about me?"

"To please you always? Perhaps. I think, above all, I cherished you, Jeanne Marie. I wanted to protect you. To take care of you, always."

"But you never knew you really loved me?"

"I always knew I loved you. You and the Father Guardian are the dearest people in the world to me. And much as I love you, I still feel my place is with the Father Guardian. Can you understand that?"

"No, I can't. When two people love each other, it's right that they get married."

"You can't believe a man can have two loves?"

"Oh yes, I believe that. But he must choose between the two."

"What would I have to offer you?" he cried. "I have no family, no money, no future. Ste. Anne offers nothing for young people. How could I support you properly?"

"God will help us."

"Jeanne Marie," he said patiently, "I know of no one who puts his trust more completely in His hands than I. Still, God can only help man to believe in himself. He can't earn his living for him. That a man must do for himself."

"You've always loved to build things. Why not study architecture? Educated men can do many things."

"It will be four more years before I can finish college.

166

Your mother would never permit you to wait. She is already concerned."

"I will wait forever, if necessary."

"But Jeanne Marie, I am not sure," he groped miserably. "I can't seem to explain my feeling about the monastery. There, I feel so safe, a peace I know nowhere else. I feel that I belong. I'm not at all sure I would be happy in the outside world."

"Why wouldn't you be happy in the outside world? I know of no one more respected than you."

"Respect isn't love."

"People do love you, Henri."

"I don't think they do."

"The point is, you get along so well with people. You could do anything. You know you could."

"I don't know. I'm not sure."

"Then I will be sure for the two of us. I'm only a simple girl, but I know one thing. You've said you love me, and I love you with all my heart. If it must be otherwise, then it's God's will."

She arose and put her hand in his. "It's time to go back now. But let's keep the love we found here, and hold it sacred."

CHAPTER
19

O N THE walk back to the Seminary, Henri felt he was overflowing with sudden joy and great confusion. His head was light, his heartbeat was accelerated, his body glowed with longing. He stopped aghast. Was it sinful to feel this way?

But how could it be sinful to love Jeanne Marie? He loved her purely, to the depth and breadth of his soul. He took out his rosary and with the thought of Jeanne Marie, his prayers seemed endowed with a new strength, a new purpose.

Jeanne Marie was right. They had found something precious, and he hoped they could keep it always.

It was not until he let himself into his small room in the seminary that the thoughts at the bottom of his head rose to the surface.

Why hadn't he tried harder and longer to find his family?

Why, indeed?

Henri imagined how it must seem to Jeanne Marie. Here he was, an educated young man of eighteen. Why did he not write to the authorities, even to the police, and ask their help?

What answer did he have for Jeanne Marie? For himself?

Henri lay back on his bed and closed his eyes.

Living within the Seminary these six years had developed within him an unusual sensitivity to sound. From the movements within the walls he could tell the time almost to the very minute.

Now the friars had completed their hour of recreation and were starting their evening prayers. It was seven thirty, the time for meditation. Peace crept through him and his inward turbulence began to subside.

He smiled at himself. This was the meditation hour for him even though he was not in the chapel with the Brothers.

Why hadn't he told Jeanne Marie what he had promised when he entered the Seminary?

How well he remembered that afternoon. In the hazy gold of the late sun, the tree branches, laden with soft green foliage, blurred into the blue sky. The Father Guardian's face seemed afloat in the golden light. He had laid aside the paper when Henri entered the room.

Henri remembered how he had spoken to him of not running away. The thought of leaving the security of the Seminary and the Father Guardian had left him breathless with fright. He had been glad to agree he was too young to try to find his family by himself.

Then he recalled how he had promised the Father Guardian he would not seek his parents until he had finished his education. That had been almost five years ago. The time was almost up. This coming summer he would be free to go.

Now that he knew he was in love with Jeanne Marie, did he still want to find them so badly?

Yes. He had to set his mind at rest.

And if he found them, would he be tempted to abandon Ste. Anne and go back?

No. Even before he realized he was in love with Jeanne Marie, he had felt the need always to be near her. Now he knew being near her wasn't enough. He had to be *with* her, always.

But he had to make peace with the past before he could go on with the future. He owed that much at least to his family. Love was a way of life, not life itself.

Each moment Henri had with Jeanne Marie was an infinite joy. He never knew he had so much love to give anyone. His days and nights became obsessed with the urge to be near her, to care for her, to cherish her. They found endless things to talk about, and became lost in a world of their own—a happy world filled with laughter. How much laughter had lain dormant within him all these years!

But with it all, he planned and thought of the future.

One night, as they sat on the steps of Jeanne Marie's home, Henri told her what he must do. "When I'm graduated from the Seminary next June, I'll go to work for part of the summer. When I've earned enough money for the trip, I'll go and try to find my family. Whether I find them or not, I'll return in the fall, and if you're still willing to risk a very uncertain future with me, Jeanne Marie, I hope we shall be married."

Jeanne Marie laid her head against his shoulder. "We'll be so happy, Henri."

And so the summer arrived and the summer drifted by. A soft look, a gentle touch of Jeanne Marie's hand, was enough to send Henri's spirits soaring. He would let no day pass without seeing her.

Madame and Monsieur Laurent saw it come about, said nothing, but smiled in pleasure to each other.

Louis Ferragne was the next to grasp what had happened, and it came as a shock. He retreated; his excuses not to join the lovers were transparent, but in their joy they hardly noticed.

One day late in August they came to the river. Henri stretched on the ground, his head cradled in Jeanne Marie's lap. Gently she brushed the heavy hair back from his forehead. It wakened that long-forgotten memory, and he felt bathed in love as he had so long ago. He took her hand in his, and pressed it to his lips.

"I love you, Jeanne Marie."

"And I love you," she whispered. Then they were silent. The white clouds gave way to gray, and a wind rose gently from out of nowhere.

"Summer is gone so soon." She shivered. "There's so little sun in Ste. Anne."

"It depends on where you look for it." Smiling, Henri rose. "For me the sun will shine all winter."

"I hate the winter," she said a trifle sharply. "It takes you away from me."

"When winter is over, spring will come, and the sun will come back."

"I'm an ungrateful girl. You know what I'll do, Henri? I'll pick up every piece of this summer, tie it up, and keep it near me all winter. When it's dark and lonely I'll untie it, and the sun will shine again."

They laughed together.

There was no fall: suddenly winter burst upon Ste. Anne.

171

When Henri went home for Christmas, he was shocked at the change in Monsieur Dupier. He was more emaciated than ever, and the feverish light shone brighter in his eyes.

"Uncle Paul," Henri said, "you look ill. You're giving too much to the church and not enough to yourself. You're not eating properly. You've made yourself sick!"

"The Lord is my shepherd," Dupier said dreamily. "I shall not want. He maketh me to lie down in green pastures . . . . "

"We must lead one life at a time."

"You think I fear death? I welcome it." Proudly Dupier drew up his bony frame. "I am prepared to face my God. Have I not done my work well here on earth?"

Henri did not know how to reply, but made up his mind to speak to the Father Guardian as soon as he returned.

The friar went with Doctor Senntierre to Dupier's house, but Dupier would not allow himself to be examined.

"I have long ago placed myself in God's care," he said stubbornly.

The doctor walked back to the monastery with the friar.

"I could not tell for certain, but he appears to have every symptom of the disease we know so well in Ste. Anne of the Prairies."

"Tuberculosis?"

The doctor nodded.

"Best keep Henri away from him."

The friar hesitated. "How long will it be?"

"Two months, two years," he shrugged. "I can't tell."

"I don't want Henri to know."

"As you wish." The doctor bowed and turned back toward the village.

Henri was waiting in the Father Guardian's office. "How bad is it?"

The friar took a deep breath. "The doctor can't say. Dupier wouldn't allow himself to be examined."

"But he looks so ill." Henri was surprised at his own concern. The distance between Dupier and himself had never been bridged from the day they had arrived in Ste. Anne. There was never a moment of warmth to remember. Yet he felt this peculiar sense of responsibility: Dupier *had* cared for him, fed, clothed, and housed him for eleven years. More than that, he was the only link with the past, and Henri had never given up hope that Dupier knew more than he had ever told anyone.

"Perhaps, Father Guardian, I should leave the Seminary and go back to Monsieur Dupier for the next term. If I took care of him, I might succeed where the doctor might fail."

"I forbid it. You could make no difference, and you might end up destroying yourself."

"I suppose you're right, Father." Henri bowed his head.

Henri was studying in his cell on a March evening when one of the lay friars called him to the Father Guardian's study. There he found Louis Ferragne, breathless and red with cold.

"It's Dupier," Henri guessed. "He's worse."

"Yes. The doctor thinks you and the Father Guardian should come at once. I can't locate Father Antoine."

Silently the three of them moved through the night.

There was a full moon bathing the snow in silver. The air was sharp and clear. Henri drew long draughts of it into his lungs, trying to feel part of all this, but unable to shake the sense of detachment, of unreality.

What was it like, he wondered, never to hear the crunching of the snow underfoot, or feel the spongy new grass, or see the setting of a summer sun?

What was the matter with him? Didn't he know of the glories of Heaven? Hadn't he himself sung their praises? He shook his head, impatient at his own stupidity.

Paul Dupier no longer knew anyonne. He lay there waxen and still. The friar took the holy oil and touched the eyes, softly murmuring the last rites. Henri looked on in numb silence.

Suddenly Dupier opened his eyes and Henri's heart plummeted within him.

"I am tired of the winter." Dupier's voice was querulous. "I shall be glad when it is over." Then he closed his eyes and died.

The next day Henri, Father Antoine, and the Father Guardian went through Dupier's belongings. There was not a scrap of paper with so much as the Fath name on it. Henri was sick with disappointment. If Dupier had held a key to his past it had died with him.

"You wish to keep the house?" the priest asked.

Henri looked around the dull gray room. No matter how much wood had been burned there, the house had never been warm. He hated it. He had always hated it.

"I see no need to keep it."

"If we sell it, it will pay for a good burial. There will be something left over."

"Sell it!" Henri said savagely. "It belonged to him. I could never touch the money."

174

Father Antoine said nothing.

All through the funeral Mass, Henri sat as if turned to stone. When the body was lowered into the grave, the tears finally fell. He felt their warmth as they trickled slowly down his cold cheeks.

Jeanne Marie helped him pack the few belongings that were still in the house.

"You were much moved at the burial," she said shyly. "You have a forgiving heart."

"Don't," he said harshly. "I didn't weep for the death of Paul Dupier."

Jeanne Marie rubbed her cheek against his sleeve.

"You'll find them soon," she whispered, "and I shall help you."

The year was over. Henri stood before the Father Guardian, a full fledged graduate of the Seminary.

"Beloved Father Guardian," he began wretchedly, "I've found a great love in architecture—I don't know how to tell you." He looked down at the floor.

"That you have decided to marry Jeanne Marie?"

"How did you know?" Henri gasped.

"One may live behind cloistered walls, but it does not affect one's eyesight." He smiled.

"I feel that I have betrayed you."

The friar shook his head. "Haven't you learned, Henri, that it's only when you're untrue to yourself that you betray anyone?" He picked up the large cross that hung on his crown, and held it in his hands as if drawing strength from its touch.

"For myself, Henri, I have often wondered how much of my life was due to divine intervention. With you," he looked up into the boy's eyes, "I seem to have no doubts.

If you marry Jeanne Marie, I am sure it is God's will. If you don't, it was something not meant to be."

"I think I should also tell you, Father, that I plan to work for part of the summer, then leave and try to find my family. It's something I must do."

The friar nodded.

"And when I return, Jeanne Marie and I shall get married."

"You are certain you will be back in Ste. Anne by the fall?"

"Yes."

"Then I will keep a place open for you in the College. There is no course in architecture, but there are many books."

"But Father—"

The friar held up his hand. "I know you expect to get married. But things may not go as you plan. It is wise to think ahead, to prepare for emergencies."

"I have no right—"

"You have every right. Whenever men seek the highest, it is holy. Go ever forward my son. Trust in Him. God's will be done."

The next day Henri presented himself at the Laurent house, dressed as well as he could manage. He stood before Monsieur Laurent. He bowed, but before he could begin, Monsieur Laurent stood up easily and grasped Henri by the hand. "No need to speak, Henri. Nothing would make us happier. To my wife and me, you are already a son!"

Jeanne Marie came out of her room in a new flowered cotton dress. Her large blue eyes glittered, and there was an unusual flush to her cheeks.

Henri looked at her with concern. "Do you feel all right, Jeanne Marie?"

"Of course. Why?"

Henri put his hand to her cheek. "You seem feverish. Are you sure you're not ill?"

"It isn't every day a girl gets engaged, Henri." Madame Laurent smiled, drew Henri to her. "Allow me to welcome my new son."

Monsieur Laurent disappeared, and within a few moments came back with a dusty wine bottle. "I've saved this for a long time. Let's drink to your happiness, my children."

Then Jeanne Marie's brothers came in to toast them also. Pierre lifted his glass high: "To our sister's husband, who has been a brother to us for so long."

The three boys downed their glasses and beamed at him bright-eyed. Henri felt overcome. If he never found that family of long ago, what love he had in this one.

They planned the wedding far into the night.

On this point Madame Laurent spoke with great conviction. "No daughter of mine will go out of this house unprepared. We must preserve much more food, and we must begin to sew immediately. There are sheets, cases, cloths, and clothes!" She threw up her hands. "Jeanne Marie, we shall have to work long and hard this summer!"

"No need to kill yourselves," Monsieur Laurent said. "The wedding can always be postponed for a month."

"No!"

There was a startled silence. Everyone looked at Jeanne Marie. She lowered her eyes, and her hands clenched and unclenched themselves. "I'm superstitious. It's bad luck to change a wedding date."

Henri walked over and took both her hands in his. "Everything will be just as you wish, Jeanne Marie. We'll change nothing. You can prepare your dowry long after we're married."

Everyone laughed in relief.

In the days that followed, Henri saw Jeanne Marie seldom. He protested to Madame Laurent: "What do I care if there are two sheets or ten, if she has new clothes or not? She will kill herself if she doesn't stop."

"It's a labor of love." But for the first time, Madame Laurent sounded concerned.

And when they were together, it was not for long. Where they once talked far into the night, he insisted she go off to bed early instead. At first she refused, then she seemed to go almost in relief.

The time to leave Ste. Anne drew near for Henri. They didn't speak of it, but each night Jeanne Marie clutched him in terror, as if he would not be back again.

Henri watched her strength seep slowly away. Yet he was not prepared, one night, to come and find her already in bed. Madame Laurent was waiting for him outside.

"Would it make you very unhappy, Henri, to wait to be married? This fall seems so soon. There is still so much to be done. Jeanne Marie is not herself. The doctor has suggested that you wait."

"For Jeanne Marie, I would wait forever." Henri smiled and frowned at almost the same time. "But we must be certain to get her well quickly. I suppose she's unhappy about the postponement?"

"She's terribly upset," Madame Laurent admitted. "She has some wild idea that if you don't get married now, she'll lose you."

178

"I'll go in and reassure her. With your permission, of course."

"Of course."

There was no doubt that Jeanne Marie had been crying. Henri sat at the side of the bed and put his arm around her. "No need to be unhappy, my beloved. We'll have a whole lifetime together. There's plenty of time."

"But you're going away. And when you remember a silly sick girl in Ste. Anne, you'll never come back. Oh Henri, if you would only wait to look for your parents. When I'm well again, I could bear it."

Henri smoothed her hair, sat silent for a long while. There was no longer the urgency, but he had waited so long for this summer. If he didn't go now, perhaps he would never go, never find them. And if he did, would they be strangers to him? Would they know him, love him as he knew Jeanne Marie loved him?

It was Jeanne Marie who mattered. Henri knew without any doubt or question that no sacrifice would be too great for him to make for Jeanne Marie. She could have his life for the asking. He knew he could never leave Jeanne Marie while she was ill when she might need him.

"I've waited so long, I can wait a little longer." He smiled down at her.

She threw her arms around his neck, and snuggled her head against his shoulder. "I know I shouldn't have asked, Henri, but I'm glad I did. You've made me very happy."

They sat quietly for a long time. Finally Jeanne Marie asked, "But what will you do instead, Henri?"

Henri had been thinking of the same question, and was ready with the answer. "I'll work through the summer. Save what I have and can earn. Then I'll return to

179

the Capuchin College. Father Guardian has saved my place. He says that they can teach me quite a bit about architecture. I'll be prepared to build a modest castle for my princess when she's well enough to climb the spiral stairs."

Jeanne Marie laughed happily. "What a silly fellow you are." She lay back with the radiant look of a woman who knows she is loved.

The war raged on in Europe. When his call came, Henri reported to the draft board in Three Rivers. There for the first time Henri realized that his eyesight had been blurred for some time. He was refused and returned to the Capuchin College.

Ste. Anne was still disinterested in the war. They were fighting their own grim battle for survival against another deadly winter.

The Father Guardian collected as many books on architecture as he could legitimately requisition from the resources of the Provincial. Henri devoured them all. He had been without a home for so long he seemed to find his greatest joy in planning them, if only for others. He turned out to have fine talent for practical building. When one wing of the monastery became so cold and drafty as to be unhealthy, Henri devised a method of insulation for it.

The Father Guardian begged God's forgiveness for his pride in the boy. And he told Henri, "You're a born builder, my son. One day you will leave a symbol here on earth that will never be forgotten."

Henri looked forward to that Christmas with anticipation. There had been no questioning of his decision: The Father Guardian never mentioned it again. He and

Jeanne Marie were free to discuss marriage openly. For some months he had worked on his present for her. It was a table, the kind to stand beside a bed. He had divided it into two sections. Under the top surface there was an opening for books. The bottom section had a door that could be locked. It was large enough to contain a sewing basket or any other small necessities.

There was a sheen to the wood that only loving hands could have put there. How many times had he closed his eyes and imagined Jeanne Marie's face when she saw it! It would be the first article of furniture for their future home. It seemed only fitting that it should be made by his own hands.

Nothing remained to mar his happiness as he loaded the table on the Capuchins' wagon. His friend Brother Armand drove him to the village, and they had a merry time along the way.

Henri jumped down in front of the Laurent house. Carefully he carried his table to the porch and set it down. With a wave to Brother Armand he knocked at the door.

Pierre, grown tall and handsome, answered. He stood and stared at Henri for a moment as if startled to find him there. Finally he seemed to recover himself.

"*Bon Noël*, Henri." His voice was barely a whisper.

As Henri prepared to answer he felt a strange sensation, as if a cold hand had touched him.

Pierre opened the door wider.

"Come in. Ah, you have brought Jeanne Marie your Christmas present." He looked at it for a moment and his eyes filled with tears.

"What is it?" Henri cried. "What's happened?"

Pierre lifted the table into the house. At that moment

181

Henri saw the doctor come out of Jeanne Marie's room. Again he cried, "What is it? Tell me!"

As the doctor cleared his throat, Henri pushed by him and opened the door to Jeanne Marie's room.

At the sound, she slowly turned her head and smiled. Her eyes were shining, her cheeks were flushed.

"Oh, my darling." Henri knelt beside her bed. He took her hand and kissed it gently. "What is it, my love?"

Jeanne Marie opened her mouth to speak but began to cough instead. It seemed as if she would never stop.

CHAPTER
20

HENRI did not know how long he sat with Jeanne Marie. But some time later there was a soft movement beside him. It was Pierre. "Henri, Monsieur the Doctor would like to say good night."

Henri arose and followed him out as if in a dream. His eyes were burning, and he ran his tongue along dried lips.

The Doctor was seated beside Monsieur and Madame Laurent at the table in the center of the room. Henri sank dizzily into a chair.

Monsieur Laurent stood over him. "Drink this, Henri." He drank the brandy in a single gulp, and choked; but it burned him back to reality.

"You see how it is, Henri." Madame Laurent clasped her hands on the table. "My Jeanne Marie will be buried before she is married."

"No!" His cry rang into the room. "Doctor, we must do something. What can we do to make her well again?"

"You don't understand," the doctor said patiently. "It's tuberculosis."

"You've said that before, Doctor. And I know that people have been cured of it."

"Diagnosed in time, yes. Then the only cure would be a sanatorium for one year, or two, or even three. For Jeanne Marie I fear it is already too late."

"God will be happy to receive her." Madame Laurent bent her head. "I know it. He will receive her with open arms."

"He's not ready for her!" Henri stood up abruptly.

"Sometimes," Monsieur Laurent said huskily, "I think you are the most beloved of all my sons."

He might not have spoken for all the notice Henri took. "I must return to the Seminary tonight . . ."

"It's begun to snow again," Madame Laurent said. "The hill path will be difficult."

"That's what I need. Doctor, if there's the slightest hope for Jeanne Marie in a sanatorium, then that's where she's going. I don't know how, but she will go."

"How can you be so sure?" Madame Laurent cried out. "Who will take her? Where will you get such a sum of money?"

"God will help me find a way."

The doctor bowed and said nothing. As Henri turned to go, he paused once more at Jeanne Marie's door, pushed it open softly.

Slowly she turned her head. Henri composed himself carefully, went over and sat down in the chair beside her bed. "You have surprised me, my little one."

"You would know soon enough," she said with difficulty. Weakly she fingered the covers as her eyes traveled over his face. "Henri . . . this dream we had. It's over."

184

Deliberately he fixed his eyes on the square of linen at her side. "It's not over, it's just begun," he whispered. "A moment, my beloved." He left and returned holding the table up for her to see. "*Bon Noël,* Jeanne Marie."

Her eyes widened.

"Oh Henri, it is beautiful." She ran her fingers over the satiny surface. "So smooth."

"You see, I've made it from the very best wood. To last a lifetime." He set it by her bedside. "It shall be here for now. And when you're in our own home, it will occupy a place of honor."

"I hope," she whispered. "I hope."

"Good! Hoping is part of the battle. Believing is another part. I ask you to believe now. Believe that you will get well. I'm going back now, to pray, returning to seek His help. Pray that I'm in His grace." He picked up her hand and held it to his cheek. "Good night, my little one."

Outside the snow stung his eyes. He pulled his cap down on his head, and drew out the rosary from his pocket. His hands fingered the beads as he started on his way.

It took him longer than usual to reach the monastery. Finally, breathless and cold, he found the gate and slipped inside. The walls seemed to embrace him. He felt welcome and cherished.

The light was on in the Father Guardian's office, but Henri crept away to his room. He sank to his knees by the side of the bed and buried his face in his arms. There he wept. He had not felt such anguish since the early years when he had been wrenched away from his mother.

"Oh God, have I sinned against Thee? If I have, punish me, not Jeanne Marie." He clasped his hands in front

185

of him and raised his head. "She's so young. Surely she would shine in Thy grace, but the earth here is so dark. It needs her smile, the glow of her goodness."

"Take me instead!" In his grief he called out, and words echoed back.

"Take me instead." Into the words he poured every devotion within him.

He stood up, walked to the window and looked out. The snow was swirling madly now; the whole world was engulfed in a whirlpool of white.

Fragments of things he had read and digested came to his mind, and from the *Imitation of Christ:* "Love is a great thing and a good

And alone maketh heavy burdens light—"

And then, "Love does not blind, it opens the eye. It is love that presents values to us, makes them flash up in our minds."

Yes, thought Henri, the Lord gave and the Lord has taken away. As it has pleased the Lord, so it be done. Blessed be the name of the Lord.

Then he said, aloud but softly, "I shall work so that Jeanne Marie shall live. I pledge myself, O Lord."

Then slowly he made his way to the friar's study.

The light was still on. Henri knocked.

"Come in."

"Henri!" A look of surprise flitted across the aging face. Then the Father Guardian smiled, removed his glasses, and began to polish them. "Come now, the table you made could not have turned out that badly."

Henri was startled. He had no idea that the Father Guardian had been aware of his Christmas preparations.

"It's something else that has turned out badly," Father Guardian stated rather than asked.

"It's Jeanne Marie! Tuberculosis. Unless something's done for her immediately, she'll die!"

The Father Guardian sat up very straight. "Are you certain?"

"The doctor thinks it's already too late."

"That poor, lovely child." The friar made a sound of sympathy.

Henri strode back and forth.

"But I know she can live. Will live, with help."

"I pray she will."

"The doctor says the only chance is a sanatorium."

"Yes, she must go. But it will cost money. The Laurents have nothing. Where can we get help?"

Henri hesitated. "I thought of going to Father Antoine."

"Father Antoine? Father Antoine." He drew a deep breath. "It's most irregular, but I don't see why not. His Archdiocese is near here. Unfortunately ours is not. It's worth trying even if you don't succeed."

"God will not fail me."

The Father Guardian looked troubled. "It is not a question of failing."

"He has already helped me to believe in myself. And to believe." He sat down and looked directly into the friar's eyes. "Father Guardian, I have decided to take holy orders. I will devote my life to His service."

The friar looked at him for a long time, then slowly shook his head. "The Capuchins won't accept you, Henri."

"Why not?"

"You don't, you can't, make such a decision when you're not yourself."

"I've never felt more myself! 'Love and do what you

will, for if you are moved by love, you will choose what is right.' You have read that Father—"

"Henri," the friar said sternly, "you are bargaining with God. Do not attempt to deceive me or yourself by hiding behind St. Augustine. We could not receive you. God bargains with no one!"

"But—"

"We shall speak of it some other time." The friar was decisive. "This is something you must think about, Henri. It is not a decision to be made lightly or desperately. You must take time. Time to examine your soul. To weigh your faith. You must know."

Henri made no answer. He knew that for him no more time was needed.

Henri was waiting for Father Antoine directly after the six o'clock Mass.

"I have come to you about Jeanne Marie."

"Ah, yes," murmured the priest sadly, "Poor child. I promise you, my son, she will go to God well prepared, well fortified."

"I came to seek your help to fortify her for life, not for death."

"I?" he looked astounded. "Certainly, Henri, if I can. What is it you want?"

"Help me get Jeanne Marie to a sanatorium quickly. That's her only chance."

The priest shook his head. "False hope, my son. There is no longer any time."

"Death comes soon enough," Henri said, trying to swallow his anger. "We needn't hasten it along."

"Blasphemy, Henri! When God beckons, we must come."

"I don't believe God is beckoning!" he cried out. "She hasn't had a chance to live. She's not ready to go. The doctor says the sanatorium is still a chance. We must find the money to send her."

"And you ask me for such money? How would I get it?"

"The Church must have emergency funds somewhere."

"Henri, I'm only a poor village priest," said Father Antoine slowly. "It's not for the likes of me to ask for an accounting of Church funds."

"I'm not asking for an accounting," Henri's voice rose in exasperation. "I'm just asking you to write to the Archdiocese to see if they can help Jeanne Marie."

"This isn't a responsibility of the Church. That's what they'll tell me. I needn't risk their displeasure or waste my time asking."

"I find this all very strange." Henri looked coldly at the priest. "Waste time, you say? It is a waste of time to try and save the life of an innocent girl." He drew in his breath. "But it wasn't a waste of time to write to the Archdiocese so that a boy would never see his mother again. You didn't mind risking displeasure then!"

Father Antoine blanched, stood staring fixedly at Henri.

Remorse, like a physical pain, struck at Henri's heart. He passed his hand over his face. "Sorry, Father, but I'm upset. God forgive me." He turned and walked out of the vestry.

"Wait!" The priest raised his hand weakly, but Henri had already gone.

CHAPTER
21

A FINE servant of the Lord I'll make," Henri observed in disgust as he paced back and forth before the Father Guardian. "I went on an errand of mercy, and all I managed to do was to lose my temper."

"Then perhaps it's wiser to use one's head instead of one's heart," Father Guardian smiled. "For myself, I've taken the liberty of speaking to Doctor Senntierre. He gave me this information." The friar rummaged about his desk, and located a piece of paper filled with notes. "The nearest hospitals are at Trois Rivieres and Lake Edward. Both are the same distance from here. Trois Rivieres has only a diagnostic clinic, which is useless to us, since the doctor has already established a positive diagnosis. And Lake Edward is desperately short of funds. They are expecting a grant from the provincial government, but have not received it to date. Unless the grant is forthcoming, they may have to close entirely."

"Only two places in all of Canada?"

"There are two others in the Laurentian Mountains: the Laurentian Sanatorium and the Mount Sinai, both at Ste. Agathe des Monts. Each has an excellent full time medical staff, but you must apply and wait your turn. There's no telling how long that would be."

"And there's no time to wait," Henri cried despairingly. "There's got to be one place that will take her immediately."

"There are two more—the Bruchesi Institute, which has fifty beds, and the Grace Dart Home, which has forty beds and cares for the most advanced cases. Both of these are in Montreal. I'm afraid the Dart Home is our only hope at this time."

"Then that's where she'll go!"

"It's not that easy, Henri. The doctor will make the recommendation, but he can't assure her admittance. He'll write, and we must wait to hear."

"We've just agreed there's no time to wait!"

The friar shook his head.

"It's about a hundred miles to Montreal, isn't it?" Henri said.

"Yes."

"I'll go there myself."

"But Henri, it's a hard journey in winter, and expensive."

"The farmers will help me. I'll walk—I'll even crawl if necessary!"

"And when you reach the city?"

"I'll sleep in the streets."

The Father Guardian looked full at him. "Yes, I can believe that. But you may never reach the city. You may perish along the way."

"When God beckons, I'll come."

"Hmm," Father Guardian murmured. "Surely there would be no harm in writing her." He seized paper and wrote rapidly, then blotted the page and slipped it into an envelope. "When you reach Montreal, Henri, you won't have to sleep in the streets."

Henri took the envelope, glanced at the name on it. Madame Elvire de la Chappelle. For a moment the writing seemed blurred, and he brushed his hand across his eyes. It was clearer then.

"Is she someone you—" he hesitated. "Is she someone you loved as much as I love Jeanne Marie?"

The friar smiled a little. "She is my sister."

Next day Monsieur Claveaux took Henri as far as St. Casimir, left him with a cousin who was going a good part of the way to Trois Rivieres. There was a long delay as the farmer prepared to leave, and Henri had a hard time controlling his impatience. The hands of the village clock were almost at noon when the two climbed into the sleigh and set off. An hour later they turned onto the main road. It began to snow long before they reached Batiscan, and Henri could barely see the houses to either side as the horses drew them steadily along through the little town and back onto the road once more.

It was close on to three o'clock when they approached Champlain.

The farmer appraised the thickening sky. "Best you remain in the village overnight."

"I can't afford the time. I must reach Trois Rivieres by this evening."

The farmer shook his head. "It's still a long way off. No one may be traveling that way today, and you'd have to go it on foot."

"If that's the only way, then I will."

"A stubborn young one," the farmer remarked. "It must be an affair of the heart to take you such a distance, eh? And in such weather!"

An affair of the heart. Yes, it was that, but so much more than that. It startled him to think his love for Jeanne Marie vied with his love for God, and if he could save Jeanne Marie by lying down under the wheels of the wagon, he would do it gladly. But life does not provide for such simple solutions.

Henri wrapped the old horse blanket more securely around his legs, and they pressed on in silence. Then the village came upon them.

The farmer climbed down before a grocery store, went indoors and made inquiries. No one knew of anyone traveling farther south this day.

Henri thanked him for his kindness, and started off down the road that he and the Father Guardian had charted together.

The cold grew more penetrating, and he buried his hands deeper into his pockets. The snow fell thicker. The wind whistled past his ears.

One hour became two; the short day yielded to night. His feet felt frozen and his hands felt nothing. In alarm he blew on his hands and rubbed them together. A little of the pain returned.

Now he was isolated in a world of dark and snow. He did not know whether he was one, five, or ten miles from Trois Rivieres.

A small farmhouse thrust its shadowy outlines against the deeper darkness of night. He made his way to the door. He knocked. A woman answered.

"Pardon me, Madame, but could you tell me—"

"Shut the door," a coarse voice bellowed.

"Trois Revieres," he mumbled.

The woman pointed to the south and slammed the door.

Doggedly he propelled himself forward. The wastes of white stretched endlessly on either side of him. In between the snowdrifts were faint traces of wire fencing, the only sign of man on the desolate landscape.

There was a ringing in his head now. He had better find shelter for the night; his breath was coming in short gasps, and he knew now he could walk no further. Perhaps if he could just lie down for a few minutes.

He shook his head angrily. Lying down in the snow would be almost certain death. He could not afford to die now. Later. Much later, when he had grasped a lifeline for Jeanne Marie.

Once more a dark outline rose against the night. Then there was a faint glimpse of light. He struggled forward, pounded on the door. Finally there came the sound of steps.

Nearby a window creaked upward, and the muzzle of a gun slid under the opening.

He turned away repeating the words of Isaiah to himself, "They that hope in the Lord shall renew their strength. They shall take wings as eagles; they shall run and not be weary. They shall work and not faint—not —faint—not faint—not faint."

He stumbled down the path to the road, began weaving forward from side to side. Finally his knees melted away, and he sank into the snow. Gratefully he yielded his tired body to it. Just for a moment, he told himself.

When he awoke, an elderly woman was bending over him in the flickering light of a small farmhouse. A stocky, bewhiskered man was handing her hot bricks from the oven which she wrapped and put alongside of Henri.

"Better, eh?" said the farmer.

Henri nodded.

"That's good. And it's good, too, that I lent my wagon to a friend down the road. He was bringing it back when he found you."

"You will try to eat something now." His wife held out a cup of steaming soup.

Henri struggled to sit up among the blankets and bricks.

"Madame, I—"

"First the soup," she said kindly. "You can thank me when you're on your own feet again."

The first spoonful burned a trail down the center of his body. As he devoured the soup, he could feel his strength returning and his cheeks aflame.

Then he swung his feet to the floor and stood up. "I do thank you, Madame. Both of you."

"God is good," she said simply.

"Where am I?" Henri stood there swaying slightly.

"You are in Trois Rivieres," said the farmer, "and the good Lord alone knows how you did it."

"I must go on."

"I think you've done enough walking for one night," the farmer said. "You will remain where you are. In the morning, we will see what we can do about getting you on the road again. You are going to Montreal?"

Henri nodded.

The sun was just rising when the farmer wakened him the next morning.

"It is the time to go to the market," he announced. "Hurry!"

Henri dressed quickly and boarded the wagon. In a short time they were in the village square. Sleighs and trucks stood side by side.

"Remain here." The farmer threw his reins to Henri and jumped down. Henri waited for some time.

The farmer came back grinning. "We're in luck. There is a truck. And it's going all the way to Montreal!"

"I don't know what to say, Monsieur. How to thank you—"

"If you don't hurry, you'll have nothing to thank me for!" He hurried Henri through the line of vehicles and stopped beside a tan truck. A slight young man stood there munching bread and cheese. When he saw them, he nodded his head toward the seat alongside the wheel and climbed in next to Henri.

"Too bad you didn't get here before I loaded," he grinned. His teeth were in bad condition, but the smile was good-natured.

Henri turned to say good-bye to the farmer. He felt something shoved into his hand, and then the farmer was gone.

Henri opened the package. Inside were several thick slices of bread and bologna.

There was a screeching noise, and the truck shuddered forward. "I always let out the clutch too fast," the driver remarked in good humor.

Quickly they picked up speed.

"We're going so fast," Henri said.

"This packed-down snow is a gift from *le bon Dieu*," said the driver. "It's when the snow melts and the roads run with mud that travel is impossible. They always speak of paving, but I don't expect to live to see it."

It was hours before they reached the outskirts of Montreal. Henri knew he'd never have made it on foot.

"Ever been to Montreal before?" the driver asked.

"Just to pass through." Henri was startled by his memory. Would he ever forget that day?

"Well then, look up ahead. They say the Pont Victoria is the eighth wonder of the world."

Henri saw the city beyond the far end of the bridge. It was crowded with buildings of many shapes and sizes. He hadn't seen such tall buildings since Dupier—but he closed his mind to the past.

"You going some place special?"

"I have a letter here." Henri removed his heavy mitten and took the envelope from his pocket.

"That's in Westmount, a very special part of the city. I won't be going anywhere near there in my truck."

"You've already been more than kind. I hope some day God will reward you for your goodness."

"He had better," the driver grinned, "for I'm certainly not receiving any reward here on earth!"

Henri laughed.

"I can let you off at St. Catherine Street. The policeman directing traffic there will help you find the way. Yes," he appeared to come to an agreement with himself, "that's the best way."

He pulled his truck up to the side of the street.

Henri jumped down. "Thanks," he cried. "Many thanks."

The driver waved as he rolled away.

Henri showed the policeman his letter, and the policeman told him which streetcar to take.

Henri had no idea of what it would cost to ride these elegant street cars, and he had to save his money for food.

"I think I'd better walk," he said.

"It's a long way," the policeman said seriously.

"It doesn't matter. Up in Ste. Anne we use what God has provided."

It was a very long way. Henri plodded on and on through the empty streets, his head drawn in and his shoulders hunched against the wind. He was beginning to feel the lightness in his head when he came upon the house, small but perfectly set in a walled garden.

The gate was locked. He found the bell and pressed it as hard as he could with his numb forefinger. At last the door to the house opened. A small fretful-looking maid stood in the doorway.

"What do you want?" she demanded.

"I have a letter for Madame de la Chappelle." His voice sounded weak and uncertain.

"If you have a letter for Madame, you can send it through the Poste!" She slammed the door shut.

CHAPTER

22

HENRI did not know how long he remained standing there, but finally he began retreating down the street in the direction from which he had come.

At the next corner he stopped. Why should he go from here? He was no beggar at this gate. He was here at the Father Guardian's suggestion. It was to his sister that Henri's letter was addressed, not to this thoughtless, ill-mannered servant. He turned and retraced his steps.

This time he pressed the bell long and steadily. When the door opened, a small slim lady with snow white hair was standing beside the maid.

"Stop that noise," Madame de la Chappelle commanded. Then in a softer voice she added, "What is it you want?"

"I have here a letter from the Father Guardian in Ste. Anne of the Prairies."

The lady spoke to the maid, who hurried to open the gate.

Henri followed her into the house, stood in the doorway while Madame examined him from his fur hat to his heavy boots.

"The letter," she said, holding out her hand. When she had read it, she looked long and hard into Henri's face. "So you are Henri.

"Mathilde, take Monsieur's things from him," she commanded.

"Yes, Madame."

"And then show him into the guest room. There is a bathroom next to it, Henri. A hot bath will feel good, I am sure. When you have finished, I will meet you in the parlor."

His vision blurred by the warmth of the house and his head reeling, Henri stumbled upstairs after the little maid. She threw open the door to a room, and he stepped in. Except for the figured rug and the high mound of covering on the bed he could not have told what it looked like. He sank gratefully into a chair and closed his eyes. For a long time he was aware of nothing but the sound of running water.

"Your bath is ready, Monsieur," Mathilde said from the doorway. "Best take it while it is hot."

In all his years in Canada, Henri had never known such luxury, but it did not occur to him to linger. He finished quickly, dressed and made his way downstairs to the parlor. At the threshold he stopped, bewildered.

He felt he'd seen this room before, but he couldn't have. The rusty wheel of his memory turned and he was again a small boy fingering the plush chairs and the great couch, looking up at the multicolored chandelier that hung over the big table. No longer could he picture his mother's face, but he knew that in just such a room had she waited for him.

"Are you all right, Henri?"

"Forgive me, Madame." He shook his head.

She motioned him to a seat and rang a silver bell. Mathilde appeared with a bowl of soup and two slices of bread on a tray. While he ate, Madame reread his letter, then sat quietly waiting for him to finish.

"My brother speaks of a young girl, Jeanne Marie Laurent, who is seriously ill in Ste. Anne of the Praries. He thought I might help. Why don't you tell me about yourself and Jeanne Marie."

Omitting his abduction, he told of his lonely years growing up in Ste. Anne. He told of his friendship with Jeanne Marie and her family. How, when they were older, he and Jeanne Marie had fallen in love. Of the shock of her terrible illness.

"This tuberculosis, how bad is it?" she asked.

"The doctor in Ste. Anne says there isn't much hope, but I *know* she will live!"

"She must go to a sanatorium," Madame said. "And they're all so crowded."

"The Father Guardian got all the information for us." He reached eagerly into his pocket. "The doctor said there might be room in one in this city—the Grace Dart Home."

Madame looked away from him.

"I know, Madame. The Dart Home is only for the most advanced cases, and many don't recover. But that's the reason why there may be room for her."

"Perhaps you're right."

"Does it seem wicked to you, looking forward to the death of a stranger so that Jeanne Marie might be given a chance to live?"

"Come, Henri, you're not wishing anyone ill; you just

want Jeanne Marie to get well. If I only knew someone connected with this place." But as Henri frowned she leaned forward, smiled, and patted his knee. "This is a time of war, however, and like all the great generals we will plan our strategy."

Henri stared at her for a moment, then said, "Forgive me, Madame, but just then you looked so much like the Father Guardian. Your smile. The look in your eyes."

"You love him very much."

"I would die for him."

Madame arose. "There has been quite enough talk of death," she said severely. "Now, if you'll pardon me, I'll go and make an appointment."

At nine o'clock the next morning, they were admitted into the office of Madame's personal physician. She wasted no time. "Doctor, there is a young girl up in Ste. Anne of the Prairies, who is desperately ill of tuberculosis. She must be admitted to a sanatorium right away. What can you do for her?"

"Ste. Anne of the Prairies, eh? Lake Edward Sanatorium near Quebec is the closest one, but it's impossible to get her in there. The Laurentian sanatoriums would take weeks. Perhaps we will find the answer right here in the city."

He took up the telephone.

The Bruchesi Institute was most cooperative but firm: there simply was no place, and they did not know when there would be one.

At the Grace Dart Home, the Superintendent could not be reached. A female voice suggested a letter.

The Doctor replaced the phone and swung around in his swivel chair. "If it's a letter they want—" His pen scratched across the white sheet. Then he folded it and slipped it into an envelope.

"For a young man of such determination," he said, smiling, "there should be no difficulty getting the attention of someone in charge."

It was just past ten when Henri reached the hospital. The Superintendent was away and another doctor in charge. He would have to wait.

Over an hour later a doctor in a white coat entered the Superintendent's office. Henri watched him speak to the receptionist, then glance through the glass partition in his direction. Finally the doctor shook his head and hurried from the office.

The secretary came out to him. "I'm sorry," she said, "but perhaps Monsieur would prefer to return another time?"

"There's no time for another time." Henri settled down to continue his wait.

Around noon time, Henri saw a youthful doctor pass by and glance at him. He disappeared down the corridor in the direction of the hospital dining room.

It was long past lunch time when Henri saw him again. As if on an impulse, the young doctor stopped before him.

"Is there anything I can do, Monsieur?" He had bright brown eyes, a nose slightly askew, and a full mouth that disclosed well-cared-for teeth.

"I hope so," Henri said.

"Do you by any chance understand English?" the doctor asked in his accented French.

"If you speak slowly," Henri smiled apologetically. "I never hear it, and what I knew is almost forgotten."

The doctor held out his hand. "My name is Dan Stern. I'm from the States, specializing in diseases of the eye. Don't ask me what I'm doing here, I don't know myself. Perhaps its your delightful climate that persuaded me to stay."

Henri could not help laughing.

"That's better." The doctor looked relieved. "Now what seems to be the matter. Are you having trouble?"

"Serious trouble, Doctor."

"What shall I call you?"

"Henri."

"Well, let's have it, Henri." He sat down to listen.

Dan whistled long and low when Henri had finished. "You are in trouble. One, you have to get her in here, where there's no place open. Two, there's no money to pay for it even if she does get in."

"I don't know what to do, Dr. Stern."

"Well, there's nothing like trying. Come on." He got up, pulled Henri into the Superintendent's office.

"Perhaps that man who is taking the Superintendent's place would not like us to be here," Henri said. "He will probably be very angry."

"Right you are, so let's make him good and angry."

To Henri's consternation, Dan put in a long distance call to the National Tuberculosis Association in New York City. "But that will cost so much money! I'm not sure I have enough with me to pay for it."

"Think nothing of it." Dan waved his hand airily. Then he roared into the telephone, "Sam, you old son of a gun."

There followed a few minutes of personal conversation, during which Henri gathered that Sam and Dan Stern were somehow related. Then: "Sam, I want you to call your pal at the Canadian Tuberculosis Association in Ottawa and slip a girl in here." He listened intently.

"Don't worry about the space, Sam. If there isn't any when the girl arrives, I'll make space. The girl's name and address?" He looked inquiringly at Henri.

"Jeanne Marie Laurent, of Ste. Anne of the Prairies."

The doctor's voice rose. "No, I'm not married yet, and I'm not going to get married!" With that he hung up. Then he snapped his fingers in irritation. "I forgot to ask him who can help out with the money."

He reached for the phone again, put in a call to the Canadian Tuberculosis Association in Ottawa.

Henri looked around nervously. Suppose someone came in!

This time the conversation was brief. As Dan hung up, the doctor in charge stood in the doorway.

"Sorry, Doctor," Dan said, standing up hastily. "This was an emergency."

"There is no emergency so great that it can't wait for you to use your own nickel, Monsieur."

Dan pushed Henri out of the office before him. "I'm sorry. I promise to remember to do that!"

Outside he said, "Wait till the old man gets the long distance bill." The thought kept him enchanted for a long moment.

"May I ask," Henri broke in hesitantly, "what they had to say about the funds?"

The doctor's face grew somber. "It's the same situation as in the States. The organization can't assume the responsibility for any individual. Up here, the sanatoriums are all public, but each patient must pay around two dollars a day. Sometimes the municipality contributes, but from what you've told me of Ste. Anne, they can't even help themselves." He looked anxiously at Henri. "You'll have to raise it somehow."

But how? He had the money he had saved for the trip

to New York. He had not touched it, even to get to Montreal. He knew he would need it for Jeanne Marie. But it wasn't nearly enough.

Finally Henri remembered the house.

Of course! The funeral expenses had left over a small sum; Father Antoine had deposited it with la Roache for him. In the back of Henri's mind was the notion to save the money against a dire emergency.

Well, what greater emergency could there be?

"I have some money," Henri declared. "Enough to last for a time. When she needs more, I'll work for it. Every cent will be paid."

"That's wonderful!" Dan grinned. "Come back tomorrow morning. The regular Superintendent will be here, and by then we'll have the message from Ottawa, or I don't know my boy Sam. The rest should be easy."

"Dr. Stern," Henri's blue eyes looked deep into the merry brown ones. "I don't know how to thank you."

For the first time the doctor seemed embarrassed.

"My thanks will be when you marry the girl and live happily ever after.—And Henri, my name is Dan."

"If Jeanne Marie gets well, I'll most certainly live happily ever after." Gravely Henri held out his hand. "I'll never forget you, Dan."

"I don't think I'll ever forget you either, Henri."

NEXT day everything went as Doctor Stern had promised. The Superintendent was kind and understanding; arrangements were made quickly and finally there was nothing more to be done.

At eight o'clock the following morning Henri took his leave at the door of Madame de la Chappelle's house. "Words are useless, Madame."

"Yes, there's always a time when they're not needed." She handed him a package of food.

"The size of it, Madame! I'll be eating this for a week."

Madame smiled. "You've shouldered the responsibility of a man; now you must eat like one." She picked up a railroad ticket from the table and added it to the package. "Before you protest, Henri, let me say this is not for you, but for Jeanne Marie. The sooner you return, the better chance she will have."

There was a small silence.

"God will bless you." His voice was heavy with emotion.

"He already has." Madame's voice was peaceful and content. "May God go with you."

Henri boarded the train, sat down, and looked around him. It was not very different from the one he had been on a little over twelve years ago.

How he had fought getting on, that time! He had known he was being taken away from everyone he knew and loved. Exhausted with weeping, he had faced the future with dread.

How eagerly, this time, he had boarded that very same train. Now he was going toward everything he knew and the people he now loved. Now he was filled not with dread but with love and hope.

When the train stopped, it was past noon. He made his way to the same market place from which he had departed by truck three days ago.

Few wagons remained from the morning's loading, but he found a farmer who was going through Ste. Anne and helped him load the wagon. It was past four o'clock in the afternoon before they finally rolled out of Trois Rivieres, and night had fallen by the time they reached Ste. Anne.

Madame Laurent opened the door.

"Come in, my son, come in." She bustled around him. "Pierre, Martin, Bernard! Some hot water. Help Henri off with his wraps and shoes. Quick!"

Henri glanced toward Jeanne Marie's room.

"She's resting," Madame Laurent sighed. Then there was the sound of coughing, persistent and steady. "Yes, Henri, the coughing, the eternal coughing. It must be God's will. I only pray she will not suffer too long."

"Madame Laurent," Henri interrupted, "we have no way of knowing God's will. We must pray to Him for guidance, then do everything possible for ourselves."

"What can we do?"

"The sanatorium in Montreal has found a place for her. When she has been cared for there, then we will know what is God's will!"

Monsieur Laurent came over and sat by Henri. Quickly Henri told his story.

"Jeanne Marie must be taken to the train. Someone will have to go with her."

"But the hospital costs," Madame Laurent sighed. "Where will we ever raise such an amount of money?"

"We'll start to do without," her husband said grimly. "Many families do not eat three times a day."

"Even so, we won't save enough."

"For the present there's no need to worry," Henri said. "Monsieur la Roache and Father Antoine hold the money from the sale of Monsieur Dupier's house in trust for an emergency. It will be enough until the spring. Monsieur Laurent, you'll have to take Jeanne Marie to Montreal. I'd like to come, but I must return to the semiary. This summer I'll work"—he turned to Monsieur Laurent as man to man—"and between us we'll manage."

Laurent lowered his head, unable to speak.

Madame Laurent burst into tears.

"Oh, Henri," she wept, "it's all you have in the world."

Henri said nothing for a moment, then answered quietly, "No, I have something much more: One who will never fail me, Madame. He is all I'll ever need."

Madame Laurent threw her arms around him.

"Oh, my son," she cried, "in truth I think you are one of His chosen ones."

Next morning Henri carried Jeanne Marie out of the house in his arms. Tenderly he laid her across the improvised bed in the sleigh. At the sight of her pale face, he was assailed by doubts for the first time. How would Jeanne Marie survive the journey? She was already so weak. Was he sending her away to die amongst strangers? Is this what he had accomplished for her?

Suddenly he was conscious of Jeanne Marie's eyes upon him. It was almost as if she guessed his doubts. He felt a faint pressure of her hand.

"I will return, my beloved. Only promise me—" He bent low to hear her. "The journey—the one that is so important to you—wait for me to make it with you."

He bent down close to her so that she could hear him. "I will not leave Ste. Anne until you return."

Jeanne Marie smiled. Slowly the sleigh moved forward, and she began her journey.

Henri watched until it disappeared from sight. Then he turned and walked back along the familiar road.

So God had decreed that it was Jeanne Marie, not he, who was to leave Ste. Anne.

Would she ever come back? Would he see her again?

He prayed that Jeanne Marie would live. He prayed desperately for her life. If she lived, he would be content to devote himself to others. He would dedicate himself to His service if only his prayers would be answered.

Then it was done, without conditions. He had committed himself. From now on, no one could belong to him, for he would belong to them all.

The sun was high in the heavens when he opened the gate and disappeared behind Capuchin walls.

The next morning, Henri woke early. It was so dark outside. This was the way it would be for him now that

Jeanne Marie was gone. With a heavy heart, he rose and dressed.

After devotions, the Father Guardian sent for Henri. "First, my son, let me say I'm glad to have you back."

"I'm glad to be back, Father."

"I'll pray for Jeanne Marie. And you must tell me how she fares."

"Of course, Father."

Then the friar recalled his purpose. "Suppose, Henri, someone asked you to explain miracles. Would you know how to answer?"

Henri looked surprised. "Probably not. Why, Father?"

The Father Guardian smiled. "I'm going to ask you to forego some of your own classes in the College for a short time. Father Martin is ill, unable to conduct his classes in the seminary. I thought perhaps you wouldn't mind taking on his work. It will be extra, Henri, because you will still be responsible for your work in the College."

"I'll do the best I can, Father. And gladly."

And he was glad. He found himself grateful for the extra work, grateful for having less and less time to think of Jeanne Marie. Gradually the heaviness in his heart grew lighter.

But the doctor's reports from Montreal to the Laurents were not encouraging. Jeanne Marie was very ill—so ill she could not write. Only time would tell.

The days lengthened into weeks and the weeks into months. Then it was May. On his twenty-first birthday Henri received a letter from the sanatorium. He stood there clutching it in his hand, unable to move. With a great effort of will he went to his cell.

Someone had written the letter for Jeanne Marie, but the words were hers.

"My beloved Henri:

For the first time I know that I am going to get well."

Get well. Get well. The words swam before his eyes. He sank to his knees before the Virgin and covered his face with his hands and the tears streamed down his cheeks.

Finally he rose and went back to the letter.

"The doctors and nurses have cared for me so well, but it is you, my beloved, you and your enduring love and faith, that have fought for my life and won. . . ."

Henri sat looking at the letter for a long time. Then he left his cell.

The Father Guardian was at his ledgers when Henri knocked. Henri entered, went to the window, and stared out. When the friar had finished his entries he joined Henri at the window.

"Wool gathering?" he said.

"One of the hazards of spring," Henri admitted.

"Spring is never too early for many things—" The friar looked intently into Henri's face. "It's not too early for winter planning, let us say?"

Henri said, "That's why I'm here—to prepare for the future. Father Guardian, if the Capuchins decide I am worthy of them, I should like to be considered as an applicant."

"Jeanne Marie—she is worse?"

"On the contrary, she's better. I realize I still have a year to go before I would be able to enter my novitiate; but the year would be valuable because she still needs my financial assistance. She will have to remain in the sanatorium at least another year."

The friar remained silent for some time. Then: "Have you thought about this carefully, my son?"

"For many months. Ever since the day I saw Jeanne Marie off to Montreal. It is true that I prayed to God to save her, and in return promised Him myself. But since then that has become a very small part of my decision."

The Father Guardian said nothing.

"I don't know quite how to say this—I've been in love with Jeanne Marie for a long, long time. But I think I loved her the most when she became ill and needed me so desperately. It seemed, then, that I could love most by helping those who need most. And then I had a love for the needs of others—of all the others—that transcended myself and my own needs." He looked directly at the friar. "To live my life within the sight of God to help mankind, that will be my greatest happiness. I believe this."

"It's been a long time since you had a home and family. One day the urge may come again. Then it will be too late."

For a long time Henri sat staring at his hands. Then he said: "Many times I pictured myself with a home and family, like the Laurents. At holiday times, when the house has been full of relatives, I have watched and partaken." He paused and added slowly, "Partaken, but not really been part of." He held up his hand. "I know that you are about to say they were not really my family. Who, then, would my family have been in a different future? To whom else would I have ever belonged?" He sat back lost in thought.

After a time the friar asked, "You feel that you belong here?"

"Yes. I've found my place here. This is where I belong."

"Then I must believe your decision is correct. It is said

213

the stronger the love, the greater the readiness to sacrifice. Having experienced such a great love as you have had for Jeanne Marie, and having yielded it in favor of Him, seeking, I hope, a union which does not end, you must know that what your heart and mind have decided is right."

Henry nodded.

"But Henri, you must know what all this entails, before it is too late. For years you've dreamed of the day when you'd be reunited with your mother, your family. You've planned and postponed your trip—this last time because Jeanne Marie was ill. But I want you to know that once you have taken your vows, you will not be free to plan another one. You will have to put it out of your mind. Your concern for the past must not be a burden to you."

Henri had faced that decision. Of late he had lain awake nights thinking of what it would be to give up the possibility of finding them again. After all, what was there to give up? Should he manage to find them, he would be a stranger to them, and they to him. The difference had been years in the making. Now it would stand between them like a great wall, unyielding and insurmountable. What good to find them again, only to discover he had lost them long ago?

"I have taken it into account, Father Guardian."

"Your parents and your past are not going to prey on your mind?"

"I don't think so. I pledge my word not to look for them so long as I'm with you."

"Then it is decided."

"Thank you," said Henri simply.

"I have dreamed of this day, my son," he said huskily. "I pray God you have chosen the right way."

"I shall pray, too."

Quite naturally neither Henri nor the Laurents wrote Jeanne Marie of the decision: her health was still too uncertain to risk the shock.

With Henri's twenty-second birthday came the news that Jeanne Marie would be home for Christmas.

That fall, Henri entered his novitiate.

Then came the last letter from Jeanne Marie:

"I am coming home, Henri. I say it over and over again. The words don't seem real, I can't believe them. Home, and for Christmas!"

The letter fell from Henri's fingers to the floor.

Jeanne Marie. Back from almost certain death.

Jeanne Marie. Whole and well again.

How would he feel when he saw her? He closed his eyes and for an instant pictured her in the blue cotton dress that matched her eyes, and her long blonde hair blown by the breeze. Would he ever forget that day when they found their love "at the beginning of nowhere," and what had lain between them?

But he was no longer in Jeanne Marie's present or future. He had begun his own future. In time she would marry someone else.

He would always love Jeanne Marie, and surely more than others, as the Father Guardian loved his sister. But they were no longer together, except as all were children in God's Love.

Then he started. There was no longer time to write her of his decision. But it was better so. When she got home her own family would tell her. The news would be more easily endured, the pain deadened. Of course, that would be the best way.

The five days to Sunday were endless.

At dawn on Monday Henri knelt before the Virgin.

Monsieur Laurent rose early to meet the train at Trois Rivieres. The train limped into the station and Jeanne Marie was in his arms. She had never looked more beautiful.

"Life has been good," he said at last. "Perhaps better than I deserve."

"Better than I deserve, dear Papa," she whispered, "but not you."

All the way home she chattered on.

"And Henri?" her voice strove for casualness. "There's another girl?"

Monsieur Laurent looked straight before him: "There is no other girl."

He heard her long breath of relief.

The reunion in the house was a potpourri of tears, laughter, prayers and praise.

"And Henri? Where is he?" Jeanne Marie whispered to her mother through all the excitement.

Madame Laurent tried to think of what to say; then there was a knock at the door.

"It's Henri!" Jeanne Marie cried. "My hair!" And she disappeared into her room.

Henri was calm as he knocked on the door, entered, took off his outer garments. At that moment, Jeanne Marie came out of her room, and ran to him with outstretched arms. For a moment, she seemed aware only of his beloved face. Then her eyes took in the brown robe, the white cord, the crown and the cross. She stood stock still. The color and radiance drained from her face and her eyes were bluer than ever. Henri felt as if he were drowning in their depths.

Her hand went to her throat.

"No!" Her scream froze the room and all the people in it.

Sᴏᴍᴇʜᴏᴡ Henri made his way back to the monastery. He was not himself again until he sank down to the cold floor in his cell.

He implored forgiveness. How could he ever prove himself worthy of God's grace? How could he expiate this awful sin?

For Henri knew that when he looked into Jeanne Marie's eyes he had felt as he did that day when they were both eighteen. Once more, he had wanted to take her in his arms, once more to kiss those lips.

"Forgive me, for I have sinned . . . ."

His prayers calmed him as they never failed to do. After a while he arose and sat on the straight-backed chair in front of his desk. Absently his gaze passed over the three shelves of books on the side wall, came to rest on the life of Benedict.

"And you, my brother," he murmured to the Saint. "Was Fancy such a one as Jeanne Marie to drive you alone into the thorny bushes, and roll your naked body in pain to forget?"

"And who was it for you?" He turned to the next volume that bore the name of Godric, the Welsh Saint. "Who had you standing up to your chin in the icy river through those long nights?"

With such drastic measures had these two mastered their fiery natures. Surely his common sense would provide as good a way as self-mortification. It must. He buried his face in his hands.

Couldn't he face the temptations of the outside world? Couldn't he love without sinning?

He would have to learn.

Daily the somber bell ringing in a new uncertainty wrenched him from his troubled sleep. But slowly Jeanne Marie's last scream grew fainter. Slowly the wound healed for him as he knew it would heal for her, in God's mercy. And Henri thought of how he could serve.

In addition to his rigid routine, he helped teach in the Seminary from time to time. He kept old Brother Armand's wood pile ready for the morning stove. He comforted new boys entering the Seminary, and tutored those who fell behind in their studies. He kept his eyes open for repairs, and with the Father Guardian's approval made many himself. And he was grateful for everything that kept his day filled.

In time he gained strength from the very irony of his life. It seemed that events conspired, and continued to conspire, to keep him from searching out his past. He had promised the Father Guardian to postpone the search till he had come of suitable age. Then, out of love for Jeanne Marie, he had postponed it again—till she was well, till she could accompany him. Now she was well but no longer his, and once again he'd pledged his word to the Father Guardian. It must mean something that he could not leave this little prairie town. His faith, his devotion to learning and God's work, his will to serve —all seemed more purposeful because he had wanted so long to leave, and still was here.

And then, in time, this too seemed false. He needed no fancies, no tempting sophistry, to give him strength and explain his presence here. He was here. He was confident.

As for Jeanne Marie, the first few months of her homecoming she shut herself away. Even when she joined her family she did not seem to be present. Occasionally she would smile, and then it was worse, for she seemed then more distant than ever.

Louis Ferragne called often. He would stay for hours, though Jeanne Marie would barely speak to him. Strangely enough, she did not seem to mind his visits. Perhaps for her he was part of a pattern of her old life with Henri—a pattern she could not bear to abandon.

Louis's love was patient. It waited until Henri received his Doctor of Divinity degree four years later. When he was ordained a Capuchin, Louis waited no longer.

He came to Jeanne Marie, and stood before her trying to seem bold, and when she saw the longing in his eyes she began to weep.

Louis cradled her in his arms as if she were a child.

"I loved him so!"

The cry cut deep within him. "I know," he soothed her. "It will not be the same. The love you had for him you must treasure forever. I could grant him that and not feel generous. After all, if it weren't for his faith and his fight, you wouldn't be here for me or anyone." He raised her head with his hand. "I'll never forget that, Jeanne Marie. And it's right that you should not forget it either."

She did not answer but wept quietly, bitterly.

"But he's gone, Jeanne Marie," Louis said, "as surely as if he had departed from this earth. You can't mourn forever. You didn't recover just to waste your life away. You're a grown woman now, and everything lies before you."

She dried her eyes.

"What good am I to you, Louis? In a way, I do love you. But enough for a wife? I don't know. Why should you risk unhappiness?"

"I'll earn your love after we are married."

Jeanne Marie's fingers twisted in her lap. "You may have to be patient a very long time, Louis."

"I've already proved I'm patient, and now I can be patient a little longer." He rose and stood over her, stretching out his hand as if to touch her hair but drew it back instead. Jeanne Marie did not notice. "Never fear, I understand."

"Please," she faltered, raising her eyes at last. "Let's not tell the others just yet."

"Whenever you wish will be the proper time."

"Good night, my dear."

Two months later, as Henri sat at his board drafting plans for the new wing to the monastery, he was called to the Father Guardian's office.

"Come in, my son," the friar said gently. "Jeanne Marie has good news."

Jeanne Marie looked up.

"Jeanne Marie," he whispered. Then he extended his hand and in a stronger voice said, "Jeanne Marie, beloved little sister."

For answer, she put her face against his hand. He could feel the tears on the back of it.

"Henri—blessed, blessed Henri."

The Father Guardian had lit the lamp. In that instant Henri felt a quick jab of pain in his right eye, saw a halo of colored light form before him. He brushed his hand over his eyes.

"Henri," Jeanne Marie said, "Louis and I are to be married."

So the inevitable had happened. Jeanne Marie was to be another man's wife. Another man would kiss her lips, smooth that golden hair.

"Louis is a lucky man," he managed to say.

"I'm the fortunate one," she said gravely. "God has rewarded you and me, Henri. I hope that He will be as good to Louis."

"I am sure He will be. I wish you both the very best from the bottom of my heart. I will pray for your happiness."

The friar rose and bowed his gray head toward Jeanne Marie. "God go with you, my child. I, too, shall pray for your happiness." He made the sign of the cross before her.

Jeanne Marie got up to go. "That journey, Henri," she said softly as she drew her shawl over her head, "does it still trouble you?"

"It was never meant to be. Within these walls I have found my true home."

"Good-bye, Henri."

"Good-bye, Jeanne Marie."

She turned and left.

Henri made his way back, not to the drawing board, but to his cell.

"I want only her happiness," he prayed aloud. "You have granted me the greatest happiness here on earth. Jeanne Marie deserves no less."

Henri prayed and then it was time for Vespers.

Time at the monastery passed in its strange, sedate, reverent way. It was neither fast nor slow nor important, and the friars, though aware of each passing hour, often lost track of the date. The daily routine was like a river, smooth and untroubled: up early for chapel; then breakfast and work until noon; an hour of recreation, and back to work; chapel again before supper; prayer and meditation before bed.

There were few changes, few interruptions; there was devotion but no drama; there was the goodness of service and faith, which were their own rewards. Henri was at peace, but yet not totally. He knew that there existed inside him a restiveness, an emptiness. Something was missing, it seemed, yet he could not determine what it was.

This mood was still new as 1925 drew to a close. It did not change when, one night after vespers, Louis came to tell him of the birth of a son. He was glad for Louis and Jeanne Marie, and he consented gratefully to their desire to name the child after him. Louis murmured, "God has been good," and he agreed with all his heart. And as Louis departed, Henri felt God's goodness the more keenly, for he was calm and quiet and genuinely happy. He prayed for Jeanne Marie, for Louis, for little Henri. His love was pure.

As usual, illness came to Ste. Anne that winter, but by February it had reached epidemic proportions. Not since 1918 had they seen anything so severe. Doctor Senntierre knew the symptoms well—the temperature, aching bodies, weakness, malaise and general prostration. But there was little he could do for influenza beyond administering aspirin and cough medicine, plying the patient with liquids, sponging his feverish body.

The illness usually ran its course in about a week: the lucky ones recuperated, and the others fell dreadfully ill of pneumonia.

Between the influenza and the pneumonia, Doctor Senntierre had to call for help by the middle of February. But the doctors in the neighboring towns were caring for their own people, and the epidemic had struck Montreal and Quebec. There were no doctors to spare anywhere, and all available nurses had been pressed into service, even local midwives, who were given refresher courses in the cities and sent to work in the outlying districts.

In Ste. Anne the situation grew more and more critical. There was no place to care for the sick, so Father Antoine had the pews removed from the Church, and long lines of cots were put up. But toward the end of February the Church was filled to overflowing, and the Doctor appealed to the Capuchins.

The Father Guardian did not hesitate. He closed the Seminary, sent the students home, and turned the building into a temporary hospital. He pressed every friar, every student in the College, into service. He sent Henri to Trois Rivieres, to the Archdiocese, and from door to door to get linens and blankets; and between trips Henri would take his place on the nursing schedule.

The local undertaker was flooded, and the friars took on the additional chore of knocking pine coffins together, and conducting funeral services.

It seemed as if the nightmare would never end. And when it did few families were left intact, and many found themselves with patients who never really got well again. And then Ste. Anne's old enemy, tuberculosis, set in.

Henri, pale and drawn from the hard work and long vigils, was deeply disturbed. One night in the Father Guardian's office, it all rose bitterly to the surface: "If we had a hospital here, so much of this could be prevented."

The friar nodded, settled back to listen.

"It's wrong, Father. It's cruel, inhuman. Why should we have to depend on Quebec or Trois Rivieres, or Montreal for our health—our lives? Ste. Anne is the center of a large, needy area. Health is always a greater problem among the poor. There should be a hospital right here, in this very village!"

"Yes, you're right," murmured the friar. "But there's not enough money in Ste. Anne to sustain a few rooms, much less build a whole hospital."

"Then let's go outside Ste. Anne for help. If each town in this district would raise the money for a single room, then a hospital could be built to serve us all."

"But the people, Henri. The people here are good and devout, but in many instances sadly ignorant. They would take much persuasion to give part of their poor earnings to build a hospital."

"Persuasion is not impossible. They gave so much to build a church."

The Father Guardian looked at him aghast. "A church saves men's souls, my son."

"And their sick bodies? There's no need to save those as well?"

"Haven't you learned, my son, that the soul is more important?"

"Yes, of course. But I insist the soul can flourish as well in healthy bodies. Better, even."

"It may be true," the friar said.

"Then why not try? It's within the province of the Church to sponsor the undertaking." Henri was sitting eagerly on the edge of his chair. "And it's been done before."

"Yes. But in larger cities, and not by monks or friars. And to build a fund would take years. Who is there ready to do it?"

"I am."

The two plain words hung there between them.

"You?" The friar was startled.

"Yes." And Henri was startled, too.

Then the friar said evenly, "You are not permitted to do such work. You forget, my son, you're a Capuchin."

"I haven't forgotten," Henri thrust his head forward. "Do you remember when I asked to remain in God's service? I felt then, as I feel now, that my greatest happiness is to serve. And yet something's been missing here. I've felt a need, a lack. I don't feel that need, that lack, when I'm working in the parishes. But just when I see how much more I could do, I must leave them and return here."

The old man was staring at him dumbfounded.

"Beloved Father Guardian, beloved friend," Henri's voice was urgent, "it's not that I've been unhappy here. It's just that the need is so much greater out there. Ste. Anne has been unhappy since Father Antoine left. They have so many burdens to carry. Perhaps in a small way I could help them."

"Are you suggesting that you leave this holy order to become a secular priest!"

"Yes." Henri's voice was low. "It's just what I am suggesting."

"No!"

Henri sat with bowed head. He was not altogether unprepared for his reaction.

For some time the friar sat there unable to speak. Then, his voice thick with hurt: "Henri, my son. I have dreamed . . . I'm an old man, not long for this life . . . No," he interrupted himself fiercely, "I have no right to plead for myself. This isn't a decision to be made in haste. We'll speak of it again. If it's still your wish, I'll write to the Provincial."

"Thank you." Then Henri felt the sharp pain behind his eye and the friar's face blurred. He brushed his hand across his eyes. He'd have to see the doctor about stronger glasses, he thought impatiently. "Good night, beloved Father Guardian."

"Good night, my son. Will it never be 'Good night, Father Guardian,' for you?"

They spoke of it often in the month that followed. Night after night they spoke of it until it became an enemy against which the Father Guardian fought with every means at his command. He must have known that in the end he would lose. Finally, one night, he surrendered to the inevitable.

The one letter grew into a voluminous correspondence. It took over a year for the decision to be implemented and made a fact. And then it was done.

Henri was thirty-two years old when he was granted permission to don the robes of a secular priest.

Henri went back to Ste. Anne in his new black robes. There was so much to be done. He felt the need of haste; he did not know why.

His first Mass in Ste. Anne of the Prairies filled the church. Not only had everyone in the village turned out to pay him respect, but they had come from neighboring towns as well. The warm summer sun lighted the stained-glass windows, casting broad bands of blue, red, and gold across the heads of his congregation.

Henri had found a family for himself. These were his people—his very own.

Happiness filled his heart and overflowed as he began to pray.

CHAPTER
25

In october of that year, 1929, the New York Stock Market crashed. Disaster spread north over the country until it reached Ste. Anne of the Prairies.

Farms were foreclosed and abandoned. The stores dealt more and more on credit. Men drifted around looking for work. Hopefully the unemployed came from Montreal and Quebec, stayed a few days, then drifted away. The lumber company closed down.

Around each house, every inch of ground was planted with vegetables against the winter. Clothes were patched, handed down, traded, and worn threadbare and the people took on the look of poverty.

But poverty was an old acquaintance here; fear was the stranger. It was some time before the people recognized the stranger, and by then he was firmly entrenched in their midst.

The door of the parish priest, like the pendulum of a clock, swung back and forth. Some of Henri's callers left him raw with fatigue. Often he sighed hopelessly, convinced they would never grow up. But whenever he was able to help or to bring a measure of peace to some troubled soul, he would feel satisfied at heart, cleansed in spirit, and restored in strength.

And far into the nights he worked over his blueprints, studied hospital administration, financing, and maintenance, wrote letters seeking information from a list of hospital directors sent him by his old friend, Dr. Dan Stern. But always toward midnight his sight blurred and he could read no more.

Doctor Senntierre had diagnosed Henri's eye condition as astigmatism. Periodically he gave him a new prescription, but the blurring persisted.

Perhaps, Henri thought, the installation of electricity would make a difference. The power company had assured him it would be very soon now. Had it not been for the selfishness of a few who opposed changes it would already have been there. Though a man of God should be above anger, such impediments to progress filled him with a cold, slow outrage.

When Henri's plans for a hospital had finally taken shape on paper, he brought the subject to the villagers.

An almost childlike excitement swept the congregation at their Wednesday night meeting. A hospital . . . a hospital . . . a hospital.

Ah, if there had been one for my Jean . . .

For my Therese . . .

For my Achille . . .

They implored their priest: "What can we do to help, Father?"

"Yes. Tell us what we must do. We don't have money, but we still have our ten fingers. They're still good for something."

An overpowering sorrow rose within Henri. He felt the sting of tears in his eyes; and it took an effort to regain control of himself.

Yes, many of them would never be anything but children. But they were his, and he loved them, and they in turn must love him. Weren't they proving it at this very moment?

Among his people he caught sight of Jeanne Marie. The years had been kind to her. With the whisper of gray hair her face had a new softness. She was looking at him and nodding her head as if to say "Yes, Henri, you were right. This is the greatest love."

The Mayor rose, proposed a church supper, and sat down amidst approving nods.

"Let's open a rummage," la Roache cried. "People will make donations from all over."

"Father!"

Henri recognized the upraised hand of Jerome Giradot, whose father had passed on, leaving him the butcher business. "Why not sell the wood we gather to give away at Christmas time? That would fetch a pretty penny!" There was a sly grin on his face as he sat down.

There were some gasps, and a few hisses, at this suggestion.

With an air of expectation the group waited for their priest to speak.

"There would seem to be little gain," Henri said slowly, "to suspend one charity for another. The poor need wood just as the sick need medical attention. It is good to care for the sick and dying but we must also provide for the living."

"Bravo!" It was François le Clerc, the same who had envied Henri's Capuchin education.

"Bravo!"

And many of the congregation joined in reproof of poor Giradot.

"Please!" Henri held up his hand in distress. "Monsieur Giradot is not to be disregarded. The sale of wood is something to think about. Perhaps some of the younger people, who have free time this summer, will try. They can cut and pile it, and when the snow comes, run the extra wood into Trois Rivieres on their sleighs and sell it there."

"That is a good thought," Pierre Laurent said.

"Yes!"

Giradot looked pleased and proud.

"I prefer the rummage sale," someone said.

Monsieur Laurent arose. "I'm an old man." He smiled at the chorus of no, no. "Perhaps because I've spent so much of my life with ledgers, it seems to be a matter of arithmetic. Add the proceeds from the supper, the sale of wood, and the rummage sales, and put them all together, and from so many little piles, one large one will grow. Why don't we undertake all these ideas?"

There was some clapping, and Laurent held up his hand. "So I move, Father, that we elect a chairman of this project who in turn will appoint the head of each committee."

The priest turned to his congregation.

"All those in favor," he began, and was drowned out.

"Monsieur Laurent. Monsieur Laurent." The chant was taken up by everyone.

"Oh, no!" Laurent sat down in dismay.

"Oh, yes, yes!" Smiling and laughing, several of his neighbors pushed him forward.

"You see," Henri smiled at him, "we've made a beginning."

Hundreds of people turned out for the Church supper. Henri walked among them pleased and excited. But when he counted the proceeds he found that the Church supper had yielded only one hundred eighty-five dollars. A bazaar and a dance left the total under five hundred dollars.

Henri felt annoyed at himself. How naïve he had been to think by such petty means he could build a hospital.

Night after night, he had studied surgical catalogues. The operating room would require drums, drum stands, Mayo tables, basin stands, back tables, instruments. Why, the instruments alone would cost over three thousand dollars! And they would need at least twenty drums at ten dollars each to sterilize the linen and gauze. Beds, linen, and blankets would run to over four thousand dollars. Then each room had to be equipped with chairs, chests of drawers, and screens. All this without the cost of the building itself—material and labor.

He had been assured that any hospital under a hundred beds for Ste. Anne and the surrounding area would be impractical. He had figured on thirteen rooms: four rooms would have twelve patients, four would have eight, and the last five rooms would be for contagious illnesses. Each would have only four patients.

He had gone over his figures time and again. The hospital could not be built for less than sixty thousand dollars.

Sixty thousand dollars! And for a winter of effort all

233

he had to show was a few hundred dollars. At that rate, they would never raise enough money.

Clearly a large part of the money would have to be raised outside Ste. Anne. After all, the hospital would service all the nearby towns. They would have to help.

Henri armed himself with detailed maps of the surrounding area. He circled and numbered the villages within reach—St. Marc, St. Casimir, St. Thuribe, St. Alban, Deschambeau—and then the ones to the west.

And so methodically he started on his quest.

But at every turn he heard: "We have so little to give. What we can spare goes to support the church. Even then it is hardly enough."

Over and over he heard it, but still he went on.

St. Jean de Baptiste was marked down for the fifteenth of March. Soon after Henri started, the snowfall started. It was late in the year for a bad storm, but he pressed on. The wind shifted and drove the snow against his face, flapped the black priestly robes around his legs.

For two hours he walked, cold and wet and angry, as if the elements at least must yield to him. Then, toward the end of his strength, a horse and sleigh materialized from out of the smothering blanket of snow. He stumbled forward, put out his hand, sank against the side of the sleigh.

"What have we here?" The words came from far away.

"It is a priest, Father!" another voice answered.

"Then we'll take him to the rectory. Here, give me a hand."

There seemed to be a shouting in his ears as Henri came awake.

"Ah, good!" said the old priest. "You can take something to eat now." He motioned; his housekeeper came quickly with a steaming bowl of soup—thick green pea soup.

The shouting Henri thought he had heard was the storm battering against the house. It tore at the window frames rattling the panes of glass and whistling through the cracks.

The priest followed Henri's eyes. "What terrible need brought you out on a night like this, Father? A man can catch his death in this weather."

"Yes, I know. That's why I'm here." And Henri told him of the plans for the hospital.

"And so," said the old priest, "over and over you find that the people want to help but have little to help with. It becomes tiresome to hear it, eh?" He shook his head and sighed. "Well, St. Jean de Baptiste is no different from the rest, and they too have lost many to the illness. But our industry here is brick, and I promise you, Father, that my people will at least provide some brick for the enterprising priest of Ste. Anne."

"Thank you, Father."

"And how much has been collected in all this time?"

"About five hundred dollars."

"Five hundred! For a hospital you'll need thousands. It will take you years!"

"I'm prepared to work as long as God spares me."

The priest nodded. "Rest now. Tomorrow we will return you to your task."

Brick from St. Jean de Baptiste, cement from St. Marc, gravel and stone from St. Thuribe—all helped to swell the total. By the fall of 1931, two and a half years after his campaign began, Henri had in cash, pledges of cash,

235

and value of materials, a grand total of seven thousand dollars. He had covered every circle on his map not once but many times, and this in addition to his work in Ste. Anne, his priestly functions, his sketches, studies, and calculations at night.

Henri knew now the hospital lay within the realm of possibility. But was he strong enough to see it through to completion?

And had he made his specifications strong enough? How many times he had checked them, drawn them, added to and substracted from his basic figures. But still the minimum of sixty thousand dollars stood firm.

He kept in regular communication with Dan Stern now, and one night in November he enclosed a recent sketch in his letter.

Some weeks later a bulging envelope returned. Eagerly Henri opened it, stared at the check for five hundred dollars, then read the letter.

"Forgive my delay in answering, old man, but I've been pretty busy, too.

"I submitted your plans to my architect friend. He says that in spite of the depression, he could use you in his organization! However, I gather you are not considering any change of vocation at the present time, so the loss is his.

"As you can see, he has taken the liberty of making some minor changes in your sketch.

"This morning I operated on a patient. His sight will now be satisfactory but his *vision* will be as poor as ever. So, being an unscrupulous fellow, I raised my fee five hundred dollars. If he won't see, it's only right he should help preserve such vision as yours. . . ."

On the bottom there was a postscript.

"I suggest you omit writing him a thank you note!"

And then a second postscript.

"A good way to raise funds is to appoint a Board of Directors. Their names go on the doorway and their money into your coffers."

Henri's heart was warmed as he folded the letter. Truly did God have many images.

In 1932 the depression reverberated all around him. Henri could not believe conditions could get worse, but they did, and steadily. Now the shop-keepers in Ste. Anne were rich in paper debts, impoverished so far as their supplies were concerned. There was next to nothing to be bought in town, even if a man could pay cash.

On February the 8th Henri lost heart for the project. On that day, after a short illness, died the person he loved most, his Father Guardian. Just before he died, he opened his eyes and said, "What a wonderful Father Guardian you would have made." He sighed, and his voice trailed off. Henri bent close to hear him. "I tried so hard, beloved Henri. . . ." And he closed his eyes forever.

But Henri could not afford to indulge his grief for long. The situation in Ste. Anne became so acute, and morale so depressed, that the little wood being chopped was left lying in the forest. Henri asked Jerome Giradot to organize the men, get them to chop wood on a regular schedule, and arrange to transport the wood into town.

Jerome was a harsh taskmaster, and the men grumbled. But they were so surprised at Jerome's unexpected zeal for the community that, for the most part, they co-operated.

In the interim, Henri kept up his efforts to get a teacher of English for the parochial school. Finally the Archdiocese sent one. But a few children complained there was no one at home to speak English with, so Henri offered to hold a class for adults one night a week. Monsieur Laurent, Louis, and Jeanne Marie were among the first to register. Each Monday night they met in another member's house, and Henri was elated at the progress they made. Soon he had fully two dozen students.

On Tuesday nights, Henri met with the Mayor, Jerome, and a committee of four, to discuss the problems of the town and how to cope with them.

Wednesday nights Henri conducted choir practice; Thursday evenings were given over to parish calls, Friday evenings to social events, most of Saturday to fund raising, and Sunday afternoons to special services for the young people. So his weeks hurried by.

But the fund grew all too slowly; the hospital seemed further away than ever.

Christmas of 1932, like the Christmas just past, seemed to intensify the misery in Ste. Anne. Desperate times called for desperate measures; and Henri, knowing interest in the hospital could not be sustained much longer without tangible results, was forced reluctantly to accept an asset he had had through all his long struggle for funds. That asset was a supply of free labor. Yes, the men had been working without wages for Jerome Giradot; he knew they would work gladly without wages to build the hospital. And yet the idea was so repulsive to Henri, seemed such a cruel blow to the men's dignity, that he had put it behind him for over a year. Now he must make the suggestion, as much for their sake as for the hospital.

Of course he would pay them something. A little would seem like so much, and that was a pity, too.

Henri did some quick calculation. He'd been figuring a quarter of the cost of the hospital—some fifteen thousand dollars—would go into labor. If the work could be done for five thousand dollars, they'd need only fifty thousand all told. With twelve thousand dollars now in the fund, plus pledges in materials adding to perhaps six thousand dollars, he might expect to be half way to his goal by next Christmas.

But it was too little, and next Christmas was too late. He needed a lump sum of money, and he needed it at once. Not the entire amount, but ten thousand dollars or more, enough to start work at once.

A phrase from Dan Stern's letter came to his mind. A Board of Directors, he had said. But Henri knew only the men of his Church. The thought startled him and he re-examined it. Why not!

Then began the first of his correspondence with his Archdiocese. The final answer came in time for Easter: the Church would match his twelve thousand cash on hand and would advance the remaining twenty thousand as a low-interest loan to be repaid by the towns serviced by the hospital; and it would be Henri's responsibility to supervise the building of the hospital. When it was completed, the Church would help staff and maintain it.

Henri put the letter down and set a paper weight on it. As he removed his glasses, he caught a glimpse of himself in the mirror. For him, thirty-six years of age was no longer young. His thick brown hair was streaked with gray. Deep lines marked his lean cheeks, and his blue eyes seemed much too large staring back at him from their dark hollows.

It did not seem possible that God was so good. He put his glasses back on and re-read the letter.

There was no doubt about it. He had read correctly.

There was also no doubt that his eyesight was getting steadily worse.

The Saturday before Holy Week Henri called a meeting. His heart ached as he saw his people shuffling in, saw how their pride was slipping away.

As Henri spoke a faint glow of hope illuminated them.

"But we can afford only the most meager wages," Henri warned, "and it will be hard, hard work. New work for most of you."

The father of seven children stood up. "It's so long since I've worked, Father, I'd do it for nothing. Just to have something to do."

He sat down, and Henri saw the people averting their eyes, as if this one man had exposed all of the shame in Ste. Anne.

A stillness filled the Church. Henri raised his hand in benediction and prayed with them.

The day after Easter Henri invited the mayors and priests of the neighboring towns to a meeting, to decide where the hospital should be built. In deference to geography and Henri's efforts, the committee voted to build in Ste. Anne, on the road which ran west to St. Ubald and beyond.

The day the ground was broken for the foundation of the hospital was like a holiday. Women and children milled about; the men bent eagerly to their picks and spades.

Suddenly his own words came to Henri's mind, and the moment of happiness was tinged with sadness. Yes, now they'd be providing for the sick and the dying. But what about the living?

CHAPTER
26

Fʀᴏᴍ the day ground was broken, Henri spent every moment he could spare with the builders. As the weather grew hot, he saw to it that the men had water to quench their thirst; in the winter he organized a squad to make and serve hot soup, to keep fires going at the building site. In and out of season he was there, talking to the men as they worked, encouraging them, joking with them during their breaks.

Spring came again and the end was in sight. The men worked harder than ever—longer hours with shorter lunches and fewer breaks.

In exactly one year, the hospital stood all but complete on a hill about a half mile west of town. It was made of yellow brick and it gleamed in the sun. The ground around it was turned for seeding, and the smell of fresh earth permeated the air. Three of the boundary lines were marked by tender young tamarack, which would break the wind and hold moisture for the land.

It was la Roache who reminded Henri that the hospital had to be dedicated; Henri, lost in ordering supplies and furnishings, had barely given it a thought.

"If you like, Father," la Roache said casually, "you may leave it all in my hands."

"Thank you, Monsieur, I'm grateful. But perhaps the villagers would like to help make the arrangements. They've already contributed so much."

"Don't forget it was I who contributed the land on which the hospital stands."

Henri bowed. "We'll never forget our debt to you. None of us."

But la Roache was only partly mollified. "What do you propose to do?"

"I'll write to His Eminence Louis Pasillon, the Bishop of our Archdiocese. When I have his answer, we'll all make final plans together."

La Roache looked his disappointment.

The Bishop replied that he would come gladly, and would be happy to have fifteen people attend him personally as he made the blessing. The villagers agreed that the priests from the neighboring towns should be invited to attend the Bishop. They insisted Henri give the benediction, and they submitted to his persuasion that la Roache should deliver the dedication speech.

La Roache was elated. "Ste. Anne knows who has been good to them, eh, Father?"

Henri smiled.

"I shall have a fine meal in my home for all the visiting dignitaries. The Bishop will also attend the meal, won't he?"

"If there's time, I'm sure His Eminence will be honored."

La Roache took satisfaction in the prospect.

243

Henri suspected that the Laurents had something to do with the date selected for the dedication: it was his birthday, May 22. But he said nothing.

Dedication day came, clean and sparkling, warm but not hot. From the neighboring villages people crowded into Ste. Anne. Children from the parochial schools in the area arrived in their uniforms.

Then His Eminence the Bishop arrived, accompanied by his secretary and twelve of the priests from the neighboring villages. He entered the small chapel inside the hospital, made a brief prayer, and came out again.

The children, carrying banners, moved solemnly around the outside of the building. Behind them walked the Bishop. He sprinkled the holy water and blessed the outside of the building. Then, attended by his secretary and the priests, he entered the building again and moved through the corridors, sprinkling holy water and blessing the interior.

La Roache's dedication speech was not as pompous as Henri feared, and Father Bernard from St. Jean de Baptiste told how he had discovered a certain young priest in the snow one night. Henri was smiling as he faced his people for the benediction. Then he began to speak the Latin words of the most Blessed Sacrament.

Everyone remained on the platform until the newspapermen from Quebec and Montreal finished taking their pictures. Then the Bishop, priests, and mayors left the stand.

La Roache led the visiting delegation proudly to his house. Henri locked the doors to the building and came down the steps after them. A little girl stood there, her lips moving.

"What are you praying for, my child?"

"I'm praying for a stomach ache, Father."

"A stomach ache!"

"Not a big one," she added hastily, and looked wistfully at the new building.

Henri grinned. "Never pray for pain, child. You'll have enough of it in your lifetime. If you wish for something very much, pray that God will help you find a way to earn it."

He took a watch from his pocket. "If, in an hour, I return to find all the papers removed from the steps, I wouldn't be at all surprised to go through that hospital, you and I, and without benefit of a stomach ache."

"Truly, Father?"

"Truly."

She darted away and began to pick up the papers.

After an hour at the banker's house, Henri excused himself and walked back to the hospital.

A small solitary figure sat waiting on the steps. Without a word, she rose and slipped her hand into his. He unlocked the door and they entered the building.

With the completion of the hospital, Ste. Anne soon returned to poverty and desperation. The men were helpless in their inactivity, and in their helplessness they were angry. The little they had earned in a year had been gobbled up by debt, and while the situation was the same as before, it seemed worse.

Five months after the dedication the Bishop came on his regular rounds to visit Ste. Anne. Over dinner, he and Henri sat talking. Henri seemed restless and distracted. The Bishop finally said, "What's troubling you, Father?"

"I'm worried for my people. I don't know what the future holds for them."

"How does anyone know what the future holds for any of us? In Europe, for instance, there is no future with this man Hitler."

"Hatred is a powerful weapon," Henri said, "especially when it's fired by hunger."

The Bishop said, "I wonder what the people think of Hitler."

"I don't think the French Canadians have been thinking very much. All they do is shrug their shoulders. *Les Boches,* they say, one can expect anything from the Germans. Their own poverty crowds everything else from their hearts and minds." Henri leaned forward over the table. "And you know something? It very nearly crowds everything out of mine. My poor people."

"They are good people. God will be merciful."

"Perhaps we place too much of a burden on Him." Henri hesitated and when the Bishop kept silent, he went on.

"If we could bring a business to Ste. Anne. A mill, a factory—work of any sort which would provide a livelihood. A livelihood, and a chance to feel like men again."

The simple meal was over, and Henri rose to pace restlessly on the worn rug. "When the hospital was being built, there was not enough work to go around. One day I found Bouscier digging in the frozen earth like a man possessed. I stopped and spoke to him. I said, 'I didn't know you had been hired for work, Bouscier.' 'I wasn't, Father,' he replied, 'but if I didn't work at something, I'd go crazy.' Then he buried his face in his hands, and cried like a small boy. Bouscier,"—Henri's voice was filled with pain—"can lift anything. He is known as the strongest man in Ste. Anne. And he has four children."

His Eminence cleared his throat. "One catastrophe out

of many. But the people of Ste. Anne have always relied on their wood cutting and farming to earn a living. I don't understand what has happened."

"People no longer buy wood. They cut their own or do without. The little that is shipped to other towns brings almost nothing. As for the farmers, they can no longer afford to buy seed or hire help, and the little they produce costs so much to ship, and sells so cheaply, that they end up with nothing."

"They have their faith."

"Yes. Faith helps keep us alive. But it won't fill empty stomachs. In the end, the stoutest faith can fail."

The Bishop walked to the window. How cheerless this land was; indeed it took faith to survive here. He turned back to Henri. "I wouldn't know how to go about creating a factory. Many factories take away the opportunities for good manual labor by installing machines. Besides, do you think a factory would bring good to Ste. Anne? It could also breed evil. It could wean the weak away from the reliance upon their faith."

"Then it is up to us to bolster their strength. If faith has survived empty stomachs, why can't it survive full ones? If the Church is to endure the people must also."

It was getting dark, and Henri switched on the light—electricity had come in with the hospital. He stood swaying for a moment, then sank into a chair, removed his glasses and closed his eyes.

"What is it?" The Bishop's voice was filled with concern.

"Of recent years, a halo suddenly appears when I look at direct light. And I can't see clearly anything that's close to me."

"Far-sightedness is the price we pay for the advancing

years," the Bishop said. "But I do not understand this halo of light. Have you seen a doctor?"

"Not recently. I did see one in Trois Rivieres not too long ago. He said it was astigmatism, but he was not altogether certain. He said I should see a doctor in Montreal."

"And why haven't you?"

Henri gestured impatiently. "My eyes—they can wait. But my people can't."

"Father, there's nothing I can do!" the Bishop said. "I have no authority to send you into the business world. We have many such villages as yours in Quebec. It's the same in all of them."

Henri kept his eyes closed, his head thrown back.

"But you, Father. They have great need of you here. You must take care of yourself. This at least you can give them—the best of you."

Henri made no answer.

"You must go to see a specialist in Montreal, and without delay!"

Henri sat up straight.

The Bishop held up his hand. "No, don't say it. I want to know only that I'm sending you on a trip for your health. May God guide your purpose."

Next morning after mass, Henri went to visit Madame Laurent who was not well.

A new mill for Ste. Anne. The idea crossed his mind again as he neared the Laurents. But why should any mill come here? What could the people offer to lure a business to their village?

As Henri walked, he saw an old woman airing her

quilts on the line in the pale autumn sun. The gay patch-work flapped in the wind.

The people here could not afford to buy blankets. Sewing together odd pieces of fabric had been their sole means of securing sufficient covering. Those in more fortunate circumstances had family looms in their homes, and wove their own blankets, many of them quite lovely.

He stopped in the middle of the road. Why not a blanket factory? Why hadn't he thought of it before? True, there were other villages further north where the people were known all over the world for their blanket weaving. But why not here, closer to both Montreal and Quebec and transportation south and west?

He turned on to the Laurent house. Jeanne Marie opened the door. "Good evening, Father."

How many times had he heard that familiar salutation! But it had never ceased to sound strange from her lips.

"Mama's not feeling well, and we brought her some broth. The little one and I were just leaving. Come," she turned to the slim young boy behind her, "we must go home. Say good night to the Father."

The boy rubbed his eyes sleepily.

"Good night, Father."

Father. Again the phrase welled up in Henri's heart. Yes, this boy *was* his son. He was fortunate to have so many children. He put his hand on the boy's head.

"Good night, my son," he said.

After Jeanne Marie left, Henri visited with Madame Laurent, then sat down to speak with Monsieur Laurent, the one man in Ste. Anne with whom he felt a personal kinship. He laid out his idea briefly and asked for advice.

Monsieur Laurent was definite. "They will come only

if they get a factory financed on a long term basis at a low rate of interest, plus many local benefits and accommodations."

"Where do I start?"

Laurent puffed thoughtfully on his pipe. "Get a firm that is well established, trustworthy, and with plenty of current business. Tell them a building loan will be provided locally at a very favorable interest rate. The town council can make the land tax free for say, fifteen years."

He reached for a pencil and some paper. "If business conditions improve, and they've got to, I would say in a little more than five years the company should be able to start amortizing the factory. Certainly in fifteen years they should have the factory all paid for. In the interim, they would in effect be paying a very modest rent; and the cheap labor—emphasize the cheap labor, Henri— helps them to meet competition successfully."

"It makes sense, except that the town council will have to vote to exempt the land from taxes. Of course we have other problems. To run a factory, you need cheap power. And transportation."

"The vacant land near the waterfalls at the river— there's one answer. Below the falls the river is navigable; perhaps with some dredging that might be another answer. The province will improve the roads and maintain them, just as they did for Shawinigen Falls."

"But the bank loan. I'm sure la Roache can't supply all the funds."

"Ah," Laurent said wisely, "there are ways. Talk to Monsieur the Banker, then let's meet again. You might ask him about his connections in Montreal, too. Now that he considers himself a public-spirited citizen, he'll be all too eager to tell you everything."

Even Henri was surprised at the cordiality with which la Roache listened to his suggestion of a factory for Ste. Anne. Yes, he had a good friend in Montreal, Paul Chevalier, head of a branch of the Royal Bank of Canada. He would be glad to write to him. Dealing in business loans, he would know which industries might be interested in a factory in a rural area. He would write immediately and let the Father know as soon as he heard.

In less than two weeks la Roache came to the rectory with news. Monsieur Chevalier had suggested five firms that produced blankets or wool wear: Dominion Textiles Limited, Royale Rugs, Belmore Blankets, Les Dames Couverts, and Duchesne and Son. He had enclosed a letter of introduction to all five. All Henri had to do was write and request an appointment.

That night, Henri wrote to all five. He asked for an appointment on Thursday of the following week. He wrote a sixth letter to the eye doctor, asking for an appointment late in the afternoon of that Thursday.

On the following Wednesday evening, Henri arrived in Windsor station, went to a quiet little hotel, and after a light supper tried to read himself to sleep. But almost at once the letters ran together. He closed his eyes and rested them. When he opened them again, the page was still blurred.

There was no doubt about it: his eyesight was failing quite rapidly now. How much worse would it get? Might he lose his sight entirely?

Had poor sight been hereditary in his family? He didn't remember any such thing. Somehow he was certain his mother had never worn glasses. And at the thought of her, something stirred within him.

His memory fumbled down the long avenue of years as

he sought to recapture his mother's face. It was in vain. He gave up and opened his eyes.

Of two things he was certain: tomorrow he'd know the worst about his eyesight, and if he ever came face to face with his mother, he would know her immediately.

Dominion Textiles occupied a large suite of offices right off St. Catherine Street, West. A receptionist brought his message to the inner sanctum of offices. A senior vice-president received him cordially and listened patiently. Then: "But surely, Father, agreeing to all that you say, you must understand that it's unfeasible to expand at this time. Our financial position would not stand it. I'm sorry. Perhaps at some later date . . ."

Royale Rugs, near the Queens Hotel, gave him a firm rejection: Ste. Anne is too isolated; it would cost too much to train help, and so forth.

Belmore Blankets was more kindly. But expand? We haven't got enough business to keep this factory busy. Perhaps at some future time . . .

Les Dames Couverts told about the same story. Yes, the Father's idea had merit, but they were just beginning to hold their own. Business would have to pick up considerably before they could think of expanding. It was possible the day would come, but impossible to say when.

Didn't the prospects for 1935 look better?

It was impossible to say yet. Only time would tell the story.

Henri departed, walked sadly down the hill. With what high hopes he had started on this journey. How bleakly it was ending. Perhaps . . . Some time in the future . . . It was possible . . . Some day . . .

But the people of Ste. Anne could not afford to wait for some day. They were hungry now.

As Henri walked down to Notre Dame Street, West, he became aware of the faces that passed him by. The times seemed little happier for the people in Montreal than they did for the ones in Ste. Anne.

709 Notre Dame Street, West, was an old building, and Duchesne and Son had unpretentious offices on the third floor. A slim blond gentleman with a wisp of mustache hurried forward.

Monsieur Claudet was elaborate in his greeting and evidently much impressed with the clergy.

Henri, his spirits rising for the first time in hours, explained his proposal.

Monsieur Claudet was properly cautious: "You say your bank will arrange financing, and the plant will be tax free for fifteen years." He leaned forward. "Now then, what have you to offer for skilled labor?"

"Our weavers have learned the craft from their forefathers. If they can produce such fine things on obsolete home equipment, how well they would do on modern machinery!"

"Yes. Yes. But modern machinery takes training time. And time is money!"

"I'm sure you've had to train much of your labor even here in this big city," he answered with spirit. "In Ste. Anne of the Prairies, the wages would be far lower. It would cut your costs considerably. And we are years—perhaps generations—away from unionizing."

Claudet did not answer. Then he reached over and pressed a button on his desk. A secretary came in.

"If you'll dictate the entire proposal to her," he suggested.

When Henri had done, the girl smiled and left.

Claudet turned to the priest.

"I can promise nothing, Father. If you please, submit

253

your guarantees in writing after your return to Ste. Anne.
If my firm gives it favorable consideration, I myself will
come for further discussions."

He held out his hand in farewell.

Henri hurried to the doctor's office, found the ophthal-
mologist waiting for him. Then came a half-hour of tests,
and in the end the doctor was still undecided: "It seems
to be presbyopia and astigmatism, but I fear something
more."

"That sounds bad enough," Henri remarked.

The doctor persisted: was there some specialist Henri
knew? He himself hesitated to give a positive diagnosis.

Eye specialist. How would he know of any such person? Suddenly a bright memory returned. "Yes, I do
know a man, one I'd trust implicitly."

"Then you must go to see him at once."

"He's quite far away. All the way down in New York
City."

"It's still on this planet," the doctor said drily. "I'll
write your Archdiocese and give them my recommendation."

"There's plenty of time for that," he said absently.

"You're wrong! There is *no* time."

But there had to be time, Henri thought obstinately.
After the factory was built. After that.

He caught the first train back to Trois Rivieres.

CHAPTER
27

T‍HE town council and the bank worked swiftly and the documents were sent out. But Monsieur Claudet's firm was apparently in no hurry. Four weeks went by and Henri heard nothing.

Then one morning in the middle of November, Henri came to breakfast and found a long slim envelope beside his plate. For a moment he stared at the return address: Duchesne and Son, 709 Notre Dame St., West., Montreal, Canada.

Slowly he picked up the letter and read it.

Soon it would be Christmas. What a gift he would have for his children!

Monsieur Claudet still promised nothing, he reminded himself quickly, only that his firm was interested and he would come. Yet he felt grateful, certain of eventual success.

Monsieur Claudet came the last week in November.

Monsieur la Roache had all the papers ready. With Louis Ferragne, Leclerc, and Geugnee, he showed Claudet about the village. Finally they returned to the Mayor's for lunch.

"Such a young man to own such a vast enterprise," remarked old Claveaux, smiling at Claudet.

"I? But I don't own the company!"

"You don't?" Claveaux peered at Claudet over his steel-rimmed glasses. "Then who?"

"Duchesne is a fine French name, but it belongs to Albert Wollenstein and Son."

The men at the table were stunned.

Perhaps, thought Henri, they feared Claudet had no authority to consummate the deal.

"Yes," Claudet said confidentially, "wealthy Jews, of course. And the good Lord seems to have decreed that the French Canadians should spend their lives making them wealthier."

A pall settled on the groups. There were no Jews within fifty miles of Ste. Anne, but hatred for them was a commonplace nevertheless.

Henri felt a strange sensation in his stomach. It took him a moment to realize that he was physically ill. These were his people—the very ones for whom he had renounced the Capuchins. And this was what he had accomplished.

"This Monsieur Wollenstein," Henri said, turning to Claudet, "he is of a Canadian family?"

"But no, Father." Claudet sat up, pleased with being the center of interest. "Monsieur Wollenstein landed in this country thirty years ago. He had nothing, only a wife and son to support. He took a pack on his back and walked out into the country to peddle his wares. I've heard that he walked to La Chute, Ste. Jerome and even as far north as Joliette.

"He was clever, mind you. He soon had a stall. And then he set about purchasing factory rejects. He sold them at low prices and a good profit, and soon he had a large store of his own. The next step, buying a factory and becoming a manufacturer himself, was not difficult. Especially since he could always hire French Canadians for little money!"

Henri ran a hand through his hair, took his glasses off and wiped them. "From the first days of creation, God has hidden in the bowels of the earth treasures which the hand of man must draw forth for his needs and for his progress. My son," he addressed Claudet, "you think God has reserved only for the Jews the right to work hard and prosper?"

A gasp went around the table.

"Would anyone have stopped you, Monsieur Claudet, from taking a pack on your back and walking to La Chute, St. Jerome, or Joliette?"

Claudet remained silent.

"Why didn't you?"

"I—I never thought of it. Mind you," Claudet added, "it's not that I was lazy. I never thought of it."

"Exactly! You never thought of it. God has given you many blessings. Do you expect Him to think for you also? Or do you wish you were a successful Jew?"

Claudet could find no answers.

"Why don't you consider that this man—he happens to be a Jew—has worked hard, and through his work has provided others the chance to work and earn a livelihood also? The Jews, in their Megilloth, thanked God for the wise men among the Gentiles. Can we, as Catholics, afford to do less?"

"But assuredly not, Father," said Claudet.

257

"Let us pray that Monsieur Wollenstein will see fit to engage in one more venture, and raise our families from despair."

When news was known to more than one person in Ste. Anne it was no longer a secret. In the weeks it had taken Claudet to come to Ste. Anne, the village stirred with excitement. When he left, the gossip swelled into malice.

Jews. They had never known any before, but in Europe Hitler considered them the cause of the world's unhappiness. Didn't he say they hoarded all the money in the world? And everybody said they always exploited the poor. And now they were coming to Ste. Anne.

Edward Rousselin, who had seldom felt the urge to work, became a very busy man. Henri saw him bustling about the village, catching people by the ear, disappearing the minute he saw Henri approach. One day, Henri found him shaking his fist at Pillon, who stood firm and angry in his doorway.

"When the Jewish Imperialists come, you'll be on your knees. Then you'll remember what I say. Then you'll remember the name of Rousselin!"

His voice heavy with disgust, Pillon said, "As if you ever give us a chance to forget it."

Rousselin was not the only one. In the distant corners of the village a few men caught Rousselin's sickness, then a few more. In all perhaps ten per cent of the people were up in arms, but that ten per cent included many Henri had known all his life in Ste. Anne. Eyes he had looked into since childhood would no longer look into his. He understood now why priests were discouraged from taking positions on sensitive subjects.

A dismal Christmas came and went. January stretched

bleakly into February, and still no word from Duchesne and Son. By now Rousselin had organized a campaign to keep the Jews out of Ste. Anne. His followers held meetings in the open, sought out converts. Henri wished all this energy could be put to some constructive task.

One night toward the end of February, Henri returned late from a visit to one of his parishioners south of the village. The night was cold and sparkling, and the crust on the snow crunched underfoot as Henri walked briskly along. Then he saw, with some surprise, that the lights in Louis Ferragne's store were still on. As he approached, he heard voices raised in anger. He grasped the handle, opened the door, and the atmosphere of anger assailed him.

Jeanne Marie was the first to see him, and sucked in her breath sharply. The seven men turned to face him stonily.

"Good evening, Father." Jeanne Marie moved to his side. Without hesitation, Louis came to Henri's other side.

Fouchette spat ostentatiously on the floor, pulled up the collar of his shabby jacket, and left.

Poor Fouchette, thought Henri sadly. He had been out of work so long.

He looked back to find Rousselin staring at him.

"Good to see you, Edward," Henri said casually. "It's been a long time."

Rousselin said, "I don't attend the church of a Jew-lover."

Jeanne Marie gasped.

There was a mumble of assent.

"You prefer looking for a church based on hate? I'm afraid you'll never find that with me."

259

"I'm looking for a church where there is no question of God!" Rousselin said.

"And you think God exists only in our church?" Henri turned on them, angry and unable to control his anger. "You, Matthew Chaumiere. Did you think I doubted Our Lord when we fought together to save the life of your child? And you, Vincent Gardeau, your mother's?" And he went on, naming them by name.

The group stood and listened. In the end they were wavering, but Rousselin cried, "You are inviting Jews into Ste. Anne to weaken and defile us!"

"Jesus was a Jew. Is there anyone here who questions what He has done for us?"

The men's eyes were averted. The only sound in the room was of heavy breathing.

Henri felt sick. His head was aching. He closed his eyes for a moment against the blurred faces in the room. He told himself he was a man of God. He must not permit himself to become so angry. These were the children of the church, he must share in their failures.

"I think it is time to pray," he said, and bowed his head.

Slowly, one after the other, they followed suit.

But the rumblings persisted. There were empty seats at mass. Despite the vigilance of his friends, Henri heard such epithets as "heretic," "defiling his robes," "misuse of authority." He flinched but never wavered.

He spoke with Laurent one night of how soon they might expect a definite answer from Duchesne and Son. "We can't afford to bother Claudet, yet how I'd love to know the answer."

"One letter would do no harm," Laurent said.

"Perhaps not." Henri sat up and leaned forward eagerly. "What if we asked him to ship one loom up here now? We could start training the workers at once. It would save time and money. It might also make a good impression, eh?"

"We could put it up in the school basement," Laurent said. "I know of a man from Shawinigen Falls who could train the men at night." Then his skepticism caught up to his enthusiasm: "I don't know. Do you think he would mind such a suggestion? Looms cost money, and the shipping would be high."

"Not so high as the time spent training men at his own expense. I'll write this very evening."

A week later the answer came. Mr. Wollenstein himself signed it. He was still pondering the general proposition, but the ingenuity and good will of the Father had impressed him; and such cooperation would certainly increase their chances for success. He expected to make a decision within a month. It would probably be a favorable decision. If all went well after that, they would be ready to break ground for the factory sometime that summer.

Cooperation. In the first flush of joy Henri savored that word. Such a marvelous opportunity for Ste. Anne. How far would his people go?

That night as Henri was working in his study there was a crash at the windows, and something hit him, knocking off his glasses. He stood up shocked, and looked at the floor. Attached to the rock was a sheet of paper on which was printed—

GET OUT JEW LOVER

The lenses of his glasses lay shattered at his feet.

He had his answer.

T HE Bishop arrived within a week.

"Didn't I say a factory could breed evil?" The Bishop sighed as he moved his bulky figure in the upright chair.

"I still think," Henri insisted, "there would be less room in their minds for bigotry if there were more food in their stomachs." Henri rose and smote his open left hand with the clenched right. "But what difference does it make what I think! The point is that I've failed you, failed the Church, and failed the people of Ste. Anne."

"You belong to God, Father," said His Eminence. "For us failure and success are rather less important than trying to do His work."

Henri walked to the window and peered out. By the calendar, spring had arrived, but for Ste. Anne it was still far away.

"The factory, however," the Bishop continued, "is not the primary purpose of my visit. The doctor in Montreal has written two letters about you. He says he will not have it on his conscience for you to neglect your sight any longer!" He paused. "How has it been?"

"Perhaps a bit worse." Henri did not add that his right eye had become all but blind.

"These are orders. Next week it has been arranged to have your parish covered by a brand new priest. Only temporarily, of course. He needs the experience."

"How can I leave? Any day now Monsieur Wollenstein will decide to come to Ste. Anne of the Prairies. The people say they won't work for him. There may be trouble."

"Nothing will happen."

"How can we be sure?"

"The good people of Ste. Anne are in for a surprise," the Bishop said drily. "The Church is financing a good part of the building."

"The Church!"

"Yes. From the beginning we've kept in touch with Monsieur Wollenstein. We have offered to lead the group that will build the plant and lease it back to him. He was delighted, since it involves so much less risk. And so much less of what you young fellows call paper work."

Henri looked at him dazed. "But Monsieur Wollenstein's company will still run it. And if the people refuse to work for him?"

"Have no fear." The Bishop's voice was grim. "After tomorrow's Mass, I myself will inform your parish of what the Church has done for them. I will remind them that if they do not wish to avail themselves of this opportunity, there is plenty of land to be had in other villages. And that the church has many children!"

"Thank God!" Henri breathed. "And yet—believe me I say this in all respect—isn't it my job to work with them, to prevail upon them, to show them the way? I wouldn't

263

want them to think I've given up and appealed for help. Do you understand, Your Eminence?"

The Bishop laughed. "Of course, I understand. But the Church is the Church, Father, and your argument is not so important as your eyes. Go and take care of your eyes, Father, so they can continue to see your flock."

Henri did not know, and could not find out, who arranged for the Ferragnes to make the trip with him. Louis said merely that they had been too many years in Ste. Anne, and he wanted his son to see something of the world. Two cousins had been pressed into looking after the store, and the four of them were off.

For the Ferragnes everything in Montreal took on the aura of a temporary miracle. It was a chore to get them aboard the train for New York.

Between Montreal and the border town of Rousse's Point, Henri studied the landscape—dull, desolate, far-flung fields from which the snow had already disappeared. As the train rolled past Lake Champlain and on to Lake George, he tried to remember if he had seen either before. But nothing stirred within his mind except a certain irony—that after all these years he was taking the long journey back for the last purpose he might have imagined.

What he would have given to have been on this train thirty years ago! And many years after that, he had still felt he must go back in order to make peace with himself. He recalled his pledge to the Father Guardian.

But he was no longer a Capuchin. His pledge was no longer binding. He was free now to look for his family— if he wished.

Henri glanced at Jeanne Marie, and found her eyes

grave with concern. She seemed to know what he was thinking. Strange: she had asked him not to go to New York without her, and now they were making the trip together. But for what a different reason.

They got off at Grand Central and waited for Dan at the information desk. A tall, easy-moving man approached them, smiled at Henri.

"I'm Sam Stern, Father. Dan had an emergency operation. It broke his heart not to be able to meet you himself."

"You're the cousin with the Tuberculosis Association!"

"I was—a long time ago."

"Eighteen years ago."

"How did you know?"

"I was in Montreal with Dan the day he phoned you for a favor. Between the two of you, you got Mrs. Ferragne into the Grace Dart Home. I've always wanted to thank you."

They shook hands warmly all around.

Sam Stern led them out of the station to a cab. He gave the driver the address, and bade them goodbye, explaining he had a business meeting that he simply could not avoid.

Dan Stern had arranged quarters for them at a modest hotel on West 72nd Street. The rooms were old fashioned with high ceilings; the food was good, the service excellent. Most wonderful of all, they were within a few hundred yards of Central Park.

Next morning they walked to the doctor's office. Spring had arrived in New York. Yellow branches of forsythia peeped over the stone wall of the park across the street. Along the avenue trees swayed their green-budded branches.

How beautiful it was here, thought Henri. And then he smiled to himself. Every place was beautiful in spring —even Ste. Anne.

"Father Henri says there's a zoo in that park!" said small Henri, his voice high with excitement.

"Then we will see it," Louis assured him.

Dan Stern's office was in the Sixties, facing the Park. A nurse admitted them.

"Good morning, Father. Doctor Stern asked that you wait in his home."

She led the way past a waiting room, opened a door, and ushered them into one of the most beautiful rooms Henri had ever seen. It was two-storied, with a flight of steps leading to a balcony. The room itself was over thirty feet square with a wood-burning fireplace, above which hung a portrait of a beautiful dark-haired woman.

Two comfortable red chairs faced each other in front of the fireplace. On the wall to the right was a beige and green couch; on either side of the couch were massive square tables with tall lamps; in the far corner of the room stood a grand piano; and the faint fragrance of perfume suggested that a woman lived here. A few other comfortable chairs were placed sociably around the room, and the rug was a broad expanse of beige broadloom.

"Such charm, such warmth," Jeanne Marie said with deep admiration.

"It's very beautiful," Louis agreed.

There was the hurried tapping of heels and down the stairs, light as a bird, skimmed the woman in the portrait.

"I'm Ruth Stern, Father," she held out her hand. "Dan speaks of you so often."

She had brunette hair, a small nose, a generous

mouth, and large green eyes. Her creamy skin showed the creases of laughter and sorrow as well. Her movements were swift and definite.

"How do you do, Mrs. Stern," Henri shook hands. "You know, eighteen years ago Dan told me he would never marry. Now I understand why he changed his mind."

"Oh, he told you that, too, did he?" She smiled and leaned forward: "Confidentially, I don't think he's figured out yet how it happened."

"These are my friends, Mr. and Mrs. Louis Ferragne, and this is Mr. Ferragne, Junior."

"Ah, another Louis Ferragne!"

Jeanne Marie moved into the tiny pause.

"No, he is Henri Ferragne," she said in her strongly accented French-Canadian voice. "He is named after the good Father here."

A door slammed.

"Where's Henri?" a voice demanded, and Dan Stern strode into the room.

He shook Henri vigorously by the hand, and pounded him on the back. "Well, Henri, you look fit enough. That nice ruddy complexion and that smile haven't changed. It's always been slightly crooked, hasn't it?" He grinned, his brown eyes twinkling.

"Ever since I was five."

"But the gray hair is new. Very distinguished, too."

For the first time Dan became aware of the others in the room. A light of recognition dawned as he beheld Jeanne Marie's tall figure clothed in the cheaply made suit. He put a hand under her chin, and looked deep into her eyes.

"It couldn't be Jeanne Marie," he said softly.

She smiled. "Yes, Doctor Stern, it is."

267

"Jeanne Marie, I'd have known you anywhere."

She withdrew slightly and nodded toward Louis. "And now I would like you to meet my husband."

"So this is the lucky man?" He turned and held out his hand to Louis.

"I have much to thank you for, Doctor," Louis said simply.

"Don't thank me, thank Henri."

"For Henri Dupier I say a special prayer of thanksgiving every day of my life."

"Petit Henri," Ruth Stern said. "I have to take my dog out. Would you like to help me?"

The boy looked at her round-eyed, then at his mother.

"It's very kind of you," Jeanne Marie said. "If you don't mind, my husband and I would like to remain for the examination."

Timidly the boy took Mrs. Stern's hand and they left the room.

"Rushing me back to work," Dan smiled to take the sting out of his words. "Come along to the office."

Jeanne Marie and Louis sat down in the waiting room; Henri entered the inner office.

"Now tell me the story," Dan said to Henri. Suddenly this gay man with the laughing mouth became an authority.

And so Henri told him of the long years of foggy vision, of the colored halo around lights, and the extreme farsightedness.

As he spoke, tiny furrows appeared on Dan's brow.

"It's serious then, isn't it, Dan?"

"I'd have to examine you before I could attempt a diagnosis," he said.

Henri never knew there could be so much complicated

procedure for an eye examination. There was an endless series of charts, and drops in his eyes, and more charts. Then he rested his face on a stand and looked through large mechanized glasses, and Dan brought forth what he explained was an ophthalmoscope and slit-lamp.

After an hour it was over.

"Would you like your friends to hear the diagnosis?"

Henri nodded.

The three sat in a semi-circle facing the doctor.

"I'm going to be blunt and to the point with you, old man," he said sharply, "so if there's anything you don't understand, please don't hesitate to interrupt me."

Henri nodded.

"In your right eye I have found atrophy of the optic nerve and a circumpapillary ring of choroidal atrophy. Also, glaucomatous cupping of the disk."

"Are you trying to tell me I have glaucoma?"

Dan nodded.

"How bad is it?"

"Bad enough in the right eye."

"And the left?"

"It's slightly affected also."

"I see."

Two simple words! *I see.* But not, it would seem for long.

Odd how he could sit there so devoid of feeling. Silent, inarticulate, empty, conscious only of the quiet room and of his own even breathing. Henri guessed Dan was far more distressed than he.

Then Dan began to speak once more: "A popular method is Elliott's operation and possibly a small iridectomy . . ."

"You believe it would help?"

"I wouldn't recommend it if I didn't think it would help."

"You said you would be perfectly honest with me. I'd like to know what you really think."

Henri followed Dan's gaze to Louis, then Jeanne Marie. He was anxious; she was leaning forward, her face deathly pale.

"I *think* there's a chance of saving your sight," Dan said. "But if there's anything or anyone you really want to see, go take a good look now, before the operation."

CHAPTER

29

HENRI closed his eyes.

If there is anyone you really want to see.

Of course, there was someone he wished to see. There always was for everyone.

He tried to recall how his mother had looked, but he could remember so little. And now, if by some miracle, he could finally find her, he might not be able to see her.

He opened his eyes and looked at the stunned faces around him. His poor friends—they needed comforting. And suddenly Mrs. Stern was there, looking stunned as well.

"Dan," he said quietly, "when will you operate?"

"You're willing to go through with it?"

"In your hands, yes."

"There are others perhaps better qualified."

Henri smiled. "I believe God gives special gifts to loving hands."

"Now look, Henri," Dan stirred, "I think I should tell you, He and I haven't been very close."

'I don't believe that. A man like you must always be in God's sight."

Dan looked uncomfortable.

"In any event," Henri said calmly, "I'm ready to leave it all to His will and your hands. There's no need to consult anyone else."

"I'll do what I can," said Dan.

"Father," Jeanne Marie smiled bleakly, "let me tell you of our conspiracy. I'll return home with Petit Henri tomorrow evening. Louis will remain here until after the operation; with me in Ste. Anne to look after our affairs, Louis can stay without worrying. It's all been decided, so you needn't argue."

She arose and looked intently at Henri. "We'll leave you now, Father. I'm sure there are some things you'll wish to tell the doctor. Things that no one else could tell."

Louis roused himself. "We'll see you back at the hotel in time for dinner, Father."

Ruth saw them to the door. When she came back, Henri was sitting in a chair, his head sunk forward.

"I wish I could pray for you, Father," she blurted.

Henri glanced up. "You can. God is happy to hear all voices."

Dan came over and put his hand on his shoulder. "Don't take it so hard, old man. We have reason to hope."

Henri roused himself. "I wasn't thinking of the operation, Dan. I have something else on my mind. You asked me a moment ago if there was anyone I especially wanted to see. There is. My mother."

"Your mother! I didn't know you had a mother."

"I don't know whether she's still alive." Henri hesitated. "It's a long story, and it all happened so many years ago . . ."

"Perhaps I'd better leave," Ruth Stern started from her chair.

"No. There's no need for that. But your patients, Dan."

"They can wait. No one in trouble."

"I'll keep it brief." He closed his eyes for a moment, then began at the beginning. "I was seven years old . . ."

It all poured out so easily Henri was taken aback. When he'd finished, Ruth and Dan sat staring at him.

Ruth Stern stirred first. She rubbed her hands over her bare arms, and drew her sweater over her shoulders, shivering.

Dan whispered, "It's incredible. The cruelty of it! Your poor mother!"

"Yes," Henri nodded sadly. "How many nights I laid awake thinking of her. How I'd love to see her once more."

"I can't seem to think straight," Ruth Stern said. "It's horrible—a little boy taken so far from home, to a strange country with a strange language. No one to help him, no one to understand."

"If it proves anything," Henri said, "it proves how desperate we all are to communicate, to find a helping hand in this world."

"Well, this time you'll have someone helping you. And we'll find them."

"I have no real reason to believe we can, after all this time."

"Of course you can!"

"It's been over thirty years."

"Father, I can't understand your attitude."

"Take it easy, dear," Dan said. "Don't get carried away."

"I wouldn't know where to start," Henri said.

"Well, I would!"

The moment Henri departed, Ruth Stern sat down at the phone. She opened the Manhattan directory. Fath. There were three of them, and two right in the neighborhood. She picked up the phone.

A woman answered. She was more than kind, but of no earthly help. The second and third calls proved fruitless, too. Ruth Stern sat and stared at the phone.

That night at dinner, she talked to Dan of nothing else. "There was so little he remembered. So little he could tell. He lived near a park. He had a brother Charles, a sister Emilie. The family employed a nurse and a tutor."

"They couldn't have been poor."

"No. Even in those days, you had to pay for that kind of service . . ."

"Is that why you didn't try phoning any Faths in the other boroughs?"

"Who says I didn't? But I could have saved my nickels." She snapped her fingers. "I know where to go! The morgue at the *New York Times*, or the library. The child of a wealthy home, kidnaped—it's sure to have been in the papers."

"Poor guy," Dan said. "From the first time I met him I knew there was something different about him."

"He had to turn out different."

"I wonder if his folks are still alive."

"Of course they are."

"Don't be too sure."

The next morning, Ruth Stern was on the steps of the

New York Public Library when the guards opened the doors.

Henri was not sure of the date of his abduction, so she started with the *New York Times* of August, 1904. When she reached the first week in September, she realized she was hungry. It was after one o'clock. She rushed out, ate a sandwich and hurried back.

About four o'clock she saw it—a small paragraph at the bottom of Page One.

"Henri, the son of Auguste and Edith Fath . . . last seen with his tutor Paul Dupier . . . two other children . . . Charles and Emilie . . . ."

She read it three times before she could believe it. Then she took down the address: Washington Square. Of course! That was the park Father Henri had mentioned, and people of means would have lived there.

She searched through the papers of the next two weeks, but there was no other clue to what might have happened.

She took a bus bound for Washington Square. It seemed forever before the bus ground to its last stop. She walked rapidly to the west, crossed the street, and stopped short.

No. 77 was no longer there. Nor was 73, 75 or 79.

Not only had the house of the Fath family disappeared, but all the other houses as well; gone, all gone to make way for the massive new apartment building before her.

CHAPTER
30

THE doorman was staring at her, and she walked rapidly to the corner. There she hesitated. Down the street to her left, and diagonally across, was a small store with a sign saying "Miltie's."

It was five o'clock, time to be getting home. But businesses were letting out, and she was in no mood to be jostled about.

A small bell tinkled as she opened the door to Miltie's.

A short, heavy-set man, with very little neck separating his broad shoulders from his round face, came forward wiping his hands on his apron. "What can I do for you, Miss?"

"Have you been in this location long?"

"Some particular reason you want to know?"

"Oh yes," she said in a rush. "I'm trying to locate a family that used to live at 77 Washington Square West over thirty years ago. Their name was Fath."

"Number 77, you say? That house went down with the others."

"Yes. I know."

"I was here before they tore those houses down, but I never heard that name. Fath, you said. No. No, I never knew of anyone by that name."

Probably no one else ever had either. Ruth Stern stood there feeling tired and uncertain.

"You know that big old apartment house on the northwest corner of the Square?"

She nodded.

"Well, they have a superintendent who must be there at least thirty years. Name of Patrick Dowling. He seems to know everything about anyone who ever lived in Washington Square."

"Thank you. You've been very kind."

The superintendent, it seemed, was collecting the garbage. An old lady with a thick brogue told her he would be back in a few minutes.

Ruth walked to a phone booth, left a message at home for her husband, and started back to the apartment. She had no idea why she was rushing—there would be other days. Perhaps it was because it had taken her so long to find that single precious lead. Perhaps it was because only a few days remained before Henri was to report to the hospital.

She glanced at her watch. Jeanne Marie and little Henri must have started for home by now. How beautiful Jeanne Marie still was, despite that miserably cut suit, and those bulky shoes. Several times in the last two days she had had to curb a wild impulse to re-dress Jeanne Marie.

Patrick Dowling tottered toward her on spindly legs. Thin straggly gray hair fell over his broad forehead, and his mouth had the pinched look of age. She wondered how anyone so old could continue to work.

He put his hand to his ear.

"The Fath family, eh? Sure and why wouldn't I know them?" He glared at her as if she had accused him of immorality. "Foine people they were. Happened right after I moved here. Seems as if I could remember them moving plain as day." He sighed deeply.

"Do you have any idea of where they moved to?"

"I never knew, but there's a lady. An artist lady, a furriner. Name of Liebling. She lives fourth house down in MacDougal Alley. Might try her. Another thing. Not that you'll be getting much help from the police, but there's a station on the other side of the Square, right on MacDougal Street. You might try that."

She thanked him and fled.

The fourth house on MacDougal Alley was already lighted for the evening when she arrived. Madame Liebling herself answered the door.

Ruth Stern stated her business.

The little old lady's mouth trembled and her voice quavered as she tried to answer: "It was a very long time ago."

"Yes, I know."

The old lady opened the door wider.

"Would you like to step in?"

"Thank you, but it's getting late. I thought perhaps you would remember where they moved to."

The old lady shook her head. "After it happened, I tried to see her, but I couldn't. She wouldn't see anyone.

Then they moved so suddenly, they didn't even tell me. And I was one of her best friends . . . I'll never forget it. I heard about their moving at the last minute, so I went over to get the address from them, but when I got there, I heard her scream." The old lady's face worked, and tears came to her eyes. "I was just outside the door when I heard it. I never went in."

"And you never found out?"

"No. I never did."

Ruth found her own eyes smarting. She thanked Mrs. Liebling and hurried away. As she walked back toward the Square, Ruth asked herself why she had become so involved. And suddenly she knew why.

A year ago, on just such a blue April day as this, she had walked out of the hospital, with Dan on one side and a nurse on the other. Her baby had been stillborn.

She had grieved for him as though he had lived and grown up with them. The doctor had said there might be more, but his tone had not been reassuring. But at least she knew where that tiny form lay. She could go and shed tears over him and come back feeling relieved of a small part of her grief.

But Henri's mother—what had it been like for her? She shivered, quickened her steps. If that mother were still alive, she, Ruth Stern, owed her that much. To see him once more.

The dusk was thickening as she pushed open the heavy door, walked into the dingy, smoky room of the precinct house.

Of the half-dozen men sitting around, the young policeman behind the tall desk noticed her first.

"What can I do for you, Miss?"

With his words, the man turned to watch her.

"I wondered if you have any record of a family who moved away from here over thirty years ago."

"I'm afraid not. Is there some reason why we should have?"

"Their boy was kidnaped."

"That's different. But it's O'Brien's last day on the force, and we're going to have a little celebration. Could you come back tomorrow? We'd have plenty of time to help you then." He grinned engagingly.

"I can't!" she cried.

"All right then. What was the boy's name?"

"His name was Henri Fath."

A man came toward her slowly. There was a trace of red left in the gray hair; lines were deep in his face, but the eyes were the eyes of a man who would never grow old.

"What name did you say?" the man asked in a strained voice.

"Take it easy, Mahoney," said a tall man from the door to the inner office. "You're only frightening the girl."

"The boy's name was Henri Fath," Ruth repeated.

Mahoney's eyes never left Ruth Stern's face. "Do you know something about Henri Fath?"

"Do you know where the Faths moved to?" she countered. "I'm trying to find the parents of Henri Fath."

"What do you want them for?" the tall man said.

"Their son Henri is looking for them."

"Where did he come from?" Mahoney demanded. "How do you know he's Henri?"

"Why are *you* asking *me* questions?" she said hotly. "I came here for information; not a third degree."

The tall man laughed. "I'm O'Brien. I was in charge

of the precinct when the boy was taken. This is Frank Mahoney, here, one of the finest private detectives in the business. He spent five years of his life looking for that boy, and it damned near broke his heart when he had to give up."

"There's a lot of money in this family," Mahoney said. "We have to be sure your fellow isn't an impostor."

"Mr. Mahoney, this man is a priest!"

"Priest or no priest, are you sure he's the boy?"

"Positive." And Ruth Stern told him Father Henri's story.

"It sounds reasonable," Mahoney said. "But five minutes with him, and I'll know for certain. Where can I reach him?"

"Let me call my husband, then I'll let you know. Do you have a phone?"

O'Brien smiled, tapped Mahoney on the shoulder.

"Let's go, my boy."

Mahoney arrived at the Stern's a few minutes before eight. Henri was not yet there.

Dan said, "What it must have been like for his folks!"

"You'll never know," Mahoney said. "They never got over it. Mr. Fath died young. Mrs. Fath, she turned into an old woman before she was thirty. Charles never wanted children. Emilie has one boy, but she's more like a bodyguard than a mother to him. Fortunately her husband is understanding. Yes, I'd say that Dupier did quite a job of destruction."

"Terrible," Ruth said.

"I wonder what the boy's like," Mahoney said.

"The boy," Dan said, "is quite a man. He's gone through hell, and now he may end up going blind!"

"What!"

"He has glaucoma. I have to operate. The chances aren't too good."

"He's going to be all right," Ruth said. "I *know*."

The bell rang; Henri came in, and Mahoney rose. The two men stared at each other.

First of all Mahoney looked for the scar. It was there—just as Mrs. Fath had said it would be!

Deep lines of suffering had made grooves in his cheeks. And yes, the eyes were blue with the dark rim around them! They looked as weary as the rest of him.

"What did you want to see me about, Mr. Mahoney?"

The voice had a decided French accent. Well, after thirty years in Canada, what would you expect?

"Father," Mahoney cleared his throat, "over thirty years ago I was hired to find a small boy who was kidnaped by a man who we can only guess was a religious fanatic."

The priest's face paled.

"The family spent a fortune looking for him. We traced him to the region of Trois Rivieres, but there we lost the trail. We never found him."

"And you think I am that boy?"

Mahoney had difficulty in hearing him, he spoke so low.

"Aren't you?"

Only silence answered him.

Finally Henri brushed his hand across his eyes. "It is all so unreal . . . "

"Take your time, Father," Mahoney's voice was rough with sympathy. "I waited so long, I guess I can hold out a few minutes longer."

Henri sat down, clenched his hands in his lap, fixed his

eyes on the floor. "He said he was taking me to see the trains—"

"And you thought he meant to Wanamaker's?"

Henri shook his head. "No. I knew he meant at the Grand Central Station."

"And you went with him!"

"I was only seven. He knew so much about trains. More than anyone. I never dreamed for one moment that when that train started to move I'd be on it."

"Why didn't you call out for help?"

Henri shook his head tiredly. "It was all so long ago. Even right afterward it was like a bad dream. I remember crying and then falling asleep. When I awoke I was in a strange country. No one knew any English. I tried"— he shook his head sorrowfully—"I tried to go home. And I got lost."

"Who found you?"

"Who found me?" Henri sat musing in silence for some time. Then he looked up and smiled. "I guess you would say it was the Father Guardian. How many nights I dreamed of finding my family again. So often I could almost touch them, and then I would wake and they would be gone."

"Do you remember the names of your family?"

"My father's name was Auguste Fath, my mother's real name was Edith, but he used to call her Dolly. I had a brother Charles, not quite two years younger than I, and a baby sister Emilie. She was almost two years younger than Charles."

He sat in silence again. How could he get the words out? Mahoney must know what he was thinking. Had God spared them? Were they still alive?

Slowly Mahoney said, "Your father died some time

283

ago. But your mother is alive, and so are your sister and brother."

"Here in this city?" Henri whispered.

"No. They moved to Philadelphia a few months after you disappeared. Your mother, well, she went pretty much to pieces. She didn't want to leave New York. She cried that if they left you'd never be able to find them again. But your father finally had to listen to the doctor. He gave up his business and moved away."

Henri buried his face in his hands.

"My poor parents," he whispered. Then he looked up, questioningly. "Can you reach my mother? Do you know where she lives?"

"Yes."

D<small>AN</small> led Mahoney to the phone in his office.

Mahoney, his hand trembling on the receiver, waited for the operator to get the Philadelphia number.

Finally a man answered, rather angrily: "Mrs. Fath is ill and can't be disturbed."

"Who is this, please?" Mahoney asked.

"This is Charles Fath, the son of Mrs. Auguste Fath."

"Well, Mr. Charles Fath, try not to get too upset. This is Frank Mahoney." Mahoney took a deep breath. "I think we've located your brother Henri."

There was a crash at the other end, then silence.

"Mr. Fath!" Mahoney called. "Are you there?"

"Just a minute," the voice barely whispered. "It can't be ... after all this time. It's impossible."

"It *is* impossible," Mahoney said quietly, "but the impossible has finally happened."

"Where is he?"

"He'll be here at Doctor Daniel Stern's, at 67 Central

Park West. Can you get here the first thing in the morning?"

"Of course. I'll take a nine o'clock train." Charles Fath hesitated. "I'm afraid I can't tell my mother just yet. After all this time the shock . . . I want to be terribly sure . . ."

Mahoney waited again for him to compose himself.

"I'll leave at my regular time in the morning. That won't rouse her suspicions. My wife will meet me and"— he paused awkwardly—"I hope you don't mind, Mr. Mahoney, but I'm going to bring my lawyer and my aunt with me."

Mahoney grinned into the phone. He had heard that Charles was a lawyer himself. He said, "By the way, I know your sister is married. Is she living in Philadelphia?"

"My sister"—Charles' voice held a certain sardonic humor—"lives just a few blocks from the address you gave me."

"When will you be here, Mr. Fath?"

"Eleven-thirty."

"Eleven-thirty," Mahoney said, and hung up.

Mahoney walked Henri back to the hotel, seemingly loath to leave him, as if the miracle might dwindle away during the night.

Finally the detective bade him good night.

Henri said his prayers, then lay back, wide awake and staring into the night. There was no moon. The room swam in a dark mist before him. Tomorrow was Thursday. Friday he was to enter the hospital for the operation. And after that, what would his life be like?

Like this? A dark mist, which the sun could never pierce?

286

His mind returned to the deep winters at Ste. Anne—to the great drifts of snow, to the blue sky above, to the spring, to the forest green, and the heather waving gently over the rolling fields.

How fortunate he was to have seen these wonders of God. No matter what might happen, no one could ever take them from him. Blind, he would still see it all so clearly.

He thought of the people who had meant the most to him in his life: his mother, the Father Guardian, and Jeanne Marie.

He loved all three. Yes, of course he still loved Jeanne Marie. A man could have two loves—many loves. Just as a man could be two men, many men.

Who could define love?

Love is devotion, loyalty, adoration, and ardor.

Through Jeanne Marie he had become one of the favored ones, for there are no real pleasures without real needs. His greatest need had been to help her, and in helping her he had found himself.

But had finding himself brought true happiness?

Attaining the ultimate truth is attaining the ultimate happiness.

The Church teaches truth, he comforted himself.

Is dogma truth?

Is mystery truth?

Yet what was it one had said?

Faith is like a glowworm: it glows brightest in the dark.

But he, who might be committed to everlasting darkness, would he be comforted by a glow in the dark?

He did not know. He knew only for himself that his faith had been a true way of life.

His thoughts returned to his mother.

Would she know him? What would it be like? Would they be strangers to each other?

Whatever happened, he knew beyond any doubt where his home was. He had known all along. And he could never leave it for anything in the world. Or anyone.

Henri rose at five, dressed, and went downstairs. There was a letter for him at the desk. Henri walked to the door of the hotel, and in the early morning light opened it and read it.

It was from his Bishop.

"Plans for the factory are progressing at a rapid rate. But there are many difficulties. We need you . . . .

"Remember, every place has its Rousselins. Success is never easy. . . . You have many anxious visitors awaiting your return, and many problems awaiting your answers . . . .

"May God guide Doctor Stern.

"As for Ste. Anne, no one will ever be able to see them as you do. So return soon, Good Shepherd, and care for your flock. . . ."

Henri folded the letter with care and put it in his pocket. Slowly he walked west on Seventy-second Street, crossed Columbus Avenue, which at this hour was strangely still, crossed Broadway and Amsterdam, continued on West End Avenue to St. Matthew's at West Sixty-eighth Street.

He prayed there for hours. Suddenly it was ten-thirty and he left for Dan's.

Ruth Stern answered the door.

"Forgive me, Mrs. Stern, I'm early. But may I speak to Dan for a minute?"

"For as many minutes as you like," she assured him. "Dan has canceled all his appointments for this morning."

They joined Dan in the living room.

"I have been so much trouble, Dan, but I want to ask one more favor."

"Anything, old man."

Henri fingered his sash, ran a hand down his cassock. "My family, they know nothing of how I have spent my life. Perhaps the shock of these robes—"

Ruth Stern found her eyes filling with tears: at a time like this he thought of others.

Dan led Henri upstairs to their bedroom, chose a dark business suit from his well-stocked closet.

"Lucky we're the same size, old man," he said.

The doorbell rang.

For a moment Ruth Stern was frozen. Then she hurried to the front outer door.

A smartly dressed woman, not too much older than herself, stood in the doorway.

"You must be Mrs. Stern. I'm Emilie Fath Wiedner." She turned to the man and woman behind her. "And this is my husband and his sister, Dorothy Wiedner."

"Come in," Ruth said, taking her hands. "I know how you must be feeling."

They were hardly settled in the living room when the bell rang again.

Two men and a woman stood there. Charles Fath stepped forward and introduced himself. He stood as tall as Henri, and almost as lean; his face had the tanned look of someone who spent a great deal of time in the outdoors. He presented his lawyer and his wife.

As they came into the living room, there was a flurry of nervous greetings. Ruth Stern looked up, and as she did, everyone stopped talking and in silence followed her gaze.

Henri was coming downstairs.

How handsome he is in those clothes, Ruth thought. And then she was immediately aware that he was like no ordinary man, and would never be mistaken for such, no matter what he wore.

As Henri descended the steps he peered at the group below. He tried desperately to make out their features, but he got only an impression of well-dressed people politely waiting.

They would know who he was, but how was he to know them?

At last he reached the bottom of the staircase. He walked up to Charles and put his hand tentatively to his face.

"Charles?"

His hand came away wet. Charles's voice tried to hold back his tears: "Yes. I'm Charles."

Then Henri turned and looked at the women in the room. He went to the woman with the dark graying hair and touched her cheek with his fingertips.

"And you are the baby," he whispered. "You're little Emilie."

"Oh, Henri!" She flung her arms around him and clung to him.

Henri kissed her and they sat down beside one another on the couch.

"And *ma mère*, my mother, is she still lovely?"

"She's past sixty now," Charles reminded him, "and she's suffered."

"Does she still play the piano?"

Emilie's eyes widened. "You remember that, Henri?"

"I remember one song in particular. I used to beg her to sing it to me. 'Genevieve.' "

"I knew that was the one!"

Henri leaned forward, his hands clasped between his knees. "She was so beautiful—like a doll."

"Yes," Emilie nodded. "And Papa called her Dolly to the very end."

Emilie's tears would not stop. Everything moved her. Henri's description of the lost little boy in the village square, the homesick child fleeing down the road to the south, his effort to learn French, and his implicit trust in the Father Guardian, and even the story of how he had turned to the Blue Lady and God.

"And so you're a priest!" Charles's startled realization brought them back to the present.

"It's been my whole life."

Charles stirred. "I wonder how Mama will feel about it."

There was an awkward silence.

"I believe," Emilie said decisively, "that no matter what Henri has become, Mama will thank God for heeding all our prayers." She rose, and smiled down at her brother. "She's waited long enough. It's time for us to go to her."

It was agreed that Charles and Emilie would go in first to prepare her. Daylight was fading when they finally drove up to the front door.

The maid told them that Mrs. Fath was feeling better today and was sitting up in a chair near the window.

Henri waited out in the hall while his sister and brother went in. In a little while they returned, obviously moved.

"You can go in now." Emilie's eyes devoured her brother's face as if she could not see enough of him.

He went in.

It was hard for him to see. Was it so dark, or was his vision failing already? His voice rang out in fright.

"Mama! Where are you? I can't find you."

And then he heard her, as clearly and as distinctly as he knew he would: "Here I am, darling."

His eyes followed the voice, and he saw a blurred figure in the chair by the window, and a blurred halo of hair. Then his mother stretched out her arms to him:

"I'm right here."

He fell on his knees by her side, and put his arms around her waist. His head lay against her heart.

She raised her arms to embrace him even as her trembling right hand lifted in that dear familiar gesture, brushing the hair back from his forehead, and rocked a little in her chair.

"My son. My son."